LOVE AND JULIAN FARNE

This novel tells the story of a group of young people and follows their careers from the early 1900's to the years between the wars. This is the world of public school, of holidays spent at summer homes and of an early assured success in politics, literature and art, taken for granted by members of a prosperous society in more spacious times.

The story is told by Julian Farne, a sensitive boy who found it difficult to face the realities of life throughout childhood and adolescence. He is to become a famous artist and although he is in love with Alison Conway, with whom he grew up, she is already engaged to another member of their group.

How Julian Farne comes to terms with life and love is the theme of this absorbing novel.

LOVE
AND JULIAN FARNE

NEIL BELL

LYTHWAY PRESS
BATH

First published 1938
by
William Collins, Sons & Co. Ltd
This edition published by
Lythway Press Ltd
Combe Park, Bath
by arrangement with the copyright holder
1974

ISBN 0 85046 541 9

Printed in Great Britain by
Redwood Press Ltd, Trowbridge, Wiltshire
Bound by Cedric Chivers Ltd, Bath

TO

DAVID WARDROP, F.R.C.S.

O sad Fraternity, do I unfold
Your dolorous mysteries shrouded from of yore?
Nay, be assured, no secret can be told
To any who divined it not before:
None uninitiate by many a presage
Will comprehend the language of the message,
Although proclaimed aloud for evermore.

JAMES THOMSON

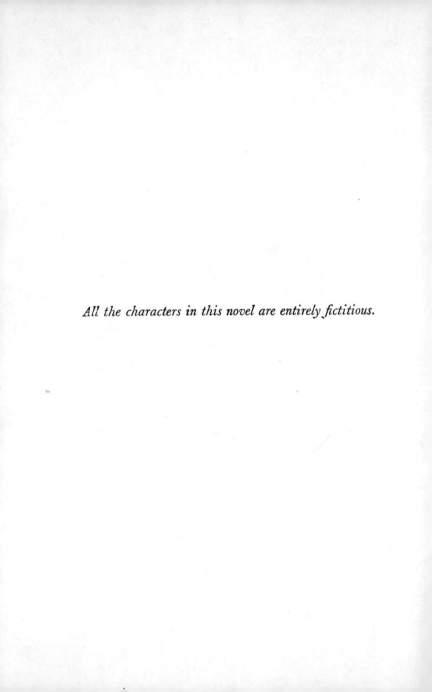

All the characters in this novel are entirely fictitious.

CONTENTS

Chapter One

STRAWS

MY FIRST vivid memory of Alison Conway dates
from the end of last century. Christmas was over and
there were but a few more days to run before year and
century closed together. I was twelve years old and
was home for my holidays from St. Benet's School near
Upnor, Kent, where my chief friend and crony was
Alison's brother Michael. That afternoon Michael
and I and Alison (who was only six) and my sister
Norah (Norrie), two years my junior, had been with
Mrs. Conway to the Egyptian Hall of Mysteries to
see Maskelyne and Cook's entertainment of magic,
and had returned to the Conways' big house in Baker
Street for tea. It was to be a sort of party to which had
also been invited Valentine and Sylvia Grey, cousins of
the young Conways. Our hansom and theirs, I
remember, drew up simultaneously at the kerb from
opposite directions and there were hurried greetings
in the rain before we all scurried indoors, I, as usual,
abashed and shy and overawed in the presence of Sir
Hereward Grey (Mr. Justice Grey), a perturbation
which Lady Grey's gentle graciousness did but little
to mitigate. But once inside the Conways' house,
with its cheerful atmosphere of invariable warm
welcome, my embarrassment vanished, was forgotten;
for some one of vastly more importance than one of
Her Majesty's judges had arrived. He was Humfrey
Conway, aged twenty, a trooper in the City Imperial

Volunteers, unexpectedly (and how excitingly!) come home from South Africa on sick furlough. How and why his coming was unexpected I cannot now recall; but there he was, big and burly in his khaki and jangling spurs, laughing and bronzed and not looking at all an invalid but as handsome and heroic a figure as ever stepped out of a sword and cloak romance.

My father was Dean of St. James's and we had a large house at 12 Portland Crescent, Mayfair. There were three of us Farne children, Faith, the youngest, being the same age as Alison Conway. The Conways were the publishing firm Josiah Conway of 3 Ave Maria Lane in the City and the two families had been friends for all the years of my recollection; but I have forgotten, if I ever knew, how that friendship began; it may have originated in the publication of my father's books, for he was the author of many volumes on ecclesiastical matters and of religious polemics, and all were published from 3 Ave Maria Lane. However that may be, as far back as my memory goes my father and Mr. Samuel Conway, then head of the firm, were close friends, and the two families on such intimate and easy terms that it was as if each family had two London houses, at least as far as we children were concerned, for we were during holidays for ever coming and going in Baker Street or Portland Crescent, so much so indeed that we would have meals at whichever house we chanced to be. This sort of mutual infiltration of young fry did not include the Conways' cousins, the Greys, whose town house in Cambridge Circus was no great distance from either of ours; certainly the two young Greys were frequently at the Conways' and occasionally with us, but any

youthful invasion of the tall stucco house in Cambridge
Circus was a rare event; it was, I imagine, generally
accepted that Sir Hereward was "not to be bothered"
and that he preferred children's room to their company.
I must presently tell something of the family histories
of the Farnes and the Conways, but for the moment
I want to revert to the homecoming of Humfrey
Conway.

I am the visual type, if that is what the psychologists
call it. Memory for me is a matter of vivid little
images, of pictures, usually all isolated from one
another as if on the walls of an infinite gallery and
waiting to be summoned at will for close inspection;
but while this visual memory is so strong that I can
recall scenes of my past life, however distant, with
remarkable distinctness, my recollection of the spoken
word, of what was said by those vivid little puppet-
images, is comparatively weak, although I think
quite up to the average. I imagine I may without
undue exaggeration put it this way: my memory of
things seen is quite out of the ordinary, I am tempted
to say infallible; my recollection of things heard is
about normal and to be accepted therefore with the
customary reservations.

This is the picture I would have you see of that
late December afternoon over thirty years ago. The
large front drawing-room, with its primrose walls
panelled in oak and silver and its remote frescoed
ceiling was, to eyes which had not known the glare
of electricity, warmly and brightly lit by six tall
pedestal paraffin lamps with immense rose silk shades,
a form of lighting which the Conways preferred to
gas, although that was used in the kitchen, the bed-

room and the servants' quarters. Heavy, tall, orange-coloured plush curtains were drawn across the four windows and the door, and a vast leaping coal-fire burnt beneath the wide chimney before whose hearth two tiger-skin rugs sprawled on the thick pale blue carpet in front of four deep, brown-leather arm-chairs. But no one was sitting down in that scene which my memory is now so clearly focusing. Doubtless, before those few moments in time which enclose the picture, some of those present had been seated, but not then. Mrs. Conway, Sir Hereward and his wife, and Humfrey in his gallant accoutrements, were standing in a group by one of the tall lamps, all but Humfrey silent, and he holding the floor, gesticulating, swept along on the current of narrative. Michael and I and Val almost holding our breaths, anxiously avoiding any movement which might draw attention to us, greedy-eared for this tale of war, hung about that small intent group. Norrie, inexplicably aloof and remote, was looking at some snapshots under one of the further lamps; Alison and Sylvia were prone before the fire, seemingly rapt away in the enchantment of picture books.

And suddenly there is a strange whimpering, half-sobbing noise; and Alison is standing upon the rug, white-faced, her hands out in front of her as if warding off frightening things, her eyes staring at Humfrey's startled face, at the startled faces of all of us turned towards her. "Oh, no! Humfrey," she screams, "no! no!" and runs to him, putting her arms round him, hiding her face against him, and bursting into crying so loud, so passionate, so alarming, that in a second those figures abruptly stricken so still by the outburst

are in swift motion all about her, soothing and comforting. And the picture fades out. I must have heard
what Humfrey had been relating but I remember
nothing of it. All that comes back to me now is a last
image of him shaking his head, looking from one
adult to another, and saying remorsefully, repeating
it several times, as if in exculpation, " I'd quite forgotten
the children, do you know."

But there is another vivid picture from that section
of my mental gallery; two, if I am to include an odd
dream, if it were a dream and not a half-waking fantasy.

It was considerably later in the evening and we
were all, with Mrs. Conway and Humfrey, playing
games in a large room above the front drawing-room
given over to the children as a play-room. Mr. Conway
had come up to join us, having been in about a quarter
of an hour, after dining at his club, so that it must
have been after nine o'clock. We were in the middle
of some round game when Mr. Conway stopped,
raised his head, and sniffing loudly said, "Isn't there
an extraordinary smell of smoke Agnes?" We all stood
still at that and Mrs. Conway said quietly "I think
there is," and then she added something about the
servants being out. But Humfrey had strolled over
to the door and opened it. I was nearest him and saw
with a sudden sense of sick terror (for I was throughout my childhood haunted by a fear of fire), a fog of
dark smoke rolling up the stairs. Humfrey darted down
the stairs, I, scarcely knowing what I did, at his heels,
and the others in a confused group behind us. The front
drawing-room door was swinging back and forth in the
draught, and the smoke was puffing out as it swung.
And then we were in the room, or some of us were, for

I do not remember Mrs. Conway or the girls being there, nor Val. The flame of one of the big lamps was flaring high above its chimney, licking out of a fume of soot-laden smoke. Humfrey walked over to the lamp and lifting it up called out "Stand clear!" There were expostulations from his father; and his mother cried out warningly; I remember the word explosion being used. And then Humfrey, holding the big lamp at arm's length, walked quickly towards the door out into the hall and saying something quietly to his father opened the door and went calmly down the stairs which led through the kitchen to the back of the house, the lamp flaring and smoking and hissing like some gigantic torch. And presently, smiling and wiping his hands on his handkerchief, he came back from the garden and said gaily, "There we are; it's all serene; it's out now; let's finish our game."

I don't know if we did finish; I have some recollection of going back in an excited hero-worshipping crowd to the play-room; but I remember how a little later we all went down to the dining-room for supper and that I was still so terrified that it was only with difficulty and with copious draughts of lemonade that I was able to swallow my food. Now that the danger was over none of the others seemed in any way upset; it was, I recall, a merry and boisterous meal; and Alison sat beside me, her face flushing and laughing, and her eyes throughout the meal in adoration upon that wonderful, heroic figure who was her very own big soldier brother. Once she drew her glance from him for a moment to look up at me and say, in a thrilled low whisper, "Isn't he brave! o-o-h! isn't he brave!" And it was all I could do to keep my voice steady (my knees quite beyond any controlling) long enough to add my profound agreement.

Sir Hereward and Lady Grey had left before the scare, for Humfrey had promised to bring Val and Sylvia home in a hansom. Norrie and I were sleeping at the Conways, I sharing Michael's bed.

My night was restless and disturbed by ugly dreams. I was terribly hot, perhaps because I had a bedfellow, or more likely I was slightly feverish. I could not find a cool spot anywhere in the big bed and my hands especially were burning and throbbing, the skin tight as if distended. But the air of the bedroom was very cold and so I put first one hand and then the other outside the bedclothes. I lay after a while with one hand stretched out in the darkness towards the half-opened window, whence came a cooling breeze. I must have dozed off with my hand like that and dreamed. There may be another explanation of what occurred; perhaps it was, as I have said, a half-waking fantasy. I do not know; but suddenly I felt small soft cold fingers grasp my outstretched hand, and screamed and tried to drag my hand away, and thrust off the bedclothes and sat up as the door opened and Humfrey stood there carrying a little lamp, shading it from the draught, and looking down with a broad grin at the tumbled bed, at me sitting up half-crying, and at Michael leaning on his elbow regarding first me and then his brother in amazement. "Nightmares! nightmares!" Humfrey laughed, shaking his head at me; "the sausage rolls, I expect; all right now?"

I nodded, looking away from his laughing face, unutterably ashamed of myself. "What—what's the time?" I mumbled.

"Five o'clock," he replied, "the rain's turned to snow and it's freezing hard. Cover yourselves up; sure you're all right now, Julian? That's good; I'm only next door; sing out if you want me." He closed the door softly and then, opening it again, smiled broadly and asked if I wanted him to sing me a lullaby; and at this I mustered up a faint giggle of relief and snuggled down under the clothes. When next I opened my eyes it was daylight; but something of the night's terrors still remained with me; and indeed to this day I can feel the clasp of those soft cold fingers upon my own.

I sometimes think that the reason my memory has chosen just those two (or three) pictures from that portion of the almost illimitable gallery is due not so much to any great significance in themselves (although in looking back upon my life their significance is, it seems to me, considerable) but to the time, the period in time, during which the events happened. I have always been sensitive to (fascinated by, is perhaps the better phrase) the abstraction time. I have always had an awareness of it as something inimical—shall I say?— to human dignity. But in writing that down I realise that it is not precisely what I mean; it does not portray time as it has always appeared to me; nor does it clarify to myself my thought about this fretting abstraction; and such a clarification ought to follow upon the act of getting down in words one's conception of a thing: or why go to the labour? The traditional, personified conception of time as an old man, bald but forelocked and carrying a scythe, has never been mine; rather has it been of a blind giant

ploughing the sand and in his unsighted progress
heedlessly sweeping everything into extinction. I
have always (or it seems to me that I have) been acutely
conscious of the flow of days and weeks and years,
and even, although possibly here I exaggerate, of
minutes, of moments. The strange bewildering
paradox of present, past and future time, that thought-
annihilating merger (if I may so phrase it) of the
three into one, that elusive frightening trinity, which
is never, and can be never, for one instant wholly
fixed and unalterable, never *still*, is always a presence
in my mind, something powerful enough to condition
my thoughts and even my actions. Even as I write these
words, a simple act which has placed the alterable
future of a moment ago upon the quivering balance
of the instantaneous present before thrusting it into
the unalterable past, I am haunted by that frightening,
that inescapable, that interminable flux. I never pick
up my brush (I am a painter) without the feeling that
it is a weapon snatched up to battle with time, to
battle hopelessly because its thrust must be for ever
too late. This is not very clear and I am all too aware
of it; perhaps I attempt a description of the indescrib-
able, as if I attempted to analyse the sudden fear that
falls upon me in an empty room, upon a solitary moor,
or, more rarely, in the middle of a motionless crowd.
And so I am driven back to my first bare statement
that I am acutely sensitive to the abstraction time.
And it is, I imagine, this sensitiveness which hooked
out of my sub-consciousness those three pictures,
because my mind at that period was, as were the minds
of most other people, charged with an even more
than usual awareness of time's passing; for not only

was the year near its end but the century also. I was an impressionable boy (perhaps impressionable is redundant); I read inordinately; I was in intimate contact with intelligent and very articulate people; and so, I imagine, just then my mind was being continually bombarded with this end-of-the-century awareness. Newspapers and periodicals must have been full of it; every day there must have been many allusions to it in conversation; every platform, every stage, every public assembly must have added their quota; my father's sermons doubtless took it for a text and I listened to his expositions both in the family circle and from the pulpit of St. James's. And so it was, quite literally, a great time; a time charged with portentous things; a time of general retrospect and general prophecy; a time therefore to me (as a being very self-centred, over conscious of my self in relation to time) of such supreme importance that it was graven more deeply upon my consciousness than any other contemporary happenings and became for all of my future the most readily evoked; and that very readiness of evocation has shouldered out other events possibly far more significant. But all this is mere hypothesis. I have stated it because while in the planning of this book it has seemed to me of first importance that I should set down the whole truth of my life as I see it, I am bound by that very sincerity of purpose to call attention to possible other sides or facets of that truth. I hope I may find the fortitude to adhere rigidly throughout to my self-imposed condition. Much that is perhaps dark here will be made light by the time my task is ended.

Chapter Two

THE FARNES AND THE CONWAYS

WHAT we make of our lives is to some extent (perhaps small, perhaps large) conditioned by our ancestors. That, whatever science may say about it, is my view of human existence and it must be my excuse (if any be needed) for giving here a brief family history of both the Farnes and the Conways.

Tom Farne, born in 1785, was a casual dockside labourer at Liverpool. He was illiterate; he never learned to read and his writing was confined to a painstaking, laboured signature in a sprawling childish hand. We do not know what he looked like as a young man but in middle age his portrait by Frith shows him as a stocky figure, very broad-shouldered, with close-cropped sandy-grey hair, little mean close set eyes and a startlingly florid (almost raddled) complexion. Apparently the most prevalent sicknesses among the dockside workers in those days were throat and bronchial troubles and the favoured specific for these with Tom and his cronies was a herbal cough cure invented by his mother, which consisted of an infusion of horehound, maidenhair and balm of Gilead, with one other ingredient, laudanum. Laudanum then was cheap and could be bought over any chemist's counter and it was to the laudanum in Tom Farne's mixture (or rather his mother's) that the cough cure owed its success, for it charmed away pain and

sent the sufferer to sleep, and Nature could usually
be trusted to do the rest, since the patients were in the
main good strong healthy material. Whether Tom
failed to see the commercial possibilities of the cure,
whether he was too lazy to bother, or whether he did
nothing for lack of knowing how to set about it, are
matters for conjecture; but it was not until he had
been working at the docks nearly ten years (from his
tenth to his nineteenth birthday) that any move was
made to prospect this gold-mine (for such it was to
prove). And the move, when it was made, was none
of Tom's initiating, but was entirely due to Harry
Day, who kept a small chemist's shop in a side street
near the docks, and whose customers were apparently
wont to belittle his own cough cures while belauding
the Farne elixir. It cannot be doubted that Tom
proved by no means wax in the chemist's hands (Frith's
portrait makes plain the mean, suspicious, petty
pig-headedness of my great-grandfather), but eventually
some sort of working arrangement was agreed upon
and in the year of Trafalgar the cough-cure was
launched upon the local market in bottles bearing from
the very first consignment that crudely-drawn label
which was soon to be almost as familiar an accompaniment of the white man's civilizing light in savage
darkness as the gin-bottle and the Bible. Not that
the natives had coughs or colds to be cured, but Farne's
Cough Cure (which now contained a considerable
proportion of alcohol—the bottles for export indeed
a large proportion) was much more palatable than
gin and made them feel twice as jolly. But this
prodigious success was far in the future, and for the
first year or so the sales were confined to the few

chemist shops about the docks. And then its sales
began to spread throughout the county, presently
were stretching out into adjacent counties, and within
ten years it was, in the matter of sales, head and
shoulders above all other cough cures in the kingdom.
It was cheap (at first only sixpence a bottle); people
liked its taste; it eased their pain and sent them to
sleep; it gave them the joys of tipsiness without
the stigma of the drunkard—remote indeed was such
a stigma, for they were able to assume, figuratively,
the shining raiment of the martyr enduring sickness
with patient fortitude. There were, by the time
Waterloo was fought, few dear old ladies in the country
who did not keep a bottle of Farne's Cough Cure handy
"just in case"; and fewer vicarages and rectories
where it did not (high out of the reach of childish
fingers) rub shoulders with Rowland's Macassar Oil
and Oliver's Brimstone Syrup.

And so the year of Waterloo found Tom Farne, then
aged thirty, making money hand over fist, but having
no ideas how to spend it, and still living in cheap
lodgings. Already his balance at Martin's bank was
large, far larger than that of many of the big merchants
of Liverpool and Manchester who, driving to business
in their landaus and phaetons, were as yet aloofly
unaware of Tom Farne's existence as a human being,
however cognisant they were of Farne's Cough Cure as
a flourishing commercial concern. But Tom Farne
was by no means a contented man; there gnawed
always at his mind like a rodent ulcer the, to him,
bitter knowledge that out of every golden sovereign
the Farne's Cough Cure earned, ten shillings of it
went to Harry Day; as much as he got, he the inventor

(his mother's share in the matter conveniently forgotten, she now being dead). That hard fact fretted
and rankled, stuck in his gills, as he would possibly
have phrased it; and it might have led to an open
quarrel and the break-up of the association, for Harry
Day was determined to have his full and just share
of the golden stream. Death, however, stepped in and,
when Tom was thirty-five, removed the former
chemist. This friendly act did not seem at first to
Tom Farne to improve matters, for Day left his share
of the business to his wife Jane, a shrewd and capable
woman of thirty-nine. My great-grandfather meditated for twelve months upon this disagreeable state
of affairs and then solved the problem very satisfactorily by marrying Jane Day; or perhaps she settled
it by marrying him. Who did the marrying is of no
great concern, but the marriage itself was of tremendous importance, not only to Tom Farne but to all
the Farnes down to my own generation. For if Tom's
mother made Farne's Cough Cure his wife made him.
She bore him three children in three years: Stephen,
born in 1822; Henry, born in 1823; and Edith, born in
1824. She took him out of his ugly Liverpool lodgings
and transplanted him into the fashionable quarter of
Manchester where they built a great house, Rockway,
which needed a staff of ten to run. She stage-managed
him, using her mother-wit and his ever-swelling
purse to hoist him into the proud position of one of
Manchester's foremost citizens. No charity appealed
to Mr. Tom Farne in vain, whether it was to endow a
cot, build a new hospital ward, found a scholarship
for a Lancashire Grammar School, or present a re-
creation ground or a library to some mushroom

township. But there was always a proviso; it had to be the Farne Cot, the Farne Ward, The Farne Scholarship, the Farne this, that or the other. And so by the time Stephen Farne came into the business the name of Farne was known and honoured (if only on the lip) throughout Lancashire and well beyond its borders.

There is no doubt that my great-grandmother Jane was a most remarkable woman and that whatever blood of hers still runs in the veins of the Farnes and their collaterals is the best part of them.

Stephen, the elder son, succeeded to the business when he was in his early thirties, his father and mother both dying within a year. His brother Henry had entered the Army, his commission as a field-cornet in the swagger Twelfth Lancers costing his father eighteen hundred pounds. Edith, the sister, married when she was twenty Mark Kendall, the only son of Kendalls the big Manchester wholesale chemists.

Stephen married blood, if not blue certainly good rich county, whatever colour that may be; the Setons were rooted in England's soil and history when William the Conqueror ravaged the north of England; and Stephen's bride Margaret ran true to stock. But that stock, rich in blood and legend was poor in drosser things, and it was Stephen's goldbags which were doubtless the deciding factor in this marriage between mongrel and thoroughbred. But whatever else it did the marriage ended the Farne connection with the world-famous cough cure, for Margaret Farne might stomach her mongrel husband for the sake of his wealth, but the smear of trade was an abhorred thing she had no intention of brooking; and so Stephen sold out for something over a million sterling, of which he took half and his brother and sister a quarter each.

That ended the Farne connection with commerce; thereafter they were county; the wealthy leisured; urban aristocracy. Thereafter their history, remote from the sweat and toil and rich vulgarity of the market-place, follows traditional lines. Margaret (unfecund perhaps by long close breeding, or lacking the wish, or cold in grain) bore her husband but one child, a boy Frederick who entered the Church and became, after his marriage, the Dean of St. James's. It is a difficult and delicate matter to write about one's own parents and I will say no more than that my father derived from the Setons rather than the Farnes. But if I am to serve truth I feel compelled to say that his marriage with his first cousin Dora Kendall was, hygenically if on no other account, a mistake. Its issue was myself and my sisters Norrie and Faith: there was a two years interval between the births. My mother's brother Luke Kendall, a medical man, married an Olive Mayne, and their two children were John and Nan, John being a year younger than I and Nan Faith's age.

There remains now what we always refer to as the army side of the family. Henry the field-cornet rose to the rank of Major, was killed in the Indian Mutiny, and left one son, Arthur, who entered the army, married (just before my father), a frail, pretty and very brilliant young girl, Alice Sade, and was presented by her with a boy, Crispin (a year before I entered the world) and a girl, Avis, three years after her brother. Avis's life cost her mother's and the two children were brought up by their grandmother, their father, a Colonel in the Seventeenth Hussars, being stationed in India.

Here then are the Farnes at the close of last century: Myself and my two sisters, Norrie and Faith; my cousins Crispin and Avis. And the Kendall children, John and Nan. Crispin Farne, the only one in his teens and he but on the first step; the rest of us one, two or more years behind. The adults: Grandmother Farne, with whom Crispin and Avis lived in Gower Street; my father, Dean Farne, and my mother; Dr. Luke Kendall and his wife Olive living in Wimpole Street.

It is a little tempting to wonder what Great-grandmother Jane would have thought of us seven children, could her shrewd old eyes have spanned the separating century. What the little, mean, close-set eyes of Great-grandfather Tom Farne, staring out of the Frith portrait, would have made of us I find a matter of indifference.

And now the Conways. And here I draw to some small extent upon the beautifully-produced little volume published about fifteen years ago from 3 Ave Maria Lane and entitled *The House of Conway: One hundred years of publishing.*

I must confess to an affection for the historical or quasi-historical tale which begins old-fashionedly, " Upon a grey blustering day in the late autumn of the third year of the reign of the first gentleman in Europe——" and in the matter of the Conways the facts allow me the fun of imitating that out-moded literary method. On a sunny morning in July (it was a Thursday and the twelfth) in the year 1821, the second of the reign of George IV., Josiah Conway, a young man in the middle twenties, stood at the open door of Messrs. Taylor and Hessey's bookshop in Fleet Street, contemplating with apparent contentment the noisy streams of passing pedestrains and traffic. Later in the day London would be stiflingly, stinkingly, hot; but at that early hour (it was barely nine), something of the freshness of summer dawns still remained in the air.

Josiah was chief clerk of the business, which not only sold books but printed and published them. Taylor and Hessey was a familiar imprint on books and a very reputable one, and their prestige in the world of letters was considerably increased by their ownership of *The London Magazine*, a monthly review to which writers as well known as Charles Lamb, Hazlitt, Leigh Hunt, Barry Cornwall, Tom Hood, Southey, Wordsworth, Wainwright (afterwards transported as a forger), Coleridge, Bernard Barton and the elder Dibdin frequently contributed. Josiah's work at that time was largely in connection with *The London*; he assisted John Taylor on the editorial side and most of the contributions passed through his hands—and very capable hands they were. He was slightly under the average height, stockily built, with thick brown hair, wholesome if undistinguished features, and bright blue eyes.

He took a pinch of snuff from a small silver box, snapped-to the lid, dabbed his nose with a large blue and red silk handkerchief, and then re-entered the shop just as John Taylor on a big grey mare reined-in sharply outside, swung himself down, crooked a yellow-gloved finger to a boy to take the mare to the livery stables almost opposite, and strode swiftly in, checking for a moment just beyond the doorstep at the comparative darkness within.

"Ah, morning, Conway, morning," he said; "marvellous weather. Have you looked over the Lamb proof?"

"Which proof, sir?"

"Lamb's! Lamb's!" impatiently; "we must go to press with *The London* to-day; to-morrow at the very latest. I mean the proof Mr. Lamb enclosed in his letter. You had the letter?"

"Yes, sir; but there was no proof."

"Nonsense, Conway; of course there was; I distinctly remember—but get me the letter. That's the one. Thank you. Now what's he say: ' Margate, July the eight, h'm, h'm, here we are. ' I do not return the proof—to save postage—because it is correct, with *one exception*. In the Stanza from Wordsworth you have changed *day* into *air* for rhyme's sake. *Day* is the right reading, and *I implore you to restore it*.' And then the postscript says: ' On second consideration I do enclose the proof.' Characteristic, hey? But there you are, Conway, we had it; now where the devil is it?"

"I'm sure we didn't, sir."

"But dammit! he says so and—and for that matter I remember most distinctly seeing it when I broke the seal as—as distinctly as I can see this paper. *Where* is it? that's the question."

"Mr. Lamb's postscripts aren't always reliable, sir. You will remember for the March number when the sonnet couldn't be found he wrote twice and then called in on his way——"

"Not on all fours at all. I had the proof here yesterday morning in my hands, here, *here*! and now where is it? Lost. And it'll take four days to get a reply from Margate and we can't wait a day after to-morrow. It's gross carelessness. It's——"

"We could print from the first proof, sir. Mr. Lamb says, as you see, that no alterations——"

"Rubbish! *Rubbish! Rubbish!* Do Mr. Lamb's proofs ever tally with his descriptions? He's incapable of telling the truth about them. He's probably made a dozen alterations——"

"But if you saw it, sir, you——"

"*I* saw it? What the devil do you mean by *I* saw it? I didn't see it; that's the whole point; not after I took it out of the letter; no! not envelope; you know Mr. Lamb won't use them; calls them modern fopperies; I didn't read it then; hadn't time; I put it with the letter over in that file and now it's not there. Where is it?"

"I don't know, sir. I'm sure that——"

"I don't want to hear any more. I've told you what I think about it and that closes the matter. We'll go to press with *The London* first thing in the morning and if the proof hasn't been found by then we'll print from the first one. Have you made a note what he said about the Wordsworth lines? All right then. I'm going out at eleven and I shall be at Harvey's Chop House at noon till two, if I'm wanted. It's unlikely I shall be in this afternoon."

For some time after Mr. Taylor's departure Josiah stood with his hands behind his coat-tails staring out through the window. His thoughts were preoccupied with a matter which had been in his mind on and off for the past eighteen months; hitherto he had balked at

coming to a decision but the breeze with Mr. Taylor
had succeeded where a combination of self-assurance,
supreme self-confidence and a large ambition had
failed. And shortly after eleven o'clock Josiah took
his hat, his stick and his gloves, informed the second
clerk that he should be out for at least an hour, and
leaving the shop strolled towards Temple Bar, crossed
over into Chancery Lane, and entering the office of
Mr. Grey, Attorney and Commissioner for Oaths,
he sent up his name by the bony, shabbily-dressed
youth who had slid off a high stool at his entry. And
a few minutes later he was closeted with Mr. James
Grey, a spare little terrier-like man in the fifties who
opened the proceedings by proffering a large gold
snuff-box. Here in that small, second-floor office
Josiah was not Conway, chief clerk to Taylor and
Hessey's, he was Josiah Conway, Esquire, of 16 Tottenham Court Road, a man of some substance and a
possible client to boot. The assiduous and excessively
courteous attention bestowed upon him by the attorney
was soothing balm after his humiliation at Mr.
Taylor's hands; and before twenty minutes had passed
the whole matter was satisfactorily settled; and a
further five minutes saw attorney and client drinking
prosperity to the new venture in a half-pint of Bristol
Milk apiece in Kearton's Coffee House across the
way.

A letter from Mr. Lamb at Margate, came by the
first post the next morning enclosing the proof which,
he said, he had quite unaccountably discovered in his
breeches' pocket on retiring the previous night.
Josiah received Mr. Taylor's not too gracious apologies
with admirable restraint, a restraint which was main-

tained when a month later he made a communication to Mr. John Taylor which left that gentleman for once at a loss for words.

And on the Monday of the third week of the following September there opened at 3 Ave Maria Lane in the City of London the bookselling, printing, and publishing establishment of Josiah Conway.

The new firm prospered from the beginning. The fine brain which had for some years been at the service of Messers Taylor and Hessey now devoted itself entirely to the service of its owner; and within five years Josiah Conway's were issuing from 3 Ave Maria Lane, books whose title pages bore such famous names as Charles and Mary Lamb, Allan Cunningham, William Godwin, Harrison Ainsworth, Robert Southey and Coleridge. And the firm's monthly review *The English Mercury* was competing and successfully competing, for public favour with such established institutions as *Blackwood's*, *The London*, and *The Quarterly*. But towards the end of those first five years young Mr. Josiah Conway achieved a feat of vastly greater significance and importance than the appearance of famous names upon the title pages of the books he published: he married on his thirtieth birthday, Rachel Hoyle, five years his senior, and the heiress of Sir Richard Hoyle, cloth merchant of Cheapside, Lord Mayor of London in the first year of the reign of George IV., and destined to hold that high office once more before the First Gentleman in Europe gobbled and stuffed and soaked himself into his grave, the royal body being tormented at the end with dropsy, intestinal and gastric hemorrhages, granulated liver, and tumour of the bladder.

Since Rachel Hoyle's marriage portion was a hand-some one, and she was thirty-six when she became Mrs. Josiah Conway, it is not unreasonable to assume in her a lack of physical beauty; and this assumption is supported, rendered indeed incontrovertible, by a portrait of her painted by Sir David Wilkie shortly after her marriage. But homely, indeed forbidding, as was her appearance she clearly brought Josiah things other than her dot and the three children she presently bore him, things no eye can see nor painter's brush portray; for the preamble to his will ran: *I would first of all return thanks to Almighty God for His great gift to me of my most dear wife Rachel to whose loving-kindness I owe all the happiness which has fallen to me in so abundant a measure.* Not that the dot had no value in Josiah's eyes; he certainly was not the man to depreciate the power of so round a sum and in later years he was ready enough to admit that the storms which inevit-ably lie in wait for a new business had, in the case of Conway's, been ridden out in the safe anchorage of his wife's fortune.

The three children of the marriage were Matthew, born in 1826; George in 1828; and Ruth two years later. Matthew entered the business; George, like the Henry Farne of his generation, went into the army and founded a military side of the family. This was not coincidence; when a Victorian family began to rise in the world it hastened to thrust roots into the Services or the Church; and first preference was, if means were available, the Army. Ruth, the daughter, married a young solicitor, John Grey, a grandson of James Grey, the terrier-like little attorney who had drunk the prosperity of the new firm with its founder.

As far as Matthew and George were concerned the new generation sprang no surprises, Matthew deriving chiefly from his father, George from his mother. But with Ruth there somehow crept in a strain of unaccountable beauty, and with it an equally unaccountable wildness. It was, one gathers, with immense relief that her mother and father saw her safely married to austere, upright, solid John Grey.

Matthew did not follow his father in the homeliness of his wife, for the Grace de Save he married was a very lovely young woman, if one may judge by the daguerreotype portrait of her. She brought him no dowry beyond her beauty, but Conway's was now in no need of gold and the beauty she brought to the Conway blood was a far more valuable contribution. True its effects were not very apparent in her only child Samuel, but it flowered fully in her grandchildren, Humfrey (the young City Imperial Volunteer), Michael (my school crony), and Alison.

Somewhat analogously the beauty of the Ruth Conway, who married John Grey, passed over Hereward Grey, the only child of the marriage, to endow the two young Greys, Valentine and Sylvia, in full measure. It may be that with the beauty there passed to them (to Val especially) other less desirable but equally inescapable heritages.

Into the army branch of the family, beauty put in a rather belated appearance in the person of Jeanette Brading, who married George's son Henry when she was seventeen and he as much again. But perhaps Jeanette's was an ephemeral, a superficial loveliness, with no roots in the blood, for Miles, the only child, was a plain youngster and as a man—but that is running ahead of events.

Let me recapitulate. Here are the Conway children (if the gallant Humfrey may, at twenty, pass for this purpose as a child) at the end of the century: Humfrey, Michael and Alison, the family of Publisher Samuel Conway, head of Josiah Conway, Son & Co., Ltd., (as the old firm was within a year to be designated); ten-year-old Miles Conway, living with his pretty young mother Jeanette in a flat in the Edgware Road, Major Henry Conway being stationed in India. And the Grey cousins Val and Sylvia. Val was eleven while Alison and Sylvia at six were the babes of our intersecting and intermingling circles.

And the Farne young fry once more: Norrie, Faith and myself; Crispin and Avis; and the Kendall cousins John and Nan.

How clear and separate and distinct they all are to me, even at this distance of well over thirty years. And (fruit doubtless of my lack of craft) how jumbled and confused perhaps to you; how much just a string of names and no more. If only I could call my brush to my aid; could paint you Crispin Farne, tall and old for his thirteen years, with his white marble-like face, his fine features (too fine, too chiselled, too carefully wrought), his pale blue glittering eyes and his thick, sweeping black hair. And his sister Avis, black-haired, olive-skinned, leggy, brown-eyed (frightened eyes, as we used to tease her). And my sister Norrie's pleasant grey-eyed homeliness; and John Kendall's apple-cheeked sturdiness; and little Nan's elfishness. And lovely little Sylvia Grey with her ash-gold hair; and Val pale, spare, yellow-haired,

languid (till sudden interest fired and tautened him).
And my crony Michael, as tall as I and broader, fresh-
faced, chestnut-haired, laughing-eyed, at twelve scaling
ten pounds for every year of his age; and Miles the
shrimp, with his plain, peaked face, his staring blue
eyes and sparrow legs; and Alison, whose beauty,
whose shy, sweet gravity, would perhaps elude my
brush. And myself? What should I see if I faced the
mirror to make a self-portrait. No, not now—God
keep me from that—but then, when I was twelve:
a tall, slim, dark boy; the mouth small, the chin
delicate, the eyes wide apart and deep-set; the expression, what?   Downcast, melancholy, bewildered,
absorbed, contemplative—which of these? Or all?

Chapter Three

ABOUT a mile-and-a-half to the south of Southwold on the Suffolk coast, the river Bly runs into the sea in a wide mouth which was once a fine harbour but is now silted up with sand and mud whose narrow shifting channels are navigable (except at spring tides) only for craft of the smallest draught. On the north bank of the estuary stand the windblown shells and ribs of the sheds and storehouses of past prosperity; on the south bank, a little withdrawn from the water's edge, are a dozen or so houses and cottages, a shop or two and an inn, making up with tree clusters and narrow lanes the much-painted hamlet of Walberswick. And there, just at the back of the inn, we had a large rambling old house which my father had bought soon after my younger sister Faith was born. That purchase seemed a sort of irritated gesture on his part, as if he said pettishly to my mother, "You've produced to my discomfiture three abominable little upsetting animals; well, here's a big dilapidated old house in extremely suitable surroundings; I trust you to make the best use of it." And so, till we were of school age, each year in April, Mother and we three children, two maids, a cook-housekeeper and an odd sort of trinity-like personage combining the duties of companion, nursery-governess and watch-dog, left our house in Portland Crescent and descended

37

upon Walberswick, where we usually remained till the end of September. My father came down for occasional week-ends and in August, or sometimes in September, stayed for a fortnight or three weeks. After we began schooling the exodus from London did not commence until the summer holidays, but apart from its curtailment the yearly Walberswick jaunt followed the lines now becoming as deep and fixed as ruts.

Even when she was there for five months on end I do not think my mother was in the least bored. She certainly did not pine for town life as, and far as a boy may judge his mother, she did not appear to miss the Dean's society. She was not intellectual; not much given to reading; and so she seemed quite happy and contented keeping us amused, joining in our games, and gossiping with the watch-dog. She might perhaps in time have got bored with so rigorously level, unchanging and unexciting a regimen; but the summer of the year I first went to St. Benet's there was a most unexpected and very welcome addition to the tiny circle of summer society in Walberswick, no less agreeable a person than young and pretty Jeanette Conway, who had bought a small cottage there in order that sparrow-legged shrimp Miles might, on medical advice, run wild in the tonic East Anglian air for as many months each year as his vivacious mother could bear to be absent from London. My mother and young Mrs. Henry Conway, despite a disparity of fifteen years and with apparently few tastes in common, somehow hit it off amazingly well, were soon Dora and Jenny to one another, and in a few weeks had, by the help of propinquity, crossed a

bridge which half-a-dozen years of previous acquaint-
anceship in London had not so much as put their feet
upon. It was quite plain to us children (as such things
always are) that my father did not share my mother's
regard for Aunt Jenny (as we called her, to his annoyance); and it was equally plain to us that his views did
not weigh very greatly with either of them. Looking
back on that period of my life I feel sure that my father
and mother had ceased cohabitation and that this was
a key to much of his conduct towards us, towards her,
and towards life.

Our house there was named *Ardvarr*. This was my
father's choice but what the name signified I do not
know. The house was almost completely hidden by
trees but from any room on the south side one could
see the sea and from most of them, across a large
meadow, the Conway's small cottage, *The Hut*, built
on rising ground further from the beach and within
a stone's-throw of the Church.

That summer following Humfrey's return from the
Boer War there was quite a gathering of the clans at
Walberswick, or of at least the young of the clans.
The Greys usually went either to Scotland or to the
Orkneys, where they had a house in Stromness; and
the Conway children went down into Cornwall to
Percuil, near Falmouth, where they owned a riverside
villa and a sort of houseboat, an extraordinary ark-like
structure hoary with years and local witticisms. But
that summer, for reasons I cannot recall, the Farne
and Conway rising generation descended upon the
Suffolk hamlet in a swarm, a roll-call of which would
have found few names missing. Humfrey of course
was not there, nor my small sister Faith, who was

staying with a school friend in Devonshire, and the Kendall children were also absent; but for the rest it was a full parade.

At *Ardvaar* we had a dozen bedrooms and could easily have accommodated every one, but Miles just then had a passion for Val and insisted upon his staying at *The Hut*; and as Sylvia refused to be separated from her brother she went too, being given the bedroom of the maid Kitty Bates, who was not at all aggrieved at having to exchange her pleasant little room for a camp-bed in the kitchen. Since every one at *Ardvaar* demanded a bedroom with a view of the sea most of the rooms were left vacant and only Crispin and Avis had rooms to themselves, Michael sleeping with me, and Alison with Norrie.

At the beginning of the holiday it had been enthusi-astically and unanimously agreed that every one (barring the adults who flatly refused) should take the first bathe of the day before breakfast; and for the first week there were no backsliders. But after a while one or more of the girls would make an excuse, especially if the morning were overcast; and one dull and not very warm morning in the early days of August none of the girls could be persuaded to come, and finally Crispin, Michael, and Val and I set off for the beach without them. Miles was also an absentee, which fact rather weakened our sarcasms shouted up at the girls' bedroom windows.

We walked along the beach for about a half a mile in the direction of Dunwich and then Crispin said, "Here, this'll do," and throwing down his bathing things began to undress. "Sun's coming out," said Michael; "it'll be hot presently." "There's nobody about," Val said; "let's bathe without any duds on; it feels grand." "You're right, old boy," Crispin said; "I was just going to suggest it myself; it's twice as good; what people want to wear the dam' things at all for I don't know; we're all made alike."

"And there are only two sorts," Val said with a grin. "Are we all ready?"

"All serene," Crispin and Michael said together and then Crispin said with a laugh, "Why, there's old Julian shoving on his suit."

"Take if off, Julian!" Val said, smiling and screwing up his eyes against the sun; "there's no one about and what's the odds if there were!"

"I prefer bathing with it on," I said awkwardly; "you please yourselves."

"Don't be sawney," Crispin said; "peel it off, old boy, and come on in with you; I'm getting cold."

I did not reply but began to button up my shoulder strap. I caught a swift glance pass between Crispin and Val and then Crispin said, "Let's take it off for him, shall we?" Val grinned and nodded. But I backed against the cliff clenching my fists, and Michael making it plain he would be on my side if there were any trouble by saying, "Chuck it, you two; Ju pleases himself same as us. Let's get in," Crispin abandoned his joke and the four of us set off slowly over the foot-tormenting shingle. Michael said just before we reached the sand, "Now the sun's out I wouldn't be surprised if some of the girls turned up and *we'd* look fools then, not Julian."

"Squit, bor, as they say about here," Crispin said, "we wouldn't. We'd look what we are. Anybody 'd think girls didn't know what boys look like to hear

you two. Daresay it's all right for Julian whose
gov.'s a parson, but——"

"Oh dry up, everybody," Val laughed, "have we
come down for a swim or a bloody sermon. Twopence
I'm in first!" and away he went across the sand with
the rest of us in pursuit. A quarter of an hour later,
as we rubbed ourselves briskly, we were all laughing
and talking away together as if nothing had happened;
but I at least felt the slight constraint behind the loud
jollity; and it was not until after breakfast and well
into the morning that the feeling entirely vanished.

In noting down those events from the past which
seem of most significance I am inclined to think that
one does not pick and choose consciously but that in
some hinterland of the mind (call it the subconscious
or the unconscious or what you will) a classification is
made as to what is noteworthy and what is trivial,
and the noteworthy or significant matter is then
presented to the conscious mind but so suddenly and
casually as to appear a quite arbitrary or haphazard
recollection of an apparently mere triviality. In no
other way can I account for my very vivid remembrance
of some quite small matter which my reason tells me
is unworthy of recording and yet which persists in
being noted down, which indeed continues to impor-
tune me until I do note it down. There was for example
the quite simple and rather silly little affair of the
Kissing Bridge; on the face of it a sheer triviality and
yet the scene comes up into my memory as bright and
clear as any other apparently far more important
event of that holiday. It may be that it is intuition
which demands that I give it a place here whatever

reason may say about it. Some half a dozen of us had been out for a walk and on our return had split up into two parties, Val, Avis and I lagging behind. Our birthdays had all occurred during the past six months so that I was then just thirteen, Val twelve, and Avis eleven. Avis, as I have said, was a leggy gipsyish sort of child with big brown "frightened" eyes which we were always teasing her about. She did not interest me and I had never bothered about her; she was just my cousin, a shy almost scared sort of kid who found the company of us boys little to her taste; or that was the impression she gave me and that undoubtedly is the description I should have applied to her.

At Walberswick there are two Kissing Bridges, small, rickety, arched wooden structures, spanning a dyke; the two, to the best of my recollection, being about half a mile apart. I do not know to this day the origin of the name applied to them, but they had interested me by their quaintness, and I had made several drawings of them. I don't know if Val were pretending ignorance, but as we approached the one nearer the river he said, "Queer little bridge that. What's it for—cattle?"

"I don't think so," I said. "It's called a Kissing Bridge. There's another over there. I've got some sketches indoors I made of them."

By this time we were on the bridge, and Val stopped, Avis by his side, and leaned against the rail. He looked at me with a faint grin and said, "A what bridge, Ju?"

"Kissing Bridge," I replied, pausing beside them. And at this he laughed and, taking Avis by the arm, faced her to him and said, "What do you think of that,

Avey?" and stooped his head and kissed her mouth. They remained still for a moment and then I saw Avis's face crimson and she pushed him away and set off at a run.

Val gave me a sly look, grinned faintly and said, "She likes kissing; so do I."

I felt embarrassed and at a loss for a light reply. "Shouldn't have thought so by the way she ran," I said clumsily."

"That was your scowling jib," he said. "What's a kissing bridge for, anyhow?"

I did not reply, and we moved off slowly. A moment or so later he said, "I'd like to see your sketches."

"I'll show you them when we get back," I replied. And then I added, knowing he was fond of drawing and half envious of what I realised was a greater facility on his part: "Why don't you come along to-morrow and draw one of them?"

He smiled. "Don't need to," he said. "But I'll draw that one when we get back. I draw best from memory." He shot me an almost malicious little smile. "And I'll bet you a tanner, Ju, mine's better than yours."

"I dare say," I replied. "Anyhow, I won't bet on it." And we began talking of other things.

Some few days (or possibly a week) later some of us planned to walk to Blytheburgh, have a picnic lunch there and return by way of Southwold. There were Crispin, Michael, Miles and I, and Norrie, Avis and Alison. It was about an eight-miles-round jaunt, and while Miles's little sparrow legs (much stronger than they looked) were quite capable of the journey, it was a long stretch for Alison, and I find it odd now that she should have accompanied us; but why she did and why Val did not, I cannot now remember. Possibly Sylvia wouldn't tackle it, and Val for once was brotherly enough to stay behind with her. We ate our food in a meadow beside the river, Crispin and I having first gone over to the little inn and brought bottles of stone ginger beer for all of us; and very delicious it was, as were our sardines, tomatoes and egg sandwiches.

After the meal we went into the church; but at the door Alison refused to enter, saying she didn't like the pictures (referring to the rather crude stations of the Cross); and as Miles did not want to go in either the two of them sat on one of the old grave-mounds to wait for us.

We three boys were a few yards ahead of Norrie and Avis and stopped at the pews directly in front of the altar to look at the wood carvings on the pew-ends. They represented the seven deadly sins, and the pudenda of one of the figures were very grossly carved. Crispin nudged Michael and said, " He's well hung, that fellow."

" Shut up, Chris," I said softly. " The girls are just behind."

" Don't be so mealy-mouthed," Crispin retorted. " What if they are? They'd enjoy the joke."

I clenched my teeth on an insulting retort and, in that moment hating Crispin murderously, moved on, fancying the others were whispering and giggling behind me. But when I turned at the lectern they were all close at my heels, looking up with grave attention at the lovely fretted roof, and in a few more minutes we had rejoined Miles and Avis in the momentary dazzling sunshine without.

But the contemptuous mockery (or what I imagined as such) in Crispin's tone still gnawed and rankled; and before long the inevitable spark kindled a blaze. We were crossing some common land making for the road. The path ran through clumps of sweet briar. I was immediately behind Crispin, and as he pushed his way headlong through a bramble swept back and scratched my cheek. I thrust it away and, beside myself with fury, cried out, "Damn you, Crispin, you did that for the purpose."

"Did what, Ju?" he said, turning and surveying me with what seemed an insolent smile.

"That bramble," I said, putting up a hand to my bleeding cheek.

"Sorry," he said. "Accident, old boy."

"Don't lie," I said and shouldered past him.

"Here, don't be dam' silly," he said, and gave me a shove which nearly toppled me over. I recovered my balance and struck at his face, and in a moment we were fighting. The fight did not go beyond half a dozen blows, none of which did any damage, for Alison burst into loud weeping and ran towards us, thrusting herself between us so that we had to stop. And presently, having shaken hands (on my part with a shame-faced embarrassment and upon Crispin's with an easy nonchalance and a friendly grin), and with a half-pretence that it was all more or less of a joke, we were leading the others in a race for the stile in the hedge which flanked the road.

I owned a fourteen-foot sailing dinghy, *Swallow*, and was rather proud of my prowess in handling her. Crispin could handle her with some skill, but not as well as I. I do not think there was much to choose between us as far as skill and seamanship went, but what small superiority I had was probably a matter of temperament. Crispin naturally did not admit that I was the better man, and his spectacular handling of *Swallow* was more attractive to watch than my cautious coaxing; and in consequence, had a vote been taken among the little world of us youngsters as to our relative merits, he would undoubtedly have been an easy winner, despite the fact that at the Southwold regatta about the middle of August he was third to my first in the sailing dinghy race for visitors, where I had allowed him to take *Swallow* and had myself sailed a strange dinghy, *John Bull*, belonging to one of the fishermen.

A week or so after the regatta Crispin suggested that he and I and Michael should go out tipple-towing in *Swallow*. Tipple-towing consisted in rowing slowly, or if there were a fair wind drifting close-hauled, with a couple of lines over the stern. Whiting was the usual catch, but we occasionally got a few mullet. As we were making our way down to the river, where *Swallow* was moored, Norrie joined us and demanded to be taken; and, since her claim to be "as good as a boy" in a boat could not be disputed, she came along.

There was a stiffish breeze as I took *Swallow* out through the ticklish channels of the silted-up harbour and we were presently scudding obliquely seaward with the huddle of Southwold coming up rapidly to port.

"This breeze is too good to miss," Crispin said. "I vote we let the fish bite each other and make for Lowestoft."

This was plainly to the liking of Michael and Norrie,

and so I merely nodded, but added: "Not Lowestoft. We'll have to do a lot of tacking coming back, and the wind may freshen."

"And it may veer, as it did in the old woman's story," laughed Crispin. "Don't be a wet blanket, Ju. Let her rip."

We were about a couple of miles out and passing Covehithe when the wind began to freshen considerably and some nasty-looking clouds came slipping up from the horizon. "We'll get back, I think," I said. "I don't like the look of the weather."

"Go on, Gloomy, you never do," Crispin said. "I'd sail *Swallow* to Holland and be there in time for breakfast."

"Well, I'm not good at miracles," I retorted, and I jerked my thumb behind me at the gathering clouds. "Look at that. I'm going about." And without more ado I swung *Swallow* round and set her on the first tack homeward. I expected a chorus of mocking criticism, but as we came round the small waves whipped by the wind burst into spray at our bow and, showering into the boat, silenced comment upon my decision. There was no real danger; *Swallow* was a seaworthy little craft; I was used to handling her, and it was simply a matter of rather wearisome tacking, made uncomfortable for the others by the spray we were shipping. But I felt (or imagined) the eyes of the others critically upon me, and it seemed to me there was a dubiety, a lack of trust in their looks. I knew they would say nothing; and perhaps because of that, or because I was acutely sensible that Crispin would have cut a finer figure at the tiller than I and that the others would have preferred him there, I began to let the affair get on my nerves, and presently was hanging on to tacks too long and losing way in coming about. And presently, when Crispin said casually, "Let me give you a spell, old boy," I thought I felt the tension, the anxious tension, of Michael and Norrie relax, and was angry with them and furious with Crispin and wanted to refuse and could find no words that did not sound unfriendly and churlish and silly; and so I nodded and gave him the tiller. And for the next twenty-five minutes (the time it took us to reach the harbour) he handled *Swallow* superbly—much better than I had been doing—better, I am convinced, than he had ever before handled any boat. Time and again he judged to a split second and tacked to a hair. It was admirable, and as I crouched under a dripping thwart I could not withhold my admiration, yet hating him for his luck and the debonair way he was carrying things off.

The mouth of the harbour looked nasty, showing its teeth on the sand-bars. I wanted to take *Swallow* in, sure he would pile her up, hoping he would ask me, but refusing to suggest it myself. But he said nothing. He just sat tight, his legs splayed out for purchase, his marble-white face dripping with spray, his blue eyes burning, a long swathe of black hair down over one eye, and a reckless grin on his lips. And he brought her in as if he had been doing it all his life; brought her in by sheer luck, for I will swear he did not see what I did, that he missed a shelf by less than half an inch. Pure ungrudging admiration brought a spontaneous "Oh, Bravo!" from Norrie and a "Lovely, Chris!" from Michael. But I could not force myself to speak. And then he said carelessly,

"Take her now, old boy; it'll look better." And again, without a word to say, I took the tiller from him and in that humiliating moment could have unshipped it and battered out his brains.

But my humiliation was not yet completed. The dregs were left and I was to drain them. Rage and shame and self-disgust had succeeded in unseating reason and skill in me, and although I saw the steam-ferry starting to cross, I held on in an impossible attempt to beat it. "Luff, Ju. You can't do it," Crispin sang out, his voice charged (as I thought) with mockery. "Shut up!" I snapped at him and carried on and gave in too late and slipped the sheet, brushed the ferry with a kiss, fouled the chain and was fast in the mud ashore. We got afloat again after ten minutes' hard and dirty work, of which Crispin did the lion's share. It was indeed his hour of triumph, as it was mine of the bitterest humiliation.

That feat of Crispin's became in time one of his legendary exploits, especially dear to the girls who had not been there.

Our uncle, Dr. Luke Kendall, was a keen and very efficient amateur yachtsman. Just after the birth of the two Kendall children, Joan and Nan, he had bought for five hundred pounds a middle-aged but very seaworthy Brixham-built fishing smack of fifty tons burden, named her *The Gallipot*, converted her hold into cabin accommodation, installed an auxiliary engine capable of plugging four or five knots, and with three men and a boy (Skipper Charles Sears of New-haven, Harry Noyce of Brixham, Tom Ludd and Ernie Jarvis of Lowestoft) he had spent many weeks of each

summer during the past ten years cruising with his
wife and children round the British Isles and occasionally going as far afield as Holland, Scandinavia and
Spain. He was a wealthy man, having succeeded to his
mother's share of the Farne money-bags. He no
longer practised as a physician, but claimed modestly
to be doing research work, a claim which his wife
(Aunt Olive) was wont to say rested on no stronger
basis than an inordinate interest in the habits of
fishermen and longshoremen as displayed in river and
wharfside pot-houses. *The Gallipot*, as any other well-
built smack, was seaworthy enough to go round the
world; and Uncle Luke was fond of pointing out to
us that she was the same tonnage as the *Pinta*, the
larger of Christopher Columbus's caravels on that
first Atlantic crossing.

And one sunny morning during the first week of
September *The Gallipot* sailed into Southwold Harbour
and anchored off Pinkney's wharf. She had come in
on the spring tide of the new moon (even at that a
difficult feat and one which brought many admiring
fishermen down to the harbour to stare at her), and
would not be able to get away till the moon was full.

The arrival of *The Gallipot* synchronised with the
coming of my father to spend a fortnight at *Ardvaar*;
but while we children welcomed Uncle Luke, Aunt
Olive, John and Nan (John especially with his apple-
cheeked sturdiness, his gaiety and his invariable good
nature which was always ready to subordinate his own
desires to the general good), my father certainly, and
perhaps my mother, regarded their invasion with, I
imagine, somewhat mixed feelings My father and
Uncle Luke never hit it off; they were oil and water;

even in town their occasional association was an uneasy one; but on holiday their utter uncongeniality was more than ever apparent. The most my father ever did as a sort of sop to the spirit of holiday was to don a black alpaca jacket and a dark grey panama; beyond that he never went. I never remember him bathing with us, and it was unthinkable to imagine him in a dinghy; the utmost he ever achieved in the way of holiday relaxation was a stroll down to the river or the beach, a sedate stroll with his hands behind his back. He was Dean Farne always. I have often wondered how he managed to stoop to the vulgarity of procreation. But Uncle Luke! My fingers itch for my brush to portray him: big and burly and red-faced, disporting himself in a hundred ways with us; bathing, fishing, boating; playing cricket or rounders; riding the horses in the fields barebacked (and once, slightly tipsy, a snorting, prancing steer which toppled him headlong into a dyke, to our shrieks of enjoyment). It was, by the way, during one of these circus-like performances that I had an agonising experience, physically and mentally. But that had happened more than a year previously at the Kendalls' house in Wimpole Street, where we had been skylarking with their two ponies on the lawn. I was riding one of them barebacked when it shied, shooting me forward against the long ridge at the base of its neck and hurting me so sickeningly that I fell off and lay doubled up, but too pudent, because of the presence of girls, to indicate to Uncle Luke where I was hurt. But he guessed and questioned me later when we were alone. But, dreading he might want to examine me, I denied it, and indeed I was no longer in pain.

The clothes Uncle Luke wore that holiday!—an old cloth Homburg, stained and tarred; a grey, much-darned sweater; corduroy trousers and rubber sea-boots, or often enough bare feet. And if his daytime exploits as a sharer in, but more often an instigator of, our wilder pranks were regarded askance by my father and with a sort of half-amused, half-disapproving tolerance by my mother, his nightly rendezvous in the taverns of the neighbourhood with local riff-raff (my father's phrase) were quite sincerely considered by them a disgrace to his position and a most dangerous example to us children. Even Aunt Olive, with her lenient eye for all the peccadilloes and shortcomings of humanity no less than of her bluff, boisterous, devil-be-damned husband, was at times moved to mild protest, a protest which always failed because so wild and ludicrously extravagant were his expressions of regret that she was defeated by her own laughter. Miles's pretty young mother (Aunt Jenny to every one, although no aunt of ours) thoroughly approved of Uncle Luke, and he greatly admired her. It was one of his jokes that they were only waiting a propitious moment to elope. But, then, as Aunt Olive said, he greatly admired anything young and feminine and would have eloped a dozen times since their marriage, except for the fact that he was never in the same mind two hours together, and also that he could never catch a train unless she packed for him and saw him to the station. But Aunt Jenny decidedly welcomed his admiration and, in order to enjoy it, deserted my mother's gossiping companionship to share in our games, in which she had hitherto displayed the merest perfunctory interest. And since Aunt Olive preferred watching her husband's and our wild antics to gossiping, my mother, bereft of her favourite pastime, had ample reason for looking upon *The Gallipot*'s presence in the harbour as a not entirely agreeable rounding-off to an otherwise pleasant holiday. *The Gallipot* did not, in fact, leave till after we had all gone, as she had to wait for the full moon spring tide on the twenty-sixth.

Aunt Jenny had thought of staying on till the end of the month, but changed her mind suddenly and the occupants of *Ardvaar* and *The Hut* returned to London together.

On the evening before our subdued and very disconsolate general exodus Michael and Miles and I went for a walk over the moorland behind Walberswick. It was dusk, very quiet, and we were apparently the only human beings for miles. And then, as we reached the top of a slope and came round a clump of gorse, we saw lying just below us, fast embraced in the sexual congress, Harry Noyce, the young Brixham man from *The Gallipot*, and Kitty Bates, Aunt Jenny's maid. They did not see us, and we crept away. For quite a while no one spoke, and then Miles said, "I can't tell mother, can I?"

"Don't tell any one," Michael said sharply. "It's not our business"

Presently Miles said, "Mother says she's flighty. Perhaps she knows."

"Of course she doesn't know," Michael said. And I added: "Shut up about it, Miles; it's nothing to do with us."

But Miles couldn't shut up. He was plainly much disturbed, as we were, too, for that matter, but we hid it better. I didn't want to talk about it, nor did

Michael, apparently. But Miles could not leave it alone. "Were they—were they," he began, and stopped, and then went on awkwardly, "were they—they——?"

"Oh, do shut up!" Michael snapped. "Of course they were! What do you think they were doing?"

That night I had a grossly erotic dream—the first I ever remember having with any vividness. It was so gross and yet so intensely alluring in a frightening way that all day it haunted my mind disgustfully yet enticingly; one moment I was bewildered and horrified at what seemed my filthiness, beastliness, and trying to thrust it all out of my mind; and the next I was deliberately recalling its images.

It was well perhaps that most of the morning was filled with the bustle and confusion of packing and getting ready for the traps which were to come for us to catch the half-past two train from Southwold.

We had a picnic lunch of cold chicken and ham and apples, and I took mine out to eat in a secluded corner at the bottom of the big garden. I wanted to be alone with my thoughts. But either Crispin had the same desire or he came there by chance, for within a couple of minutes of my arrival he strolled up, chewing an apple, gave me a grin, said, "Hallo, dodging the work?" and sat down almost facing me. I felt his eyes searching my face, and for an instant the appalling thought came to me that he was aware of what was in my mind. But his words relieved me. "Sickening having to go, isn't it?" he said. "By God, Ju, you look about as happy as a rabbit in a gin."

I looked at his handsome marble-white face (for the sun never tanned him; at the most it lent his com-

plexion a faint olive tinge, but then, as I recall the
scene, his face was its usual almost startling whiteness).
And as I watched the slow smile on his lips I felt a
sudden urge to unburden myself, not of my dream,
—nothing on earth could have wrung that shameful
thing from me—but of the affair which I realised had
been the cause of it, or had been at least the finger
which pulled the trigger. But I did not know how to
begin. I was, I always was, half afraid of Crispin's
mocking tongue, of his cynicism, of his way of carrying
things off so that one felt inferior and looked a fool.
And so I adopted an almost flippant manner, an
attitude which is really quite foreign to my nature,
no matter what the subject may be. I am, in fact
incapable of flippancy. "We had a bit of a shock last
night, Cris," I said .

"Who's we?"

"Michael and I and Shrimp."

"What was it?"

I told him and he tossed his apple-core into the air
and laughed and said, "Good old Noyce; that's one
for him, anyhow. She's a saucy little cat, Kitty is.
But what's the shock about?"

"Why—er—hang it all, Cris," I stammered, "you
don't expect to see that sort of thing——"

But he interrupted, "You don't *expect* to see it anywhere, my boy; but it's going on. My God, Ju, I'll
tell you what's the matter with you: I believe you're
pi. Is that it?"

In my relief I grinned and shook my head and said,
"Not likely."

"No bloody fear, you mean," he said. "Let's hear
you say that and I'll believe you."

"No bloody fear!" I said with a laugh.

He nodded. "That's it." And then he screwed up his eyes, grinned and, pushing the long black hair off his forehead, he said with a quick, sly glance, "I had a cuddle with Kitty the other morning."

"Don't lie!" I laughed.

"Fact. Week after the old *Gallipot* arrived. I got up one morning and went mushrooming on my own. You remember that, don't you?"

I nodded.

"So you dam' well ought, considering how many of 'em you wolfed for breakfast. Well, my boy, as I was coming back about half-past six I was passing *The Hut* and squinted in through the kitchen window, which was open; and there was Kitty getting up, about half dressed.

"I said, ' Good-morning, Kitty. Want some mushrooms?' and held up the basket; and when she said she'd like a few I went in and we sat down together on her camp bed. Her hair was down and her arms were bare, and she looked as pretty as you make 'em, and I kissed her. She pretended to be cross and slapped my face, but not hard, and then she looked at me and smiled and then, Ju, old boy, I suddenly got all lit up and wild as if I were tight and I put my arms round her and began kissing her like mad and she kissing me back. She fell over on the bed and I lay cuddling her——"

"But," I interrupted incredulously, "you don't mean, Cris, you—you——"

He shook his head. "No, old boy; no such luck. There was a noise up aloft and we heard Val talking and Aunt Jenny singing and Kitty pushed me away

again and pretended to box my ears and said, ' You're
a real bad boy, Master Crispin, that's what you are,
and you can keep your mushrooms, for I wouldn't
touch one of them for anything.' And then she smiled,
gave me a quick kiss over the eye, took three of the
biggest mushrooms and bundled me out." He
chuckled. "I went mushrooming again next morning
but the window was shut and the blind drawn, and
although I tapped on the pane it was no go."

"She preferred Harry Noyce," I said.

He gave me a quick glance and smiled. "Not bad
for you, Ju," he said, getting up and stretching.
"You're not such a fool as you look."

The sequel to the Kitty-Harry Noyce incident may
be recorded here, although it did not fall in that
holiday. Crispin did not go back to his preparatory
school at Croyde, but went, being now turned fourteen,
to Carchester, the famous Hampshire school; and
during the following Christmas holidays Michael and
I, who were not going to Selborne till the summer,
found ourselves considered by our circle very small
potatoes beside him, the first of us all barring Humfrey
(who was too old ever to be really one of us) to reach
the tremendous eminence of a public school. And
indeed he cut a fine figure, as even my critical envy
had to admit. That one term at Carchester seemed to
have removed him far from our orbit, given him a
poise and an added swagger which I at least found
magnificently intimidating, however attractive it was
to the girls. He had grown too in those twelve weeks
and, while Michael and I were both tall for our age,
he topped us by several inches. He looked almost a

man. He drew our attention to the thick golden down on his upper lip, boasted of more intimate virilities, said he was taking a razor back with him next term, and showed us a stumpy little briar pipe which he claimed to have smoked with great enjoyment—a feat, however, which I do not remember him performing. But, looking back on those days and calling up an image of him as he was then, I must admit that he took the eye. "Almost a man," indeed, barely does him justice, for he was quite five feet nine inches and weighed over nine stone and a half. And he was slim and straight-backed; he held himself beautifully; his head was finely modelled and well set on his shoulders; and with his sweeping black hair, his handsome features, marble-white face and burning blue eyes he was a gallant and debonair figure. Old Tom Farne might well have stood in stupefied wonder before this fruit of his loins of the third generation.

Young John Kendall and Miles Conway were still at Crispin's old school, St. Stephens; and, talking about them to me one day during that Christmas holiday, Crispin said, "Has Miles told you about Kitty Bates?"

" No," I said. "What about her?"

"You're sprucing. You must know."

"But I don't."

Crispin grinned. "That's your Gov," he said. "I expect he gave instructions you babies weren't to be told. Well, she married Harry Noyce three weeks ago."

"Pooh!" I retorted. "Is that all?"

He gave me a sly look and screwed up his eyes in an amused grimace. "They had to get spliced in a hurry," he said.

"Whatever for?" I asked.

"Oh, for God's sake don't be sawney, Ju," he said. "She was in the family way."

"The family way," I repeated blankly, and then I said, "Oh, yes," and must have flushed, for he stuck an elbow into my ribs and said, "Going to Selborne next September, aren't you?"

"What's that got to do with it?"

"Well, old boy, if you're so damned innocent or pi or mealy-mouthed, or pretend you are, when you get to a real school you'll have a hell of a time. Are you going to tell me you didn't expect it?"

"Expect what?"

"My God!" And he threw up his hands in pretended incredulity. "Expect what?" he mimicked, and then went on: "Why, Kitty Bates being in the family way. Didn't you see the deed done, you prowling Paul Pry?"

"Don't be a swine, Cris," I said uneasily, and at last aware of everything: "You know very well we stumbled on—on it by accident."

He laughed. "Don't get woolly. Of course you did. I was only joking. Well, that was it, and now Mr. and Mrs. Harry Noyce are expecting, as old Martha says." Again he screwed up his eyes and grimaced. "The facts of life, Ju, my boy, which we are not supposed to know anything about; or so they pretend. Bloody humbug, if you ask me. Why, if I were a nigger and lived in the Sandwich Islands I'd have a family by now."

But there I was on surer ground. "Oh, no, you wouldn't, Cris," I said. "I do know that. I've read a lot about native races, and the boys aren't allowed to have anything to do with the women till they're a lot older than you are. They aren't allowed near them;

mustn't go near their compound, or whatever it is, and——"

"And so they never do!" he mocked. "Rats! I don't believe it."

"Well, they don't, anyhow," I said emphatically; "and if they're caught trying to they're—they're, oh, half murdered. I can show it to you in—in, well, I've forgotten the name of the book, but it's about African exploration, and I'll find it for you if you like."

"Don't bother. I'm not interested in niggers. And if you showed it me in a hundred books I wouldn't believe it." He turned to face me, put a hand on my shoulder and said with startlingly unexpected gravity, "Look here, Ju, I'll tell you what I think."

"About what?" I asked, disconcerted by the change in his manner and tone, and by the sudden almost brooding expression in his eyes.

"Oh, about life and—and all the rest of the dam' business."

"Yes?"

"People are ashamed of it."

"Ashamed of it?" I repeated blankly.

He nodded. "That's it." And then his eyes blazed. "Ashamed of it, and try to hide it from us as if it were all a dirty business. But is it, Ju? Is it? And if it is, why is it? Oh, good God! don't stand there gaping like a stuck pig. Don't you ever think about things?" And then, his manner changing as swiftly again, he laughed boisterously and said, "Oh, well, to hell with it all. Been to the panto?"

I stared at him. We had been (seven of us) to the Lyceum the previous afternoon and he with us. But before I could speak he laughed again. "Panto," he said. "Good old panto; so nice for the children. Pah! They make me sick." And then, as if dismissing every-thing from his thoughts, he said, "Let's go and see if we can collar Michael and go for a mooch."

But I was unable to dismiss things so easily, either at the moment or during the next few days and nights. The matter occupied my attention and, if but inter-mittently, with disturbing frequency. I realised in myself an intense curiosity to know all about these things; I felt I was old enough to know, had a right to know; but I did not know how to obtain this information whose lack was for the first time in my life obtruding itself upsettingly into my waking and sleeping consciousness. I began to consider possible sources of this dark knowledge, passing in a slow assaying review all the people of my circle. My con-temporaries were no use. They knew no more than I did, and if they claimed to do so, I did not believe them; I was already aware that it is one of the subjects about which most people are apt to lie; boy-knowledge was mostly smut, and I knew all that side of it. What of the men? I dismissed my father without a second thought; he was indeed unthinkable. My masters at St. Benet's were almost in the same category, and Humfrey seemed himself too near to boyhood. I came at last to Uncle Luke; he was certainly the best of the bunch; he seemed to have all the qualifications for an ideal confidant; he was a man of culture and knowledge; he was a doctor; and best of all he was as much one of us as any adult can be to a lot of youngsters. But I rejected him also, and with this rejection I came upon the truth of the matter that the thing could not be done by any human being without embarrassment, and that what was needed was the impersonal help of a book, something one could read in the quiet of one's own room. And at once I thought of the books I had seen displayed in a chemist's shop in Piccadilly Circus; and without more ado I set off there alone one afternoon immediately after lunch. I stood and stared in the window for a quarter of an hour, and slowly it dawned upon my consciousness that not here should I find the help I needed. Here were books in plenty; but as I read their titles and looked at their covers I realised that they were published in the service of smut and not of knowledge; they were akin to the tales we told each other; they were in the class of writings which I learned years later was known as *graffiti*.

And so I wandered away and came after a time to the bookstalls of the Charing Cross Road; and there in the sixpenny box I came upon what seemed to me the book I was seeking. It was called *The Truth About Your Body*; and there was a sub-title: "What a young man should know about sex." Well, I was fourteen, and I felt I was enough of a man to be told all about this disturbing mystery.

I took it from the box and entered the shop with it, timid, shamefaced, blushing, I dare say, but grimly determined to see the thing through. I was prepared for a rebuff, prepared to be told I couldn't have it; prepared, indeed, for anything, a grim picture of the police being sent for not being excluded from the possibilities. But I kept my courage to the sticking-point and went up to the man behind the counter, holding out the book, title side underneath, and my sixpence. But I needn't have worried. He merely glanced at it, nodded, and took the coin; and I thrust it into my pocket and hurried away so overwhelmed with relief that I was half in tears.

And then I did a foolish thing. Instead of waiting till I went to bed where, in the solitude of my own room, I could have read in unmolested peace, I went straight up to the library at home (so eager, so avid was I to plunge into this well of truth) and, finding no one there, sat down to read it. But I kept a copy of *Punch* behind it. And the worst happened. My father came in, slippered and silent, and was upon me before I was aware of his presence; and in my confusion I dropped the book and he picked it up and looked at it. The disgusted, contemptuous glance he turned upon me is even now as vivid and clear as it was in that overwhelming moment. "Where did you get this filth?" he asked.

"I bought it," I said, and dredged my mind for words to make clear to him my need, and failed to find them, and knew hopelessly that no such words existed.

He tossed it into the fire, stood watching it blaze and consume; and then he said slowly and harshly, "It is a shocking thing, Julian, for me to find you reading such dirt."

"It is not dirty," I burst out.

"Indeed. Then why do you think it necessary to hide it behind a copy of *Punch*?"

I had not the wit nor subtlety to confute him, to extricate myself from that dilemma; and while my thoughts went stumbling about my mind he gave a glance to the heap of ash in the grate and saying, "Such vile trash undermines the health of the body and destroys the soul, thrusts out God in you and replaces Him by the devil; in future have nothing to do with it," he turned and walked slowly away to the far door, his hands clasped behind his back.

Perhaps that incident more than any other, added to the fact that I left St. Benet's and went to Selborne the following September, seems to make that year one of the milestones in my life. But "milestones" will not do; it is too trite, too hackneyed; nor has it the illuminating quality my meaning demands. But I fear the vivid arresting metaphor is beyond my reach. Something more pedestrian must serve my purpose. One's life in retrospect is a long darkness variegated by short twilit periods, and sudden brilliant flashes revealing clear-cut pictures which the years cannot fade. Here, then, was one of those flashes of revealing illumination—an unfading picture.

Chapter Four

SELBORNE COLLEGE in South Devon did not, I imagine, greatly differ from other contemporary public schools. It was famous. But which is not—or at least does not claim to be? It was old, its foundation dating from 1601 when Thomas Leigh, a rich City of London merchant and a native of Selborne, died and left half his fortune for that purpose. Its scholars (there were not in my time, nor had been for a hundred years, any day boys) numbered over six hundred, of whom one hundred were Royal Scholars, twenty Thomas Leigh Scholars, and four Henry Burdett Scholars. If there were anything to mark Selborne as in any way different from its contemporaries it was these Henry Burdett boys and, possibly, the school motto.

Henry Burdett had been a scholar at Selborne from 1812 to 1819, and apparently a completely undistinguished one, for apart from an alleged carving of his signature in one of the old dormitories (Hen Burdett 1815 Waterloo, was the odd way it ran) he left no mark upon the school records. But Henry Burdett was clearly no fool, for he came to London, made a fortune, in of all places the East End (East Ham), out of hardware; and when he died in the sixties he left a sum of money to found four scholarships, of a somewhat extraordinary type, to his old school. Two

66

of these scholarships were for biennial competition by boys who had not passed their fourteenth birthday, attending the national school at East Ham, and two for boys of a similar age and class at Selborne town. And they were well worth the winning, as they not only provided for a period of four years at Selborne, but a further period of four years at either Oxford or Cambridge; in other words, they were worth in terms of money alone something like two thousand pounds. Perhaps, because of the value of the prize, the examination was a stiff one, and as often as not no competitor obtained the requisite percentage of marks for a scholarship to be awarded. In my time at Selborne there were no Henry Burdett Scholarship boys from Selborne town and only two, Frank Beamish and Tom Frankell (of both of whom I shall have more to tell) from East Ham.

And now the school motto. It was: *ab uno disce omnes* (from one judge of all the rest) and I can imagine no school motto more proudly insolent, more plainly farcical; and indeed, if it could possibly have been true, implying a more damning criticism of the school itself.

But naturally it was not true, and at Selborne in my time (as in any other time) there were as many varieties of type as there were boys; and of all of them the one who most immediately concerned myself (and played no small part in my future) was Piers Rowland. Michael Conway came with me to Selborne that September; Val Grey came the next year; and Miles the Shrimp twelve months later. But by then he was a shrimp no longer; years of running wild had put inches on his stature, a stone or so on to his weight, and muscled out his sparrow legs to normal proportions.

Piers Rowland had been at Selborne three years and was then seventeen. He was my second cousin, but had hitherto been a name and no more; and it was a name of somewhat mysterious (or perhaps I should say intriguing) connotations. A few years before Olive Mayne had married Dr. Luke Kendall in the late eighties, her sister Esther made a runaway match with an odd fish named Quintin Rowland. He had a fine handsome appearance, but apparently little else. He was a young man-about-town living in style upon no one knew what; he was a dandy of some notoriety; a dabbler in the arts; an æsthete who ante-dated the Oscar Wilde circle by a decade. When he eloped with Esther Mayne they went to live at Arcachon in the south of France and never returned to England. Piers, their only child, was born a year after their marriage, and until he went to Selborne had been educated in France. Quintin painted unsaleable pictures, published small books of erotic verse, and did a certain amount of translation work. None of these activities brought him more than enough to pay for his cigars; and the small family lived (and in considerable luxury) upon his wife's private fortune.

It is difficult for me in words to portray Piers Rowland, for by the circumstances of our earliest association he inevitably comes into my memory as a being vastly more than life-size. When Michael Conway and I went to Selborne Piers was not only captain of the school and captain of the first rugger fifteen, but in academic achievement head and shoulders above all the other boys. It is hard for an adult mind (unless it have the vividest recollections of its school days) to realise just what this meant in terms of Piers's position relative to the rest of the school, and particularly to Michael and me as newcomers. A king at the head of his troops; a famous actor in the centre of the stage; the Pope in audience; a prima donna taking a frenzied call. All these I have seen and they are not in the same category; they are not, quite literally, in the same world. And perhaps because of that there is no precise analogy in the adult world; there is nothing by which the stature of Piers Rowland at Selborne can be measured by. For that appraisal one must go back to the days when the gods came down for a while to earth to walk among the sons and the daughters (especially the daughters) of men. Add to all of this that he was six feet tall, broad, with a truly magnificent head and fine handsome features, and my difficulty in reducing him to human proportions at that period will be realised. And indeed for years afterwards he retained in my mental picture gallery something of those god-like attributes; possibly he never entirely lost them, whatever verdict my adult reason came to pass upon him.

He was one of those rare beings in whom are apparently brought together all the graces, all the talents; there was seemingly nothing he could not do; one could not imagine a situation of which he would not be completely the master; and in his person and his talents he gave the lie to the school's motto in as downright a fashion as could only be equalled, on the reverse of the medal, by the school's biggest blackguard or most abject witling. That he had no serious rival there either mentally or physically would not have been questioned by any of his contemporaries.

The boy who most nearly approached him in intellectual achievement was Frank Beamish, one of the two Henry Burdett scholars from East Ham. Squitters Beamish (for that quaint nickname had completely replaced his Christian name and it is as Squitters and not Frank that I always think of him) was in his last year at Selborne and six months older than Piers. His father had been a small shopkeeper at East Ham and had fallen romantically in love with the child of a neighbour, and when she was old enough had married her; and Squitters was the fruit of that love-match. But these facts were not known at Selborne until the arrival at the school two years later of Tom Frankell, another Burdett scholar from East Ham. Squitters was a brilliant boy and had been the prodigy of his home district and, but for Piers Rowland, would have undoubtedly ruled the intellectual roost at Selborne. He was above the average height, but rather frail and pasty-faced; he was hopeless at games of any sort, and it must have been a particularly bitter pill for him that the one boy who outshone him intellectually was also the star athlete of the school. Beamish was, of course, a prefect and was the editor of the school magazine *The Selbornian*.

Tom Frankell, a postman's son, had been at Selborne a year when I went. He was a finely built boy, a trifle on the stocky side, with a fresh face of, strangely enough, almost girlish beauty, a laughing eye and an expression of most engaging camaraderie. He was clever, as his possession of a Burdett Scholarship attested, but it was not this which had won him in twelve months a position of some celebrity in the school. He had played association football before coming to Selborne but no rugger, and rugger was the only football game we played. And he took to it like a swallow to the air. He played from the first with that strange inexplicable aptitude which is so often called genius; and it was therefore inevitable that there should spring up between him and Piers Rowland (the captain of the first fifteen and a player of great talent) an association which quickly became a warm friendship. But it was a friendship and nothing more; a friendship based upon a mutual admiration for each other's prowess at the game which was a passion of both; and if there were added a liking due to congeniality of temperament and tastes, there was not also lacking full realisation on the part of both of them that their relative positions in the school demanded that a strict limit should be placed upon their association; and that this understanding was honoured by them in spirit and letter is best explained by the fact that the school view of their friendship was one which did not need to be mentioned with winks and nods or behind metaphorically cupped hands.

Nevertheless within a month of my going to Selborne a violent row blew up suddenly over Piers and Tom Frankell. At the time of course none of us small fry knew much about it; but as time passed a bit here and a bit there of the affair was picked up until all were sorted out and pieced together into a fairly coherent story.

Briefly, then, there was held about the middle of October a meeting of the school sports' committee.

Piers Rowland, as captain of the school, presided *ex officio*. Beamish, as senior prefect, was also on the committee. There was a vacancy for a scrum-half in the first rugger team and the names of three boys were before the committee for consideration. All three boys were in the fifth form and over sixteen. As soon as the meeting opened Piers Rowland said that he had a proposal which he wished to put before the committee; he was, he said, aware that it was a revolutionary one, but that a special circumstance warranted it. That special circumstance was the fact that they had in the school a player of such outstanding ability that it was expedient, even imperative, to abrogate for once the unwritten Selbornian law that members of the first fifteen should not be under the age of sixteen. "There is," he ended abruptly, "no need for me to name that player; but to have the thing in order I put it to you, gentlemen, that the vacant place be given to Tom Frankell."

So great was Piers's prestige, and so obviously true his estimate of Tom Frankell's abilities, that there was a general murmur of assent; and Piers was about to close the matter without the formality of a plainly unnecessary vote when Squitters Beamish interposed, saying, "Isn't the business open for discussion?"

"Of course it is, Beamish," Piers said. "But I took it we were all agreed."

"I dissent and most strongly. A law, whether written or unwritten, cannot be abrogated to fit a special case, if it *is* a special case."

"Do you mean that Frankell isn't a special case?" Piers asked. "If I tell you he is the best scrum-half I've ever seen and probably the best the school has ever had, will you still deny that he is a special case?"

Some one on the committee interrupted with a sort of casual contempt: "Shut up, Squitters. Of course Rowland is right and Frankell's the right choice, laws or no laws. What the hell do you know about rugger, anyway? Sit down and let's go on with the other business."

Beamish, stung, said with the crassest indiscretion, "I'm not prepared to say Frankell isn't a special case, but not as a footballer." And he shot a savagely lubricious leer at Rowland.

There was at this an intense silence of such duration that Beamish suddenly lost his nerve, licked his lips, and hurriedly sat down, muttering, "Have it your own way."

Piers leant forward with his arms on the table. "How do you mean, Beamish?" he asked quietly.

"I mean I withdraw my objection."

"Never mind your objection. What are you driving at?"

"Nothing."

"Don't lie. You're accusing me of having an affair with Frankell."

Beamish again licked his lips. And then amazingly, as if from some hidden source he drew strength and courage, he said slowly, venomously, "Well, aren't you?"

In the silence the ticking of the watch on Piers's outstretched wrist could be plainly heard. After a long strained minute he got up from his chair, went over to Beamish, jerked him from his seat by his collar, flung him over the table, wrenched down his trousers and thrashed him with his hand. And then he carried him to the door and, opening it, tossed him into the corridor.

Beamish went straight to the Head.

The Head sent for Piers.

Probably only three people—the Head, Piers Rowland and Squitters Beamish—knew what happened at that interview; but rumour went round the school that the Rev. Henry Clough metaphorically flayed Squitters. That rumour even added, with schoolboy snobbishness, that the Head told Squitters his filthy mind could only be ascribed to his low and mongrel antecedents.

However far from the truth rumour may have been, two facts emerge: Tom Frankell was given his place in the first fifteen, and Squitters left Selborne at the end of the term and went up to Balliol six months sooner, so it was said, than he had intended. But, of course, Beamish may have decided before the affair happened to go on to Oxford at the beginning of the year, for he was eighteen in that November.

That was, as I have said, in the October, during my first month at Selborne. Towards the end of my first year—I think it was late June or early July, I had been playing in a Muffs and Duffs cricket match (the terms are, I fancy, self-explanatory) and we had afterwards gone over to the plunge-bath. A number of us were standing naked on the end preparatory to taking a header when one of the Duffs, a scrawny overgrown fellow named Cossett, who was lounging on the side, yelped out a waggish indecency. There was a roar of laughter as I plunged in, reached the far end with fewer than a dozen swift strokes and, climbing out, made for the dressing-room in a sort of half-blind stumbling embarrassment.

That incident crystallised to the point of action the many vague, half-formed thoughts that had been for some months occupying my mind with regard to sport. I was a very indifferent player, and the compulsory games were more and more becoming an intolerable boredom. I determined to take part in them no more if it were in any way possible to avoid them. I pondered the problem then for some days but without finding a solution; there did not in truth seem to be one; not one which I could take without landing myself into what I realised might be worse humiliation. And then sheer luck stepped in and saved me. Or maybe it was not luck, unless one's gifts are luck; perhaps they are; but if so, their cultivation cannot surely be so ascribed, and decidedly for some years now I had been assiduously cultivating my one gift, that of painting. I was not an exceptionally good draughtsman if my line work were compared with Val Grey's (but, then, his drawing was remarkable, talented almost to the point of genius); but I had a highly-developed sense of colour and a real feeling for form. Now by a piece of great good fortune (and luck does enter here) there had just been appointed as art master at Selborne R. L. Sims, the man whose War pictures were later to enrich the War Museum with their terrible realism. Sims even then was recognised as a fine artist by his brother painters, but he was unknown to the public, his pictures did not sell and, having no private means, he was glad to take the post at Selborne. For some time before his coming there had been under consideration by the governing board

of the school the question of re-decorating the chapel;
and shortly after his arrival one or more of the
governors, with a rare percipience, realised what a fine
artist Sims was, took him into consultation about the
matter and finally (after no doubt taking further
opinion) commissioned him to take charge of the work.
He was given a free hand and he planned to do a
number of the frescoes himself while others were to
be done by well-known artists.

Sims was of course aware of my ability and we
were on as friendly a footing as our relative positions
allowed. I need not be charged with vanity when I
make the simple statement that I was the only boy
then at Selborne who could paint, as a painter under-
stands the word. Sims wanted some one who would
always be available and whom he could trust with
little unimportant jobs of assistance; a sort of apprentice to prepare surfaces, help with a background, and
so forth; some one who because of his own gift and
knowledge could safely be entrusted with such minor
but necessary work without any fear of the real work
being spoilt by ignorance. I was the one obvious
choice (Val, with all his slick draughtsmanship, had
little feeling for colour and pretended to despise it).
And while I was fretting and worrying over my
apparently insoluble problem Sims sent for me to his
room and, as was his way, almost thrust his offer upon
me without any preliminary explanations. I was
pleased and a little proud but by no means overwhelmed, for I did not realise what it would mean
until he said in his vague way and with an almost
flapping gesture of his stub-fingered hands (for he had
the most inartistic-looking hands I have ever seen,

thereby confuting the popular notion), "You'll have to be the assiduous apprentice sort of thing, you know, Farne: at call when you're wanted. That of course won't be during lecture time and only occasionally during prep, but I'm afraid your leisure can't be your own: games and that sort of thing, you know," repeating his flapping gesture. He must have noticed my sudden agitation and misread it, for he said, almost sharply, "Of course, if you prefer hurling yourself about in space with a lot of young animals, well, by all means do it; but——"

I burst in, unable to restrain myself, saying, "But, sir, I don't. I don't; I loa——" and bit back the word and in my excitement was conscious of tears behind my eyes. He seemed a little startled at my passionate vehemence, noting perhaps more than I gave him credit for, and alarmed lest I slipped my control (such excesses being, as I was to learn, his abomination); and so he said with a quick, almost nervous smile, "Glad to hear it; then that's all right. Can't talk any more now; I've some letters to write. Come along to-morrow evening at seven."

"That's prep, sir."

"So it is." And then he grinned and for an instant became a boy. "Well, it won't matter—for once. Cut along, now." But seeing I hesitated he added: "Yes, what is it?"

"It will be necessary to obtain leave for me to dod—er—be excused games, sir," I said hurriedly.

"Of course; mustn't do anything to upset the traditions. I'll see to it."

And see to it he did. I played no more games at Selborne, and indeed took no exercise at all except occasional walks. And during those three remaining years my health was perfect. Perhaps exercising one's gift is the best exercise of all. And I was tremendously happy; I dare say that counted, too.

It is no exaggeration to say that R. L. Sims not only solved an immediate and distressing problem for me, but made me a painter; previously I had been merely a talented amateur. And when I came to leave Selborne he gave me some sound advice about my future career.

.   .   .   .

It was perhaps this special work of mine, cutting me off from much of the school life, which was the chief reason I formed no new friendships at Selborne. Michael and I remained cronies, and when Val came along the year after us he fitted in easily, although he soon had a circle of his own into which we did not enter. Miles, by his juniority, was debarred from being with us much at school. Certainly I count my association with R. L. Sims as a friendship, and Tom Frankell and I became eventually on very friendly terms; but neither Sims, whose age and position in the school prevented it, nor Frankell, whose sporting interests closed part of his mind to me, ever occupied that place in my school life that a crony does, a place that Michael possessed since we had first gone to St. Benet's together as urchins of nine.

There were sides to Val which appealed to me and with which I was in sympathy; and this was I think mutual. But his character was more complex than mine, which is an essentially simple one; and there were those others sides to him with which I could make no contact, nor did I desire to; and it was precisely those sides or perhaps facets of his character which made him a popular figure among a coterie, and by no means a small one, which included most of the wilder spirits in the school. They were, in short, something of a rackety crowd; they were those boys to whom authority is so irksome that it becomes a matter of honour, if that is the word, to rebel either openly or covertly; coercion, and school life is little else, had the effect on them of bottling-up their energies, their vitality, their spirit, until relief could only be obtained by an explosion. Or so it is that I read them. These explosions took multiple forms, from such mild manifestations as smoking and ragging to the wilder exploits of nocturnal expeditions and visits to pubs (usually single-handed affairs) from which the roysterer frequently returned tipsy. Discovery might have entailed expulsion, but they were not discovered.

But during my last term, within a week, in fact, of my leaving Selborne, an affair happened about which there could be no concealment. It must have been pretty near the middle of July, and already the manumitting spirit of holidays was afoot in the school. For me the time was memorably exciting; I was approaching the end of my schooldays and was about to launch out on my chosen career; and I was also looking forward to a holiday which promised to be more than usually interesting, for the Farne and Conway circuses (as we called ourselves) were going to Stromness in the Orkney Islands to spend six weeks with the Greys, who had a big house there.

The first inkling we had that something was afoot was the summoning of the chief prefects of each house and the school Captain to the Head's study nearly a week before our usual end-of-the-term meeting with Mr. Clough. I, as chief of Randall's, Michael of Danton's, were present.

The Head, as was his way, came to the point immediately. "I have had an interview with the proprietor of *The Red Cow* public house at Waring." (Waring was a village about two miles from the school.) "He tells me he has had to dismiss a barmaid. The unfortunate young woman was gravid. More than one man has been associated with her; many, in fact; the matter of affiliation proceedings does not arise; but the man tells me that a Selborne boy is alleged to have been seen with her on several occasions and that the young woman has confessed to intimacy with him but refused before she left Waring to identify him or assist in any way. I feel it an unnecessary question, but I put it to you formally: Is that boy among you?" He waited a moment and, as there was no response, his face cleared and he said, "Thank you." He looked over to the Captain. "Vickers," he said, "you will call a general meeting of all prefects at seven this evening. You may have the library. Please discuss the matter and report to me at the close of the meeting. That is all now, gentlemen."

But the general meeting was not held. Shortly after tea the Head sent for Vickers and told him that the boy had been to him and confessed. He then told him who the boy was and asked him to say nothing about it for the time being.

But there is no keeping secret such matters; somehow or other they leak out to the grave embarrassment of those charged with keeping them; and by bedtime it was known throughout the school that the boy was

Val. And the fact that he did not occupy his bedroom that night clinched the matter. But none of us knew that he was sleeping in the Head's house.

Val came into my room the next morning just after breakfast, for as a chief prefect it was my privilege to have all meals except dinner in my study. He was leaving by the ten-thirty train and was wearing town clothes. He looked adult, mature, a smart young man-about-town; and this appearance lent a perhaps specious validity to his frankly-expressed view of the affair.

He sat down in one of my arm-chairs, leant back, crossed his legs, offered me a cigarette (another privilege of my office) and having lit it for me took and lit one for himself, as if by that action at that moment (for he had not that privilege) he symbolised his severance from the life of the school, of any school.

He smiled gaily at me and my heart warmed to him. Although utterly unlike Crispin, he possessed the same debonair gallantry of appearance with his slim, tall figure, his yellow fine-textured hair, and his facial beauty, about which there still remained something almost girlish.

"Chuffy gave me the option of a thrashing or expulsion. Said he was stretching a point owing to his great respect for my father and so forth. Seemed surprised and hipped when I told him I preferred expulsion. Surprises you too, Ju, eh?"

"Well, a bit. A thrashing strikes me as the lesser of two evils, although I admit," and my eyes went over his tall grown-up figure, "it's a damned humiliation. But won't the other be worse? What will Uncle Hereward——?"

He shrugged his shoulders. "Raise merry hell, of course," he said; "but mother'll put things right. As a matter of fact they needn't know anything about Dolly. Chuffy was decent enough there. He said he'd leave that to my conscience, but as far as he was concerned I was being expelled for breaking out of school at night and being on licensed premises. But I'll probably own up; to mother anyhow; queer I can tell her things I wouldn't tell the gov. But it's always been like that." He paused a moment and then, to my amazement, his eyes twinkled with merriment. "You know, Ju," he said, "it was my sense of humour dictated my choice. I really don't care twopence about a belting as a belting; the pain, I mean; and as for the humiliation, well, I don't know; can't say it'd bother me much. No, it wasn't that. But I simply couldn't stomach—my sense of humour wouldn't let me, being belted for merely doing what every man does whenever he gets the chance. Consider the humour of the situation, Ju. There would have been Chuffy lamming me good and hearty for doing the very thing he does every night, or however often married men *do* do it. No, I couldn't swallow that. You don't agree? You needn't say you do, for your phiz gives you away."

"Well, I'm afraid I don't, Val. Hardly on all fours, is it?"

"What?"

"Well—er—marriage and associating with—er—with——" I hesitated, but he laughed and cried:

"Spit it out, Ju. Don't be mealy-mouthed. With a whore. Is that it?"

"Well, yes."

"What's the difference?"

"There's such a thing as love," I said slowly.

"And the other's just lust. Love and lust. ' Love gives itself and is not bought,'" he quoted. Again he smiled into my eyes and again my heart warmed to him. "Have it that way if you like," he said, paused for a long moment and then went on slowly, and now with a touch of gravity which at first I thought might be mockery. "Ju, old boy, I'll tell you something I'd not tell any one else. And I'll tell you because I think you're a cut above the rest of us; a bit better than the average; you've kept clear of the general dirtiness. Well, old boy, I haven't. And what's more I'm dam' glad I haven't. I like it. Honestly, on my soul if I had one, there's something in me that hankers after —after—oh, well, dirt, if you like; the sordid, if that's the better word; I like whores; I do, Ju, upon my honour; they attract me, attract me just because of their whoreishness; and they have done for years; and I've hankered after their company. But it's not just whores; they're only one aspect; the bias of my mind or my spirit or whatever it is, is to the—the degraded, I suppose you'd call it. I prefer a dirty tap-room to a saloon bar; that's just a concrete way of putting it; but everything in me is apiece with that." He paused as if hesitating upon a final denuding revelation, and then said, "It'll make you sick, Ju, but I tell you that the stink of human sweat allures me; the unwashed body of a whore inflames and entices me. You don't believe me, Ju. Of course you don't. I wouldn't myself. I *don't* myself when I'm out of the range of the attraction, the the damned magnetism, I suppose. But it's God's truth, and perhaps you'll believe me if I tell you that the very thought of sleeping with some clean, shy little virgin fills me with disgust, a disgust that demands relief by shouts of laughter."

He sprang to his feet and held out both his hands and took mine. "So long, old boy," he said, smiling again, "perhaps I'll write in a day or so; perhaps not; anyway, see you at Stromness round about the twenty-second. 'Bye!" and he had gone with a clatter, leaving the room strangely quiet, strangely empty.

Chapter Five

I WONDER if I delude myself in thinking that the Orkney Islands once visited remain in one's memory with that nostalgic quality which is usually confined to thoughts of one's birthplace. If it is a delusion it is one not peculiarly my own. Sir Hereward Grey had spent a summer there when he was a boy of eleven and when, thirty years later, he passed in mental review the whole of the British Isles for the purpose of choosing a summer residence he had no doubts at all about the spot which called to him so strongly that no other seemed worth consideration; and at Stromness, on Pomona or the Mainland, he had built the big house where he and his wife, and later his children, had gone every year during the long vacation, and where I was to spend six weeks that summer, six weeks of not unmixed pleasure perhaps but for all that unforgotten and unforgettable in much the same way as the streets and lanes, the shops and houses of one's native town or village, leave bright and permanent images in the memory. Nor again was Sir Hereward's choice an idiosyncratic one, for at Stromness, at Kirkwall, at Birsay, at Ratwick on to the Isle of Hoy, and at Burwick on South Ronaldshay Island, there were other English, Scottish, Irish (and one French) families with summer residences there to which they had come again and again year after year until their babes were themselves men and women.

Do the Shetlands exercise this strange enchantment upon visitors? I do not know, although I have heard it said that once one has been to Fair Isle, that tiny speck of rocky earth midway between the Orkneys and the Shetlands, that small solitude twenty-five miles from its nearest neighbour, no other place in the world will oust it from the heart. But it was a Shetland man told me that. The Orcadians would laugh at that tale, laugh in the tolerant way in which one possessed of Eden might listen amusedly to the eulogies of a suburban garden.

They are a laughing race; or so I found them. They are of pure Scandinavian descent, as they boast, in their ever-ready and perhaps over-fond fashion of relating their history to stranger ears. They will say, with their bantering smile, "Orkney was put in pawn and never redeemed," and will then relate (every man, woman and child of them, or so it seems to me in recollection) how in 1098 (and they know the salient dates of the story as they know their own names) they became subject to the Norwegian crown and so remained until, in 1468, they were given to James III of Scotland as a security for the dowry of his wife, Margaret of Denmark, and were (and at this point of the native jest they inevitably chuckle) never redeemed from this pledge; and finally in 1590, on the marriage of the Danish Princess Anne, Denmark formally resigned all pretensions to the sovereignty of the islands. They will also tell you that they were famous in far more ancient times, were known to the old geographers, Pliny and Ptolomy, as Orcades and that many wise men (including themselves), believed and still believe them to be the fabled Fortunate Islands, dismissing the claims of the Canaries to that happy designation with the tolerant good-humour of men possessing inside information.

Sir Hereward and Lady Grey had already gone at the beginning of the third week in July, taking with them Sylvia and Alison Conway, who were school-fellows at St. Felix School, Southwold. Val followed immediately after his expulsion, wanting, as he wrote to me at Selborne a few days after he left, to get the breeze over with his father before the joint holiday began. Michael, Norrie (who was at Roedean School) and I decided to go by boat, sailing from Tilbury at eight o'clock in the morning of Saturday, July 23. The Greys all went by train to Thurso and took the boat there. Faith, my younger sister, then just turned fourteen, had gone into Cornwall with the family of a school friend, and Crispin and Avis our cousins had joined the Kendalls (at John's invitation) for a cruising holiday on *The Gallipot* and there was some talk of them calling at Stromness. John was now in his third year at Osborne Naval College. Crispin had been at Balliol a year; writing to me just before they joined *The Gallipot* at Newhaven he said there was a possibility Piers Rowland might also be with them. Piers was at Wadham and was already making some-thing of a stir in the small academic world of Oxford. Miles would have been with one or other of the parties but Major Conway was home on furlough from India and he and "Aunt" Jenny were having their first holiday together for five years and had taken Miles with them to the South of France.

As far as Aberdeen the trip was a pleasant one. Norrie had just turned sixteen but looked older and her "quiet grey-eyed homeliness" (the phrase was Aunt Jenny's and rather apt) was apparently very much to Michael's liking. He was now as big as he was going to be and it was a pretty respectable size, in the neighbourhood of six feet, broad and deep-chested; he could give me an inch and a stone, and I too was to grow no more; indeed my weight to-day is considerably less than it was then.

They had always got on well together as children and now they seemed to find each other so congenial that during those thirty hours between Tilbury and Aberdeen I was left to amuse myself, which was precisely what I desired, and I spent most of the time painting on deck until after we passed the Firth of Forth, when the weather changed, the wind getting up and the sea rising so choppily that painting became impossible. R. L. Sims had that Spring sent in three pictures for the Royal Academy Exhibition and he had suggested I should try my luck with an oil and a tempera. His three were accepted and, to my surprise and excitement, my oil. He warned me that acceptance did not necessarily mean hanging and so I was more or less armed against the disappointment when my oil was crowded out, as was one of his. But I did not greatly care; my work had been considered acceptable in the eyes of painters of recognised achievement and I looked upon this early recognition (for I was only eighteen) as a promising augury for my future. I was not going to the university but first to The Slade for a year and afterwards, on Sim's advice, to the Carsten Raven atelier in Paris.

We reached Aberdeen shortly after two o'clock on the Sunday afternoon and the weather was by then very unpleasant, rain falling, a strong wind and a nasty sea. But it was only the rain which bothered us for we were good sailors, had never been sea-sick and considered ourselves immune; we were to learn the rareness of immunity.

There was a boat leaving at seven that evening for Stromness and another at nine the next morning. We were in no great hurry and in view of the rain decided to wait for the morning and the chance of a sunny passage.

We certainly had the sun but its presence did little to mitigate our woes, possibly indeed adding to them by the mockery of contrast. I think if we had known what lay ahead of us we should have waited another day. It must have been our cocksuredness in our sea-legs which decided us to go ahead, for when we went down to the docks after breakfast we had to fight our way against a gale and the pounding of the heavy seas was like continuous thunder. More ominous still, had we but known, our boat, the S.S. *Faroe*, a clumsy pot-bellied little five-hundred-tonner, was three hours late in sailing and it being so near luncheon time we immediately went into the saloon and stowed away a big meal, the best preventive of sea-sickness, according to all we had heard. We retained faith in that hypothesis barely half an hour, and it was the last morsel we had on board. By the time Aberdeen was thirty miles astern, there was not one passenger of the fifty or so who was not down. That ubiquitous voyager whose prehensile finger awaits in every corner of the world to hook an auditor while he tells how he was the only one not sick during some terrific passage was certainly not aboard our wretched tub. By the time we reached the Pentland Firth a number of the crew were snatching odd moments to be sick, while most of the passengers had dropped off into an uneasy and intermittent sleep of exhaustion. I have been on most of the world's seas since then but I do not recollect any experience to match that night-crossing of the Pentland Firth. The *Faroe* behaved like some wild, frantic, tortured creature in a nightmare. Is there any orchestration of sound more appalling, more unutterably miserable and frightening, than the vile noises of vomiting, the hawking and groaning, the crying of children, the howl of the wind, the thud of engines, the creaking of timbers, the clatter of flung gear and the crashing of crockery?

And suddenly I seemed to wake out of this bedlam into calm, or comparative calm; we were in Scapa Flow. I got up, washed, drank some water and went up on deck. It was barely an hour after midnight yet already the sky along the eastern horizon was glimmering with a wan light. On deck half a dozen sailors were mopping and sweeping, all of them smoking pipes.

A hand took me by the shoulder and a deep voice said, "Come and have a drink." I turned and saw an immensely tall and rather stout man wearing a long rough tweed ulster and a cap to match. His face was red and weather-beaten and he wore a brown clipped moustache and a close-trimmed pointed beard.

I shook my head. "No, thanks," I said; "I've just had some water and I don't feel keen on anything else now. Pretty tough passage."

He smiled faintly. "The toughest I've known and I've done some tough ones. And never been sick before." His smile vanished abruptly. "That poor young thing died," he said, and noting my expression he explained that a young woman in the second-class, or steerage, had given birth to a baby during her violent sickness and had died from exhaustion. "She was travelling alone," he said, rasping his finger through his beard; "scandal she was allowed to; and no doctor aboard; all devolved on the Captain. Damnable business altogether. Well, I feel like a peg; sure you won't? All right." He turned to go below and then looked over his shoulder. "The babe's all right," he said rapidly and disappeared jerkily.

I leant against the rail and watched the eastern light broadening fast, my mind tossing up into my consciousness a continual jetsam of disconnected thoughts. I was half-aware of some one at my side and then Norrie laughed softly and said, "You look the picture of misery; still feeling sick?"

"Do I?" I said, and smiled; "no; I'm fine; what a grand morning."

"We're nearly in, aren't we?"

"About half an hour, I should think."

"What's worrying you?"

"Nothing's worrying me, Norrie; except life."

She laughed. "What! on a morning like this?"

And so I told her about the dead young mother. "There's something damnably wrong somewhere, Norrie," I ended sententiously; "why should birth cost a life? It's a natural process."

Norrie regarded me thoughtfully. She had long

ago decided on medicine as a career and was already
studying to that end. "It was the sea-sickness, wasn't
it," she said slowly, "rather than the birth."

I shrugged my shoulders. "I dare say; but thousands
of woman die of it every year. D'you know, Norrie,
I'd never thought about it before; the—the murderous-
ness of birth, I mean. It's really the first——" but
she grasped my shoulder and swung me round and
cried out gaily, "Oh, look!" And then she laughed and
pushed her blown hair away from her eyes and linking
her arm in mine said, "Isn't it lovely; I wish Michael
would come."

It was indeed a sight to take the eye and fill the
heart, Stromness in the dawn of a summer morning. I
was to paint it many times and it was to form the
background to one of my pictures, Ultima Thule,
purchased by the Chantry Bequest in 1923. I can close
my eyes and see it as clearly as I then saw it. But I
hesitate to sift out words to make that picture for you
and it is a hesitation based on the knowledge that by
means of the written word alone no man may impart
to another the full beauty of something which has
moved him. But there it was, clusters of grey little
houses scattered about the hillside in a wide arc above
the small harbour; a dozen boats or so; a tiny brick
jetty with a flagstaff upon whose truck a sea-gull
perched; and over all the newly-risen sun sparkling
on the faintly-wind-rippled water. That is the enduring
picture in my mind, always the same, even to the sea-
gull, head to wind, perched upon the flagstaff truck.

But memory is, perhaps luckily, subject to the spell
of other things besides beauty; and closely linked
in my memory with the loveliness of that morning

picture is a grosser matter. But how tremendously enjoyable it was, that breakfast to which we sat down in the Greys' house *Graemsay* less than an hour later and to which we brought appetites made ravenous by the sea-scour of our bellies. Lady Grey and Val came downstairs to sit and gossip with us as we ate. And how we ate! and what we ate! porridge, ham and eggs, fish not an hour out of the nets (as Val told us), toast and butter and marmalade and little flat floury three-cornered scones that incited repletion to one more and yet one more, until even gluttony might well have fled shamefaced. And then, suddenly overcome with a vast drowsiness, we went to bed and slept till nearly noon, when we were unceremoniously dragged out by the others for a swim and returned for a mighty luncheon. Indeed, in retrospect, that holiday seems compact of mighty meals with delicious unfamiliar dishes, or familiar ones strangely yet appetisingly cooked.

It was obvious to me at that memorable first breakfast that Val had made his peace with his people; he looked radiantly happy and with his yellow hair tumbled, and wearing an old grey sweater and a pair of slacks, he seemed to have shed a year or two of his age and all his cynicism and was become again a schoolboy. I could not believe as I glanced ever and again from my plate to his animated face, and listened to his light gay chatter, that he was the smart young man-about-town who but a week ago had sat in my room at Selborne and so startlingly, so nakedly, bared his heart to me.

We bathed from the Greys' small yacht *Chloe*, a trim five-tonner anchored about six hundred yards from the shore. It was about nine months since I had seen either Sylvia or Alison and I was struck by their young grace and beauty and by the contrast too between Sylvia's fair skin, ash-gold hair and laughing vivacity, and the grave sweetness of Alison with her dark hair, brown eyes, her fine features and a certain quality of stillness about all her movements. How contradictory that sounds and perhaps how foolish. And yet it is true; about every movement she made there was a quiet gracefulness which had the effect of stillness. Words, words; how feebly they serve my purpose. But where my pen fails my brush has succeeded, as a dozen pictures of Alison Conway (one painted on that very holiday) bear witness. And one, perhaps the best of all (or so I thought and would not part with it), painted only five years ago, is facing me where I write in this little room. And in it, caught by my brush, is all that grave loveliness, that gracious quietness, of which I have sought to tell you and failed.

This is not the book of that holiday, no daily record of all we saw and did. A peak or two and a few hillocks are all I feel solidly justify their noting; and to some even of these few I perhaps ascribe an importance, if but a small one, they did not possess. But they must possess it to me, to my intuition, else they would not so stand out from all the rest.

The second largest island of the Orkneys is Hoy, separated from Pomona by Hoy Sound which Graemsay Island splits into two channels, each about a mile and a half wide. Hoy, viewed from Stromness on a bright day (and very bright and intensely clear most of the summer days are), seems within easy swimming reach; but few swimmers have made the crossing, for currents are bad and the sweep of tidal water straight from the Atlantic into the neck of the sound irresistible.

By its proximity to Stromness Hoy was clearly the first choice for a picnic; but it had another claim to interest in the tall, black, isolated rock poking up out of the sea and called the Old Man of Hoy. Imagine the Cenotaph in Whitehall three times taller, tapering to the base rather than the summit, and almost black in colour, and you have a rough picture of the Old Man. Sooner or later every Orcadian says to the visitor, "Have you seen the Old Man of Hoy?" If your answer is a negative one and your stay already longer than a week you will be regarded as having treated your hosts with contumely; and they are all your hosts, wherever you happen to be, ready to offer you the hospitality of a rest and a meal at any hour of the day or night; and in high summer so little is there of night that you may find yourself breakfasting at 3.0 a.m., and lunching at 9.0; you call a meal by whatever name takes your fancy, irrespective of the clock.

And so about a week after our arrival Val, Michael, Norrie, Sylvia, Alison and I set off in *Chloe* for a day on Hoy. Val was a chancy hand with a boat and had never taken to the sport; Michael was not much better; Norrie fairly good but with no knowledge of the finer points of sailing. I was therefore skipper and Sir Hereward paid me the compliment of saying that he had watched my handling of *Chloe* for some days and was satisfied she was safe in my hands. He said this

while we stood alone looking out through the windows
of the sunny breakfast-room just before we set off.
I was to wish before the day was out that he had said
it before the others, for any doubt of my ability,
perceived in the eyes of others, does not, as it does with
some, put me on my mettle; rather does it drain away
my confidence, confusing and troubling me, so that
I commit errors impossible to me in normal circumstances.

We took plenty of provender with us and proposed
to skirt the island to the north-west, passing the Old
Man, rounding Rora Head, mooring *Chloe* in the tiny
natural harbour of Rackwick, and going ashore in the
dinghy to begin our explorations, taking the provender
and our swimming things with us in rucksacks carried
by the men of the party; for if we had any secret
doubts about our manhood at home we were indubit-
ably men in Orkney where boys of sixteen were,
we noticed with some pride, considered grown-up,
and where urchins of ten and eleven smoked their
briar pipes with all the nonchalance of habit.

It was a perfect day for sailing, bright and sunny,
and although if I had been alone I should have preferred more wind there was, I considered, quite enough
in view of my responsibility; what there was blew
steadily from the north-west so that we were able
to set a fairly straight course for our destination. It was
Val's programme and being familiar with the coast he
acted as a sort of combined navigating officer and
look-out man. He had brought his sketch-book, I my
easel and paints.

We reached Rackwick about ten o'clock and from
there, having plugged along on foot over the rocks to

the Old Man, or as near as we could get to him, Val led us after some rather difficult climbing down to a small beach shut in by the rocks on three sides, and suggested a rest, swimming and a meal. It was a shallow basin rather than a beach, for the bottom was smooth, flat, pale-grey rock. The water was so clear and still that there was full visibility to the bottom even in places where the depth was as much as five or six fathoms. It was a perfect swimming place and we had it to ourselves; we had not in fact, after leaving Rackwick, met any live thing on two legs or four, and down there in that lovely basin we felt as delightfully isolated as if we were the sole little community in the world.

The three girls went a little distance off behind a ledge of rock to undress and Val and Michael began throwing off their things. I began to set up my easel.

"Come on, Ju," Val said, dragging his tennis shirt over his head; "by God! I'm in a muck-sweat."

"I'm not bathing," I said, shifting my tripod about on the uneven surface to find a flat place.

"You're not!" Val exclaimed; and Michael stopped a moment, his swimming suit crumpled about his loins, and stared at me. "Feeling off colour?" he asked.

"No," I replied; "just don't want to; don't feel like it; I'm going to make some colour notes." I smiled and added, "I'll do one of all of you in the water as a first sketch for a picture to be called Children Romping."

"Oh, but dam' it all, Ju," Val said slowly, massaging his long slim legs, "you must come in. Look at the water. Mean to tell us you aren't dying for a plunge after all that mountain-goat business?"

I smiled again. "I'd rather paint."

"But you can paint afterwards," Michael said, regarding me in a puzzled frowning way, which made him look almost ludicrously boyish.

"You'd be all out by then."

"We'd stay in. Come on; the girls 'll be here in a minute."

I shook my head. "You wouldn't," I said; "water's too cold. Now dry up for God's sake both of you. I just don't want to. And here are the girls and I suppose I'm in for more blether about it." And to forestall their questioning I sang out to the approaching little group, "You needn't wait for me; I'm not going in; I want to paint you all. In with you and try to survive the temperature long enough for me to do two or three sketches." To my relief the girls made no attempt to persuade me and in another second, five almost simultaneous splashes marked their swift headers from the rocks.

They came out some twenty minutes or so later and stood looking at five or six impressions I had done quickly in colour and which were lying on the rocks to dry. I watched Val as he regarded them, arms akimbo, head exaggeratedly cocked on one side, and a grin upon his lips. I envied his draughtsmanship and thought the grin betokened a derisive criticism. But he only said, "Dam' good, Ju; you'll be P.R.A. one of these days." And picking up a towel he added to the girls, "hurry up, you fillies; let's have some grub; I'm famishing."

"We're not fillies," Sylvia said; "it's a horrid word."

"Highest compliment I know," Val smiled; "if there's anything more graceful than a young filly show it me." He screwed up his face. "You're as lovely as the three graces; will that suit? But do buck up, there's good children."

The meal over and our cigarettes smoked, Val who seemed restlessly unable to settle down to loafing, suggested exploring the island. The others were willing enough but I preferred to paint; and they presently went off in one party, giving me a final mocking halloo from the summit of the rocky slope before they disappeared inland. "We'll give you an hour for art," Michael had said, "and then we'll come back for you."

Left to myself I smoked a couple of cigarettes and then, finding the water suddenly enticing, I undressed and went in for a swim. I lay about for some time afterwards drying in the sun; and then, looking at my watch found I had been alone nearly an hour. I dressed hurriedly, contemplated a blank board on my easel, fingered my paint and suddenly decided to climb up to the top to see if the others were in sight. But there was no one to be seen and I set off slowly, wandering haphazardly, unmindful of direction. I found a path after a while and followed it until it neared the cliff edge when I lay down in the short stiff grass. On an impulse I moved to the extreme edge and looked over and for a full minute stared down at a small beach some hundred or so feet below but a little to the side and over which the cliff hung like a pent-house. Down there below, just visible beyond the angle of the overhanging cliff, Val and Norrie were dancing. They were both naked and the strangeness of the spectacle held me there like Paul Pry at a keyhole. Had they been embraced or dancing together I might have been startled but no more; but there was a queer unnatural quality about the scene which I found unpleasantly disturbing, for they were dancing in a slow, elaborate sort of rhythmic motion, separated by a considerable distance from each other, and with so preoccupied an air as to suggest each was oblivious of the other's presence. And abruptly I realised what I was doing and wriggled myself backward until I could safely stand upright, when I set off hurriedly back to the other beach. I found it with little trouble although I had walked much farther than I had any idea of and by the time I got back to my things nearly three-quarters of an hour had elapsed since I had set off. I quite expected to find Michael and the two younger girls there but they were not, and I picked up my paints and began working at the blank board. But my mind was not in my brush; nor could I see the scene before me; instead, merging into what was being presented to my physical vision—the quiet sea, the basin with its deep translucent water and the surrounding rocks—was the picture of Val and Norrie gyrating slowly in grotesque rhythmical motion which, as I watched it now in recollection, seemed fantastic, ludicrous and somehow, although I thrust away the thought as nonsense, unpleasant to the point of nastiness. And, as if it were in some fashion linked up with it, there invaded my mind again and again the picture of Val sitting in my room at Selborne that morning and unburdening himself (or was it boasting) of his secret, of that irresistible attraction for him of the dirty and the sordid. I thought of what I had read of the old beliefs in possession by devils, and for a while that unhappy superstition which had been responsible for so much inhuman torture inflicted upon the unbalanced, the hysterical and the insane, seemed almost credible; but it was a credibility due to the fact that the mere surface of my mind was engaged, and realising suddenly how my thoughts were drifting about in a sort of formless fog I laughed and put the old tales back into the dark little cupboard where they belonged. But there was no dismissing Val; no putting him into a cupboard and locking the door on him; he was here out in the open, a living being with powers and potentialities; some one demanding perhaps to be understood; and I could not understand; a problem demanding solution; and I could not find one; all I could do was to repeat tritely to myself "There are more things in heaven and earth, Horatio, than are dreamed of in your philosophy" and try to persuade myself that this was, if not an explanation, a clarification. But I knew that I was merely dodging, sheltering, behind words—and not even my own words.

And then there came a hail in Val's voice and a coo-ee in Norrie's and I jumped up to find them scrambling down the rocks towards me.

"You were asleep," Norrie said, smiling.

"I wasn't; merely drowsing and browsing; where are the others?"

They both shook their heads and Val said, "If they're scrambling about all this time the girls will be dead."

"Michael wouldn't do that," Norrie said; "they're probably resting at a farm or have found up something exciting." She smiled over to Val. "Is there anything in Hoy really thrilling?"

He smiled back at her, screwing up his nose and eyes, but made no reply. Instead, he walked away, hoisted himself up the rocks, and began to leap from one to another round the rim of the basin. Wet patches still marked where the tide had receded and some of these were made slippery with sea-moss. Suddenly his feet went from under him and he half toppled and half dived into the deep water. We jumped to our feet, laughing; but he came to the surface, rolled over on his back with staring eyes and went down again. Norrie screamed and would have plunged in but I pushed her away and saying "must have hit his head" I flung off my shirt, went in with a splash and in a few strokes reached him as he came up again. As I put my hands under his arms to get him over he grimaced at me, spat out a mouthful of water and said, with affected surprise, "What made you come in?"

I was momentarily furious and snapped at him, "Dam' your idea of a joke!" and swimming back climbed out, Val a few paces behind me. Norrie, who was now laughing, but looked, I thought, a bit ashen about the mouth, said, "It was too bad, Val."

He pulled off his shirt and began to wring it out. "If you think I went in purposely," he said with a grin, "you must have a poor opinion of my abilities as a joker; but once in I remembered poor old Ju hadn't had a swim and the rest followed."

I saw their glances cross and as they both smiled Norrie said darkly, "That makes it even worse." And then they both laughed as if they shared a secret joke.

I soon learnt what it was. As we sat leaning against the rocks with towels round us, while our clothes dried in the sun and Norrie went off to look for the others, I said, "So I had a swim after all, Val, thanks to you, dam' your eyes."

He turned his head a little towards me and watched me through his lashes, a faint smile on his lips. "Two," he said; "two, old boy." And as I stared at him he went on, "two swims, I mean." He laughed, opened his eyes wide and looking at me impudently said, "Norrie and I watched you from the top of the cliff; I was coming back for my sketch-book." He watched my face closely. "You're a queer bird, Ju."

Embarrassment and a sense almost of fear blurred my mind and in my groping I blurted out, "And I saw you and Norrie."

"You saw what, old boy?" his voice drawling languidly.

I might perhaps have drawn back then but I went on, "I saw you and Norrie dancing naked."

"How did it look?"

"Dammit all, Val," I began but he flapped his towel at me and said, "Don't get hot; nakedness isn't worrying you, is it? a painter an' all an' all."

"Hang it," I said, "Norrie's my sister and she's only sixteen."

At this his manner changed and he leaned towards me. "It was just a joke, Ju, and I persuaded her; I told her a lot of lies about a dance to Pan and she at last took it seriously and by the time I'd got her to agree that there was nothing in nakedness for sensible people like us to be ashamed of she was willing enough. But she insisted we kept to our own—er—orbits, as you must have seen we very strictly did." He paused, but I said nothing. I was watching his face, my mind more busy with its changing expressions than with the words he was speaking; and indeed as he spoke the affair seemed to lose its importance and to be just what he was saying it was, a joke. But as if my silence and my watching eyes had altered the drift of his deeper thoughts, those thoughts behind and so different from the words being spoken, his own eyes turned towards me suddenly clouded, and his fleeting expressions became fixed into one I had seen before, and he spoke with a sort of brooding flippancy. "She's about as innocent as a lamb." And then, grinning and slapping my bare shoulder he added, the grin a sneer for all his bonhomie, "and little white lambs don't appeal to me, Ju, as I've told you before."

A few moments later we heard Norrie's Coo-ee and she and Michael with the two youngsters in tow came scrambling down to us. Both Sylvia and Alison were tired out; they had not been at a farm nor had they found anything exciting; Sylvia, as knowing the island, had been guide to their little party, had lost the way (easy enough in Hoy with its few paths and fewer roads) and for the last two hours they had been engaged in finding it again. And there was still the scramble over rocks to Rackwick to be done. "The sky's looking horrid," Sylvia said to Val; "oughtn't we to go?"

"Our duds aren't dry yet," he said; "how do you mean, horrid?"

"Well, all crowding up with clouds over Mainland."

Val grimaced and Michael said, "Wind's getting up."

Val looked at me. "We'll skin out, I think." he
said; "wet togs or not." He turned to the others.
"You get along to Rackwick," he said, "and we'll
catch you up."

At Rackwick there was a bit of a popple on the sea
and the wind was stronger, but nothing, I thought,
to worry about; and we were soon aboard *Chloe* and
making for Rora Head. "Wind's veered a bit," I said.
Val nodded, "Pretty nearly due west; we'll get a
slapping as soon as we get round the Head."

It was nearer a bludgeoning than a slapping; the
popple had become a procession of nasty little waves
and the wind seemed getting stronger every minute.
By the time we hummed by the Old Man the sun had
disappeared behind a leaden wrack and in the tacks
our gun'le disappeared hissingly, the spray soaked
us, and the younger girls squealed with fright at the
angle of the boat. I smiled at them reassuringly, but
perhaps a trifle wanly. So far things were not too
bad but it was clearly going to get worse and already
I could feel the doubts and fears assailing them as to
my seamanship. The sea continued to get nastier and
I suggested to Val we should go round by Graemsay
Island, which would treble the distance but would be
in comparatively protected water.

He shook his head. "Take too long. And this is
going to blow up to something pretty foul within
a few hours. And if we were not home by then they'd
be in no end of a stew. We'll go straight across the
sound; it'll be a fair wind by then; *Chloe's* all right;
like me to take her for a spell?"

I shook my head and we scudded on. By now we
were all thoroughly wet and chilled. Presently Main-

land came into view round the curve of the coast. "Half an hour 'll see us in with this wind," Val said; but no one responded; and as I looked across the sound and noted the ugly seas, sheer funk suddenly turned my stomach sickeningly. I felt Val's decision was a mad folly and was inclined to ignore it and go my own way. The end of a tack brought us round an elbow of the coast so that the wind was almost dead astern and *Chloe* heeled over under a tremendous gust till we shipped water over the gun'le and I thought for one unnerving instant that we were over. Even Norrie uttered a gasp and Alison cried out, "Oh, if we had Crispin!" which moved Michael to snap at her savagely, "Shut up! you little fool, Crispin's not in the same street as Ju," which had the effect of giving me back my nerve and restoring my confidence, while it set Alison crying softly, hiding her face and with her arms clutching Norrie. It must have been the first time in her life she had ever heard that note in her brother's voice, and it frightened her more than the sea.

I was now again in possession of myself; I felt supremely confident and would have refused a suggestion from Val that we should go by the longer route. We were hissing along at a great rate but soaked and chilled as I was so great an exhilaration came over me that I began to laugh and then to shout a shanty at the top of my voice. I no longer had any fear or doubt; I knew nothing was going to happen and in those exalted moments I would have put *Chloe's* bow at an Atlantic roller. I felt then as I suppose brave men always feel, supremely confident of the issue, utterly indifferent to the encompassing peril. Never again was I to conquer so completely the inadequacy of my flesh, the frailty of my spirit.

As some twenty-five minutes or so later we walked slowly and stiffly from the quayside up the lane towards the Greys' house Alison came beside me and took my arm and looked up into my face and said softly, "I did not mean that, Julian; I—I was so frightened." I took her cold little frog of a hand in mine and glanced down at her with a smile. Her eyes were wet and the smile she gave me wan and tremulous. But her glance held and kept mine a long moment and with an overwhelming suddenness I loved her.

In all the years since I have not ceased to love you, Alison.

There occurred a few days later one of those odd events of pure chance which lend support to the view that human life is a haphazard business without reason behind it and without meaning; and further, that as is human life so is the whole universe; that cosmogony rests ultimately upon a chemical accident, a mere fluke, and upon no fixed and ordered law. There are people who can look back upon their lives and see them as a pattern, orderly, complete, and designed. I think they delude themselves. My own life has no such pattern, and if I may judge from what I have seen of the lives of others of my circle they are equally the result of blind hazard. That some philosophers affirm that it is merely the inadequacy of the human mind which interprets inscrutable purpose as blind hazard seems to me just a parading of words to hide an unpalatable truth, somewhat analogous to the drum beaten by the quack's assistant as the tooth is drawn. I think Edward Fitzgerald said once for all everything needful to be said concerning philosophics:

> *Myself when young did eagerly frequent*
> *Doctor and sage and heard great argument*
> *About it and about but evermore*
> *Came out by the same door as in I went.*

There was a small steamer, the *Hoy Head*, which ran every day between Mainland and Hoy, and one morning after breakfast Val said he was going to do the return trip to make some sketches of any of the crew or passengers who took his eye. He suggested if I'd nothing else to do I should accompany him. I agreed and we went off together. I have forgotten what the others were doing.

We did not land on Hoy but came straight back. A number of passengers had been waiting at Hoy for the boat and among them was a man who because of his tremendous build attracted considerable attention. He was quite six and a half feet in height and very broad and immediately he loomed up out of the crowd I recognised him as the man who had asked me to have a drink with him as we were nearing Stromness on the morning of our arrival. Val noticed him and said to me, "Wonder who he is; grand-looking old cock, isn't he! By George! do you see what he's doing? Knitting! By God! what with his bulk, the cut of his noble jib and his hobby he's a gift. This has been a dud trip as far as anything worth drawing's concerned, but he'll make up for it."

For the next ten minutes or so, Val prowled about

stalking the knitting giant, who made the circuit of the steamer's small deck about once a minute. After a while Val came back to me and showed me a half-dozen or so sketches so slick and clever that envy smeared my admiration with its beastly fingers. A voice (one I instantly recognised) behind us said, "May I be permitted a glimpse or is that the unpardonable intrusion?" and we both turned to find the big man smiling down at us amiably. Val laughed, gave him the sketch-book, and told him he was welcome to look through it. Having done this he introduced himself as John Stone, a Londoner of Orcadian stock, and asked who we were. When we got off the boat he said he should very much like to call on Sir Hereward and Lady Grey during his tour and Val, in his casual but engaging fashion, said he was sure they would be delighted.

He did call about a week later, had luncheon with us all and stayed until just before tea. He was a good talker and entertained us with tales of his adventures over the globe, for he had been something of a traveller.

Before he left he took Val aside, asked him about his plans and ambitions and hearing that his intention was to make an immediate attack upon Fleet Street with his pencil he disclosed the rather extraordinary information (or so it seemed to us) that he was the controlling power (financially) behind that bright little humorous weekly *Touch and Go*, gave Val a note of introduction to its art editor, Lawson Gale; and said he would also have a talk with Gale on his return to Town. Thus was Val launched upon Fleet Street without any of the struggles and disappointments which have attended the early careers of equally fine black-and-white artists. A piece of sheer luck, he always called it himself and he was not given to the pretence of belittling his own powers and merits; indeed he usually went on to point out, quite truthfully, that what persuaded Gale to accept his work and afterwards to give him the weekly centre-page cartoon was his ability; that was the baited hook; the luck was the casting of the line in Gale's direction; and this was entirely due to the good offices of the big man encountered so haphazardly that morning upon that little tub of a steamer the *Hoy Head*.

About the middle of August *The Gallipot* dropped anchor in Stromness Harbour and the Kendall horde descended upon *Graemsay*, which for the remaining month of the holiday shared with the smack the hospitalities. She arrived in the afternoon and that evening everybody crowded into her dining-saloon for dinner and afterwards we lounged about smoking and gossiping over our affairs, past, present and future. But it was to Piers Rowland that all eyes were continually turning, all ears listening. Big, dark and handsome, and looking more than his twenty-one years, he was the dominant figure, as he always was in any surroundings. Most of the men present would have stood out in a crowd as personalities, would have taken the eye and held the attention: Sir Hereward Grey's aloof austerity and fine presence; Dr. Luke Kendall's noisy vitality and almost piratical appearance; Crispin with his marble-white face and burning blue eyes; Val's strange mocking languid beauty; the apple-cheeked sturdiness of John Kendall; and the

wholesome good-looking bigness of Michael. But
Piers Rowland took the colour from all of them; he
made them seem second-rate, commonplace; he
levelled them all down; gave to each of them something of the effect of being unnoticed units in a crowd.
Perhaps I exaggerate, but the impression remains
very vividly of Piers holding the centre of the stage,
the spot-light over him, and the rest of us a sort of
retinue of dim figures coming and going about him.
And certainly, in the girls' eyes, he was the sun of the
system of which we were merely the planets. That
I have no doubt about whatever, but why it should
have been I do not know. It was not appearance,
for both Crispin and Val were more striking-looking;
not achievement, for while Piers was, it is true, making
something of a stir at Oxford, Crispin was a prominent
member of the O.U.D.S. and more, far more, had had
a one-act play put on as a curtain raiser at The Haymarket; there was Val's *Touch and Go* business still
rather in the clouds but investing him already with
something of the halo of genius; there were Michael's
poems which had appeared in the *Pall Mall Gazette*;
there was John's fine dignity as a naval officer—he
was just posted as a midshipman to H.M.S. *Acheron*
and was, he said, volunteering for the submarine
service; and, if I may lug it in as a tail-piece, there
was my picture accepted by the Royal Academy that
year. Small things all of them, no doubt, but still
notable achievements for a lot of youngsters. And
were there not into the bargain, Sir Hereward's
prestige as a Judge of Assize, and Uncle Luke's exploits
with the old *Gallipot*? But in comparison these were
little even to ourselves and still less in the eyes of the

girls. Piers, as I say, was the sun; the rest of us re-
volved about him.

Nor were the girls fluffy and indiscriminating
nincompoops; there was no soothing our hurt
vanities (if they were hurt) in that way. All had
something in the way of achievement to their credit.
Norrie was gobbling up prizes at Roedean, and a
career of distinction was plainly in front of her;
Avis was writing stories and had had one published
in *Tit-Bits*; Nan was stage-mad and was already one
of the star pupils at the famous Granville-Forbes
School of Dramatic Art. And Alison and Sylvia were
by no means ordinary youngsters.

No, I am not deluding myself; nor am I writing
with a pen influenced by the knowledge of future
years; Piers Rowland stood out head and shoulders
above us all; and he would have done so in any
company, higher or lower than ours. He could mix
anywhere; but wherever he was, pot-house or palace
(and although alliteration suggests the antithesis it is
true enough), he was the centre of interest.

There was a public-house abutting upon the harbour
and there, every day before luncheon, Piers, Michael,
Crispin, Val and I used to go for a schooner (or perhaps
two) of beer; a schooner was, I think, two-thirds of a
pint. It was a long bar at which everybody stood up
to drink and it was usually crowded with men off
the trawlers from the Dogger. One morning about
a week after *The Gallipot's* arrival we were drinking
our beer, jostled and elbowed by a score or so of these
big hefty fishermen, when Piers began playing with
Crispin at putting the hand down. It is a common
schoolboy game for two; each rests an elbow on the

table and intertwining fingers tries to force down the hand of his opponent. Crispin was no match for Piers nor, when we tried, were Val, Michael and I. A number of the men from the trawlers gathered round and Piers invited them to a trial of strength and in a few minutes had put down the hands of six or seven of them in quick succession. And within a few more minutes he was the centre of them all, beating one after the other (much of it was perhaps knack although he was tremendously strong), laughing with them, standing them drinks, and being stood drinks in return. He must have put away seven or eight schooners in the twenty minutes or so before we came out but he was quite unaffected by it (and it was potent beer in those days) and when we sat down with the Greys a few minutes later he showed not the faintest trace of having just been engaged in a trial of strength, of which the drinking was by no means the less arduous, just as it had plainly been the one the men were reckoning on to beat him. Whenever afterwards he went into the bar he was welcomed by hearty greetings, laughter and invitations to drink. Just a pot-house affair admittedly but he dominated it; he was the central figure; the rest were the supporting crowd; the supers to his leading part.

A dance in a fishing smack sounds grotesque to those accustomed to acres of floor space but there is in fact plenty of room, and on a warm summer night with only the riding-lights for illumination they can be very and intimately enjoyable, with a fair amount of give and take and a wary eye for deck fixtures. We held several, impromptu little affairs suddenly suggested on the spur of the moment; and after one of these, quite early in September it must have been, we were all lounging on deck smoking when Piers said lazily, "A swim would make a perfect close to a jolly night."

Before any of the others could speak Val said quickly, "Let's make it a race, men only."

"What about us?" Avis asked.

"You can give the prizes," Crispin laughed; "grand idea, Val; what's the course?"

"Round Laing's *Althea*," Val said pointing; "about six hundred yards there and back. You coming, Father?"

"I'm not, my boy!" Sir Hereward laughed; "I'll be time-keeper and Dr. Kendall can be starter unless he's set on competing."

"Not after the supper I've eaten!" Uncle Luke chuckled; "I'll get my revolver; no back-sliders, I hope," glancing round at the group of us about the wheel.

I did not feel any great keenness but I had no strong objections and the six of us were about to troop below when Michael suggested it would add to the fun if we swam as we were, in flannels, but without our pumps.

This being acclaimed as "Grand" we were within a few minutes lined up somewhat precariously balanced on the bulwarks waiting for the shot. The revolver cracked with startling loudness and we caught the echo ricochetting round the harbour as we came up from our dives. Before we had gone a hundred yards we were well strung out, faintly audible to each other but invisible. Another hundred yards and a sharp stabbing pain ran down my right leg and all the muscles seemed to contract into a hard lump in my thigh. I had had cramp before but never so sharply and with so swiftly draining an effect upon my strength. I suppressed a cry, turned over on my back and floated. I could see the riding-lights of *Althea* and once or twice thought I heard some one swimming towards me. The tide was clearly taking me to the right of the turning-point but my hatred of a humiliating rescue, perhaps by Piers or, worse, by Crispin, momentarily overcame my fear and I let myself drift, hoping the iron-like contraction of my muscles would soon pass and that I could at least get back under my own steam.

But the pain grew more intense and began to pass upward into my belly muscles, and the chill of the water (rarely over 55° round the Orkneys, and certainly at one o'clock in the morning considerably less), was slowly creeping over me. *Althea* was now two hundred yards away to my left; and beyond me, in the direction of my drift, was a great expanse of dark water uncheered by any lights. I regretted my folly in not singing out for help; but I still kept silent; I was suddenly overwhelmed with panic, turned over, struck out wildly, was gripped with pain and nausea and went under. I came quickly to the surface and again floated, my pain easier, my thigh feeling a little freer; but I dared not attempt swimming and kept still, drifting it seemed to me rapidly on the tide into the blackness ahead. I was intensely miserably cold. And suddenly, except for a faint not unpleasant numbness, all sensation left me and I found myself drowsily wondering how long this would last, what would be the end of it and, incredibly, not caring at all.

That was my last conscious thought; I didn't care; not a bit; it did not seem to matter at all; if this were dying how easy it was and how great a folly the dread of it.

But my next sensations were intolerably unpleasant. I was retching violently, shivering uncontrollably, my feet beating a spasmodic tattoo upon something particularly hard, my head held in a constrained position and a burning sensation in my lips and throat. I wanted to thrust things away with my hands, to shout resentful, threatening words, but found I could not; and then a warm drowsiness came in waves over me and I surrendered to it utterly.

I woke and looked round me; I was in the small cabin used by Uncle Luke and Aunt Olive, and the sunshine was bright over everything. My wrist-watch was gone, my body was naked, the bed piled with blankets, and a hot bottle at my feet. There was no clock in the room and I could make no guess at the time, nor were there any sounds overhead to give me a clue.

I must have lain there awake half an hour, my body deliciously comfortable, but my mind fretted with a single question: who had put me to bed? How and by whom I had been rescued did no more than hover upon the fringe of my consciousness.

A knock came at the door and Aunt Olive entered with a tray of tea and some biscuits. She smiled at me, asked how I felt, poured me out a cup of tea, and sat down on the bed beside me.

She told me of the rescue; how three search parties had set out immediately the alarm was raised; Piers, Val and Norrie in an eighteen-foot four-oared boat borrowed from its sleeping owner; Crispin, Michael and Avis in *The Gallipot's* sixteen-foot four-oared dinghy; and Uncle Luke and John in a twelve-foot two-oared dinghy we had been using that evening. It was this small dinghy which had picked me up and brought me back to find a messenger from the yacht *Sybil* waiting to take Uncle Luke to an urgent case of appendicitis on board. "And so," Aunt Olive said with a faint smile, "your Uncle dosed you with brandy and he and John carried you below and then rushed off, John to search for the others and your Uncle to his case." She must have misread my expression for she said lightly, banteringly, but a little shyly I thought, "and so I had to pop you into bed and tuck you up, Julian." Then she added with a sort of smiling but understanding apology, "there wasn't any one else." Relief must have leapt into my eyes, for she stared at me a long moment as if puzzled; and then she nodded her head and returned my smile as I said gratefully, "Of course you did, Aunt Olive."

"You don't want to know who won the race?" she asked.

"I can guess. Piers first and the rest a procession."

She smiled at me. "Crispin was back first."

"Crispin!"

She nodded. "But he hadn't been round *Althea*. He said he thought he heard a cry, swam to the spot, couldn't see any one and so swam back at once to get help. Piers was really first; the others came in anyhow; I've forgotten."

"He didn't hear me cry out," I said sharply.

"Then you didn't?"

"No."

"Why on earth not?"

"Oh, well, I hate people who—who muff things up and have to be rescued."

She laughed. "That was very silly of you, Julian. It's nine o'clock. Do you feel like breakfast?"

I nodded. "I feel fine now," I said.

There were other sorts of dances at Stromness, but the only kind favoured by Val was what he called "local hops." These were organised by the younger natives of the town and district and held in any available hall. All of us (except the girls and myself) had sampled them, but Val had been to nearly all. About a week after the swimming-race fiasco he asked me to come along with him to one being held in a hall belonging to *The King's Arms*. Crispin also agreed to come.

It was a wild affair, reminiscent of a rugger scrum rather than a dance; there was plenty to drink and love-making was open and unabashed. What with the heat, the press, and the stink of scent and sweat, I had had more than enough by midnight and left. Crispin had already gone, but Val was dancing riotously with a vivacious little animal of a girl, black-eyed, red-lipped, olive-skinned, wanton looking, with whom he had spent most of the evening. His face, as closely-embraced they cavorted together, glistened with sweat and wore an expression of enraptured sensuality. He did not see me; I doubt if he was capable of seeing anyone clearly; but it was not drink that dimmed his sight and fuddled his wits.

Crispin said to me next morning about ten, "Val's

just got up and gone off for a swim. He was looking a bit pale about the gills."

"Too much exercise," I said, "of the wrong sort."

"What did you think of the little wench he was running last night?"

"All right, if you like that sort."

Crispin grinned. "He told me they went for a walk about two o'clock over towards the Standing Stones and just after daybreak he tumbled her in a field all among the dew and clover."

"Tumbled her? Do you mean seduced her?"

"Good God! Seduced? Hardly the word, is it? She was hungry enough for the tourney; an eager target for love's rosy arrow. But what's the matter with tumble? Grand word, I think; lends colour to an act that sometimes lacks it. Don't you think so?"

"I dare say."

He grimaced. "But not your line, eh, Ju? Tumbling little doxies in a field or on a bed isn't your meat. Too fastidious. Or what?" He stared at me, his hot blue eyes laughing; but there was, it seemed to me, a sneer on his lips.

"Just that I don't want to," I said.

"Time you did, then, old boy." But now his lips were smiling pleasantly. Suddenly he laughed. "The way of all flesh. When you come to die, Ju, it'll be the things you haven't done you'll regret; those things you might have done with your body and didn't. Don't humbug about it; it's the only thing a man is faithful to from puberty till he collapses into the grave; the one bit of warm reality in a world of lies, in a world which cheats us of most things." He clapped me on the shoulder. "But it can't cheat us of the girls we've tumbled; nor can death." He smiled at me and repeated gaily, "Don't let's humbug, Ju; it's the alpha and omega; the first prize and the last. Sans teeth, sans hair, sans everything, but never sans that, old boy; not the hunger for it. Didn't old Cato at eighty tumble his daughter-in-law's serving-maid and then incite the puss to sauce her mistress?"

"I don't know," I replied, "but I do know he said to a grey-bearded lecher, ' Old age has deformities enough of its own without adding to it the deformity of vice.'"

He smiled. "His hypocrisy, Ju; damn all hypocrites. No, no, old boy; tumble your wenches while ye may; carpe diem, and all the rest of it. But vice; what the devil did he mean by talking of vice? Vice is a filthy affair; cruelty, betraying a friend, stealing brains, underpaying work, lying to children about God; that's vice if you like; but this business of rumpling a puss; that's not vice, Ju; don't make a mountain out of a wen; it's just an animal pleasure, like a good feed or a hearty joust in the haha. You'll be preaching me a sermon on love and lust next."

"I'm not preaching, Crispin; you're the preacher; preaching to yourself and shouting to convince yourself."

Chapter Six

I HAVE perhaps lingered over-long on that Orcadian holiday, ascribing the significance it appears to have in my mind to itself rather than to the fact that it came at a period in our lives when most of us were finishing with tutelage and were about to take the reins in our own hands, or sincerely believed we were, which amounts to the same thing in terms of responsibility. And perhaps for that reason, therefore, the immediately following years have become oddly telescoped so that in recollection there was but one stride, a giant's stride, if you will, between that year (it was 1906) and the spring of 1913. As I look back I see a very vivid picture (many pictures) of that party gathered together at Stromness, and then the next series of pictures that have any real distinctness belong to the time, seven years later, when we were all successfully launched, each at the helm of his or her own small craft.

And so I shall take that stride forward with just one swift backward glance at two happenings that followed quickly after that summer holiday. Before the end of the year Crispin's and Avis's grandmother, with whom they had lived since early childhood, died in her sleep at the age of ninety-two. There was nothing for tears in that enviable close to a much-enjoyed life; and my two cousins, sole legatees of her large fortune, could not sincerely have regarded it as anything but a happy event. But the other affair was a saddening one. I have mentioned how Major Conway home on furlough from India had spent, with Aunt Jenny and Miles, that summer in the south of France. There they met and became friendly with a London ship-broker, George Stenning, and he and Aunt Jenny fell in love and went away together. Major Conway returned to India and there was a divorce, the case being undefended. Miles, who was then nearly seventeen, returned to Selborne and afterwards went to Sandhurst. I do not think I take a sentimental view of the matter or exaggerate in the least when I say that the affair struck a deep and lasting wound at Miles. He was in love with his young and pretty mother, as a boy of sixteen may well be with nothing but benefit to himself, despite the œdipus rex rubbish and so much else of the modern claptrap. And he tremendously admired his father, the tall grave soldier who had been his first hero, and had not lost that high place in his heart. And he saw the intimate lives of these two people, so closely linked with his own as to be inseparable from most of his thoughts, suddenly broken apart; he saw that small warm intimate world of the family, so solid, so real, so invulnerable to a child (and what else is sixteen behind its bold and manly front?) disrupt before his eyes; saw his mother go away and every circumstance of her going portraying it as something vile and smirching, giving it the air of a guilty and ashamed evasion; saw his father thus humiliated, for to a young mind, unwise in the world's casuistries and sophistries, his father's position was one of profound humiliation;

and could give him no comfort, was perhaps too shy, hurt and bewildered to proffer it. And all this coming literally out of the blue, the blue of summer skies, in the middle of a holiday long anticipated and, till the disaster, rapturously enjoyed. No. It is no sentimentality which views that event as tragical, whatever joy the two lovers had of each other.

But by 1913 childhood and adolescence were far behind us; we were all, as I have said, launched and well afloat. I had had my year at the Slade and two in Carsten Raven's atelier in Paris, had been back in London nearly four years and had a studio at Clifton Hill, in the north-west of London. Since returning to England I had had each year a picture in the Royal Academy Exhibition. I do not think I am boasting when I say that if I had been without private means I could have made a fair income with my brush. But not an income anything like Val was making as political cartoonist on *The Peepshow*, the sixpenny illustrated weekly to which he had gone on leaving *Touch and Go*, where he had made a reputation spectacular enough to cause a dozen well-baited hooks to be dangled before him. The bait on *The Peepshow's* hook was not the largest; but he took it, he said, because of that journal's influence and prestige, and of course money was no matter of consequence, as both he and Sylvia inherited handsome legacies from grandparents when they were twenty-one, and would have more when their parents died.

We were indeed all doing very much what our youth promised; for in the main the clever youngster becomes the clever man or woman and the dull are dull for ever. Piers at twenty-eight was the Tory member of Eastwich, was one of the P.M.'s Parliamentary private secretaries, and was considered by the knowing (and justifiably considered) as marked out for early preferment and a brilliant political career with only, as Crispin said, Heaven as the limit.

Val had a large flat at Hampstead, Piers a smaller one in St. James's.

Crispin was only two years at Oxford, being sent down after a ragging affair in which Squitters Beamish's furniture and person had both suffered damage. He had travelled for two years (part of the time in America) and had returned to London in time for the production of his first full-length play (*So This Is Life?* at *The Royalty*), which had been damned by the critics but had been a box-office success and had run over seven months. He lived in a cottage at St. Margaret's Bay and when in town, which was frequently, stayed at his club, *The Pagans*.

Beamish himself (who had edited *The Isis* at Oxford) was now assistant literary editor on the radical *Morning News*, while Tom Frankell was associate editor of the socialist weekly *The Call*.

The wide gap between a young man of twenty and children just beginning their teens is apt, with the passing of a decade, to close up completely and bring them into line as contemporaries. But this somehow had not happened with Humfrey Conway and ourselves. Approaching the middle thirties and in control at 3 Ave Maria Lane, where his father now rarely put in an appearance, he seemed to be nearer his father's generation than ours; responsibility no doubt had its share in that loss of youth, but he had allowed himself to get fat; the one-time soldierly stride had become a sedate pacing; there was nothing about him now of that gallant air which had so captured us a dozen or so years previously; he looked a prosperous city man; you could have matched him a hundred times over at nine-thirty o'clock on most mornings of the year between Temple Bar and St. Paul's Churchyard. Viewed from behind (as Val was fond of caricaturing him, often indecorously), he might have been one of the younger aldermen; a grave fellow of substance with a family of adolescents.

Michael had been with him since leaving Oxford, and the old firm was now Joseph Conway, Sons and Company, Limited; the trade, however (and the term may be taken to include the whole book-world) still knew it as simply Conways. But publishing was not Michael's main interest; he was a poet, a frequent contributor of verse to *The English Review*, *The Academy*, *The Pall Mall* and *The Westminster*, and was considering the publication of a volume of his verse with the Bodley Head. I am tempted to dawdle for a moment or so on this matter of Michael's poetising, because it was a side, an aspect of him quite unguessed at by any of us. That Crispin, Val, Piers, Miles or any of the girls should suddenly become metamorphosed into that strange oddity, a poet, would not have surprised any of the rest of us (Sylvia indeed as Hazel Fayre was already writing song-lyrics), but Michael somehow did not seem to fit the part; and indeed when his first published poem appeared in *The Pall Mall* it was so utterly unlike our conception of the Michael we all thought we knew moderately well that we suspected its authenticity, despite the evidence of his name. The measure of our surprise will I imagine be better realised if I give here that piece of flamboyant rhetoric which in matter owed something to Rupert Brooke, in manner a little to Stephen Phillips and cannot, I dare say (although I am no judge), lay any claim to be considered as poetry. But it was not the pros and cons of that difficult question which concerned us in the slightest; *The Pall Mall* printed it on a page headed New Poems, and that was good enough; what was stirring us all up was that this piece of self-revealing bombast had suddenly been shot not only at us, but at any Tom, Dick or Harry (to say nothing of Mary and Jane) who could read; and by, of all people (so we said sapiently), dear old matter-of-fact Farmer Giles Michael. But judge for yourselves. The title doesn't seem particularly apt.

SWORDS AND PLOUGHSHARES

What can you place upon the other scale,
Death said to me in dream, that shall weigh down
The pain of being? And my final stroke
Which overwhelms you with eternal night?
Nothing at all, I said, except the sting
Of brine upon my lips; a sea-gull wheeling
Above a cliff-edge over breaking seas;
The solitude of little ships at dawn
Moored in a rocky harbour. All the bright
Windows of houses with tea-tables spread
Seen from a passing train; the slow down-floating
Of snowflakes in a garden; the first flowers
On sudden barrows in a winter street.
A dog that drowses blinking in the sun.

Laughter of children; the cheering of a crowd;
Toast hot from the fire; and the foam of beer;
The smell of coffee roasting in a shop.
The calling of birds at dawn. The rich sweet
Bodies of young girls. Earth after rain.
The dew on the grass—Enough! Death said, you fool,
This is the catalogue of little lusts
And hungers, toys and pictures that have been
Ever the ignoble solace of mankind.
Have you then nothing worthy of your dreams
To set against this littleness? Naught beside
These hankerings and itchings of the flesh?
I laughed at death and spat upon his face,
Mocking him for a cheat. You lie, I said,
Was it not with such little human things
You built the empires of tremendous kings?

But enough of Michael for the moment; he was to write less explicable things than that piece of juvenilia.

There remain but two of our little circle, John and Miles, called by Crispin "our service members." John was already second in command of H.M. Submarine M7 and Miles was a second lieutenant in the Coldstreams. But that little circle had lost something of its solidarity, more than it was bound to do in the normal way of things; for if Crispin and Val had not entirely withdrawn from it, they both moved chiefly among a rather rackety crowd with whom we did not come into contact.

It was, I suppose, in the nature of things that as we grew up together there should be some tentative love-making, emotional trial trips, amongst us. Val

and my little sister Faith (not that she was little, but
the epithet of former days clung) became engaged, but
she had broken it off very abruptly and had departed
for Manchester and the stage, where as Faith Darblay
she acted for some time with the Repertory Theatre.
Nan Kendall was also there for a short while, but
came south to do film work in one of the earliest
English studios.

Of all of us Alison was the only one still living at
home; the only one, according to herself, not making
a stir in the world. But if the slums of the East End
of London have any claim to be of the world, her
work there with the Selwyn Mission was in terms of
human usefulness worth all ours tossed together.
Piers Rowland loved her and she, in his regard, was
I think (and I write this with the utmost diffidence)
at war with herself; her flesh subject to his tremendous
physical allurement; her mind, her spirit, completely
at odds with most of the things he stood for—power,
success, the strong arm, all that is perhaps summed up
in that stirring yet lamentable phrase: "My country,
right or wrong."

Romantic love, with its tender raptures and honied
saws, would have found among all that little crowd
of us none to contemplate with any satisfaction,
without indeed misgiving, had it not been for John
and Sylvia, who were walking very happily step by
ordered step along that path of love which, in despite
of the proverb, runs with enchanted smoothness.
They were engaged to be married; they were so
joyously and unaffectedly in love that all the old tales
and legends of true lovers, all the passionate songs of
poets and the romantic lays of minstrelsy might well

have found resurgence of warmth and ecstasy in the inspiration of their happiness. They were going to be married when Sylvia was twenty-one. No one doubted that for a moment; it was impossible to doubt it. All the trite immemorial sayings (which curl the lip of cynicism, cause sophistication to yawn, and stab the heart of the unloved) seemed meet and right to apply to them; they were made for each other; a marriage made in heaven; a true-love match; and they two shall be one flesh; two hearts that beat as one—so they have been said how many thousand times! Do you suspect my tongue in my cheek as I write them? You have but ill understood me if you do; and I counsel you to read no further lest the end find you cheated of everything but laughter.

Chapter Seven

ON April 12, 1913, Crispin's play, *The Tree of Know-ledge*, was produced at *The Marlow Theatre* in the Strand. It was not a good play and its moderate success (it ran till the autumn) was of scandal rather than of any more solid worth, as it was well known that the Lord Chamberlain had refused to licence the play until the last scene of the second act had been so recast as to remove entirely any suggestion of an incestuous association. Crispin had by then so considerable an experience of the English stage that it has always puzzled me why in the first place he should have written the play at all, and in the second that he should have dreamed a licence would be granted to the play as originally written. If he did dream that! His own explanation, that he flung the play in the Lord Chamberlain's face as a challenge and an indictment, seems a little thin. As first written it might well have had a success upon the French stage (with a lighter treatment), but it was impossible upon the English stage.

But it was the play's theme, and his breeze with the Lord Chamberlain, which served Crispin as a text, or rather perhaps a jumping-off place, for his violent outburst at the first-night supper party at *The Savoy*. What provoked him into the delivering of that unbridled diatribe is hard to say. But such affairs are always rather incomprehensible, so superficial is one man's knowledge of another. I can only record what happened and in that record keener insight than mine may discover motives; or if not motives, at least the trigger which exploded the charge.

There was outwardly still friendship existing between Crispin and our old circle, so that all of us who were in London received invitations to the show and the supper party. Besides myself, Piers was there with Alison; Michael was with Tom Frankell, and Norrie came with me. Val was with three or four odd fish in velvet dinner-jackets; and there were about half a dozen men and women of Crispin's own particular set. Wilson Rodway, lessee and manager of *The Marlowe*, and the small cast of six players, were of course much in evidence; but Beatrice Stevenson, the star, had developed a temperamental headache and had at the last moment refused to come.

I do not know if her headache were due to the fact that young Tom Sholto had stolen the play, and that his recalls before the curtain were more numerous and vociferous than her own; but certainly her absence seemed to strike a discord which, if I may put it so, set the tune for the whole sorry affair, which somehow went wrong from the beginning. What should have been the jolliest of meals proceeded in a chilly atmosphere of unease which the champagne, far from exercising its usual dissipating glow, served only to intensify. And that very fact, I suppose, incited most of those present to drink deeply and to keep on drinking.

I watched Crispin throughout the meal. He seemed preoccupied, moody; his glance, I thought, went continually to Alison, and he gave little attention to what he was eating and drinking or to the women on either side of him.

There were the usual healths drunk with some noise and clatter, but without enthusiasm or cordiality; and after Tom Sholto had proposed Crispin's health there were cries of "Speech," but even these had no ring of sincerity in them. Or so I imagined. Perhaps I am imagining a great deal, and an account of the affair by one of the others present would wear a very different complexion. But I am not mistaken about Crispin's speech, nor do I rely upon my memory for what he said. Tom Frankell took it down in shorthand ("a good newspaperman is a newspaperman all the time") and afterwards gave me a typed copy.

When Crispin rose to speak he looked, I thought, a magnificent but a rather (to us who had known him so long) saddening figure. His intensely blue eyes blazed out of the white-marble of his face, but they seemed to blaze out of deep pits. The beauty of his fine features was marred by a hint of haggardness which the sweep of the long dark hair across his brow served somehow to accentuate. All the while he was speaking his fingers fidgetted with a tiny gold seal hanging from his fob. He smiled once, when he began speaking; thereafter his face was a mask (and no pleasant one to watch) and for most of the time his glance remained fixed straight in front of him, over our heads. It had about it something of the vacantly staring quality of a blind man's eyes. Just at the end he smiled again.

"Thank you, my dear Sholto," he said, "for the very generous things you have said about me; and you, ladies and gentlemen, for the generous applause you accorded them. Perhaps fortunately we all know they are not true. Whether I should be happier if they were I really don't know; probably not; they might prove something of a burden. If I am now capable of the emotion of surprise then decidedly I have felt surprise at the enthusiastic reception given to *The Tree of Knowledge* by the public." It was then he smiled. "For the play is a true transcript of life, and nothing is so intolerable as truth.

"But let me in support of my text, for that is my text, pass in a brief and I hope not too boring a review, this civilisation of ours in the year of Our Lord one thousand, nine hundred and thirteen.

"The refusal of the Lord Chamberlain to licence my play is in keeping with our pretence that what is happening all about us is simply not happening. We know very differently. We know that many wives are unfaithful, and that most would be if the opportunity offered; we know that many husbands are promiscuous, as all men are in desire; we know that old men buy young girls, either within or without the marriage fold; and that old women keep youths as Lucrezia Borgia kept her human stallions. And incest! against the faintest hint of which the Lord Chamberlain adamantly sets his face and we avert ours in horror, while the thing itself is rife in every slum in the kingdom. We no longer avert our glances from the homosexuals, the Lesbians, the pederasts, lest we should find nowhere to look. And all over the land those two prosperous practitioners, the procurer and the abortionist, ply their rich trade, the latter gentleman with his accommodating scale varying from

fifty guineas in a West End nursing home to ten
shillings in some dark East End attic.

"Tell me one honest thing in our civilisation to-day.
The law? You smile; no one, you protest, expects or
has ever expected honesty in the law. Nevertheless our
judges and our magistrates, you will tell me, are not
venal, whatever may be the state of affairs abroad.
Here justice is not bought and sold. We do not sell
justice to the rich; we are too honest; we merely
withhold it from the poor. Our judges are not venal;
but neither do they administer justice; they administer
their own prejudices, their own inhibitions, their own
starvations; they are vicarious flagellators. Let us
look at medicine, the healing art, and at quackery;
but it were well not to look too closely or we may
discover that they are one and the same thing; there
is no basic difference between the Harley Street special-
ist who stuffs your hundred guinea cheque into his
fob and the quack at the fair who pockets your sixpence; both are devotees of the god Mumbo Jumbo
above whose altar is written the golden word abra-
cadabra.

"But the Church, the Church of God; surely
is truth and honesty; sincerity, charity, and goodwill
to men. There is nothing here for smiles; the joke
is too old. It is impossible to feel even a faint indigna-
tion that the Church is the landlord of one-quarter of
the slum property in the land; impossible to raise the
eyebrow of mild surprise when our agnostic bishops
and deans hew away at the foundations of the Church
which richly clothes and feeds them while the hungry
flock go by unfed.

"Politics? But that is too easy; no one expects it

to be anything but an offence to the nostrils, and it deserves our encomiums if only for the work it does in the service of laughter, and its production twice annually of that fine humorous periodical, the Honours List.

"But surely there is one class which is clean, which keeps itself pure and wholesome and uncontaminated. Sport. The clean sportsman. Clean boxing, clean wrestling, clean football, clean cricket; how discordantly the words chime together; even a child's ears might note that something is wrong. So wrong indeed that epithet and substantive supply in each case a contradiction in terms.

"There is nothing at which one may look with pride, glad of one's humanity. Better look away and not think about it. Thought must at all costs be avoided; it is hell and the devil and all the torments. It is not difficult to avoid, most of the time; there are distractions: hunting and fishing; golf and shooting; theatres and entertainments; cocktail parties, night clubs and secret cinema shows; intrigues and philandering; straight adultery and crooked fornication.

"But these stale; one is sated; a time comes when one needs seek for comfort elsewhere. And indeed comfort is to be found; our civilisation is wonderful; its resources infinite. For the sated, the world-sick and the weary, there are comfortable words, there are soothing places of rest, sanctuaries where one may hide from the garish light. There is the Church of Rome. There is spiritualism. There is astrology. A new trinity of three in one; most blessed comforters. Better far to rest upon their drowsy comfort than to face the truth."

Crispin paused, and for one instant his glance went

flickering round the circle of faces about him. And then his eyes took on again that fixed, almost blank stare and he went on: "The truth; the unpalatable truth. The truth that there is no reason behind human existence and no meaning in our lives; that it is a childish folly to ask of the human race whence? And whither? There is no whence, no whither. Nothing, we came from nowhere, and to nowhere, as nothing, we return. We will not face that; anything but that. We will face unmoved all the infamies of history down to this ignoble civilisation of our own; but not that. Truth? That is a toast I would not ask you to drink. Let us have a sweeter draught. What shall I give you?" He paused, stooped and lifted his glass. And then, for the second time, he smiled and his glance, it seemed to me, went over to Alison. "Our superstitions: may they never desert us," he said and emptied his glass.

I do not remember drinking the toast; there was a sudden stirring and movement; a few chairs scraped; voices rose to a confused noise. I noticed two waiters leaning against the wall, their bodies drooped, their faces greyly impassive; I wondered what they were thinking, if they were thinking at all; I wondered how long they had been on duty; and the thought came into my head, and seemed grotesque, that they had a home and wife and children; that they were fathers and husbands; that they were known to some one as Bert or Alf or Daddy; that unbraced and smoking a pipe they lounged in a chair and read the paper, joked with the missis, or played with the children.

And while my mind, a little sleepily and hazily,

busied itself with these odd thoughts, the noise became a hubbub; and I saw at the far end of the table from me Tom Frankell upon his feet, his mouth opening and shutting in speech, although no words reached me. He looked fresh-faced and queerly boyish beside the haggard figures about him, or perhaps the lights tricked me, or the contrast existed only in my imagination. And abruptly the hubbub died away and I heard him, caught his words midway in a sentence with the effect of a gramophone record set going in the middle: ". . . Every faithless wife there are a thousand, a hundred thousand, true to the men they have married. All men promiscuous if only in desire? I deny it; all life denies it—life as I have known it. Life? What do you know of life as the common people, the ordinary normal people, live it? Your picture of our civilisation is false. Your panders and procurers, your pimps and old lechers, your abortionists and homosexuals and perverts are no more England than the horse-droppings outside in the Strand are London.

"You look upon the broad flowing river of life, and because of a patch of scum upon its surface you cry out that all its waters are polluted. You know nothing of life; nothing of the millions, the innumerable millions, of ordinary normal decent people who make up the everyday world and upon whom our civilisation, which you mock and condemn, rests and rests securely.

"You forget, or you wilfully ignore, that for every ignoble and unworthy judge there are a hundred trying to perform their unhappy task with fairness; for every agnostic dean and episcopal lying sophist there are ten thousand parsons of the rank and file doing their job with sincerity; for every cheating physician and unscrupulous surgeon there is a legion bringing something to the sick and in pain, if it is only alleviation and hope, in countless hospital wards and in innumerable cities and towns and villages throughout the world.

"Count your old women with their kept young stallions; number your adulterous lights o' love, and I will find you for each a host of women going about their daily job of caring for a husband and bringing up a family.

"The great mass of the nation is like a fine spreading oak-tree; those of whom you tell us are a mere small stinking fungus upon its bole. And if a testing time should come, and we in Fleet Street know that a testing time may soon be upon us, the fineness, the richness, the sterling worth, the decency of the common man and woman will shine out like the noon sun in summer.

"The truth that we dare not face? And if it is the truth that life has no meaning, that we come from nothing and from nowhere and to these return, dare we not face it? You underestimate our courage and our common sense. If there is only this life, then, given normal health and the common faculties, is not life in itself, just the living of it, worth while? Is there not happiness in the little everyday things, in the love of woman, in children, in doing one's job, in eating and drinking and sleep after toil? You tell us we dare not face, humanity dare not face, the unpalatable truth of one life and one only, of this life and no more, of nothing before and nothing after; I

tell you that if the time comes (and it has not yet
come) when humanity must face that as inescapable
truth, that time will not be one of despair, of railing
and cursing, of despondency and soul sickness and
spiritual death; it will be a time of new hope and
aspiration for the millions of common people who are
the world; it will be a time when the common people
will say: If there is only one life, this, then it is not
good enough; it must and shall be finer and fairer;
it must give to all in generous measure of the earth's
abundance; in those days will be ushered in a new
life, a new existence, for all, a life in which a starving
child no less than a rich and idle man or woman will
be as unthinkably impossible as the burning of an old
woman for sorcery is to-day. And the first to go, the
first to be swept away, will be that patch of scum on
the surface of the water at which you have stared so
long that you can no longer perceive the broad, deep,
clear-flowing expanse of the great main stream of life.
You gave us the toast of our superstitions. I give
you a better one: the world set free from superstition."

There was some slight laughter, half ironical; there
were comments, audible but unintelligible; there were
a few half-hearted raisings of glasses; and a flush-faced
young man, with the gesture of one performing a
symbolical rite, turned down an empty glass. And
then Val stood up and, swaying slightly, glanced
round the table through half-shut eyes, a tipsy smile
on his lips. He mumbled a few words and some one
beside him tried to pull him down into his seat. He
made a grotesquely flapping gesture with his hand;
and then his face changed, his tall figure began slowly

to subside, he slumped across the table and was loudly and catastrophically sick.

The affair then acquired the quality of an absurd dream, in which there was much aimless, jostling, shoving movement and a confusion of voices; and then, some five minutes or so later, without, at least on my part, any clear recollection of how we got there, Michael, Norrie and I were walking along the Embankment and finding the fresh night air very pleasant on our hot faces. We must have walked a fair distance before I paid any attention to what was being said, and then I picked up the talk as abruptly as if plugs had just been removed from my ears. ". . . Mad," Norrie was saying; "but I thought Mr. Frankell the least mad of any one."

"He was probably the least tight," I said. "I liked him," Norrie went on. "Wholesome's the word; like a nice crusty roll that's tumbled into a tray of Viennese pastries."

"Tom Frankell's a dam' good sort," Michael said, with the effect of one having to choose his words carefully, or as if he were controlling his breathing so as to avoid a hiccup. "But it was all a bit clap-trappy and—er—childish, wasn't it?"

"How was it?" Norrie asked. "I thought it very good sense after Crispin's nonsense."

"Well, I don't know," Michael said; "but really, has humanity ever bothered much about another life? Man's obvious business and preoccupation has always been with this world. Has the great mass of human beings ever really believed in any other?"

"I'm sure it has and still does," Norrie said. "What do you think, Julian?"

"A lot have; strongly enough to die for, anyhow," I said, wondering if my words sounded as foolish to them as they did to me.

"Well, I don't think so," Michael rejoined, "and therefore Crispin's hypothesis of the world's refusal to face an unpalatable truth, and Tom's about the ushering in of the Golden Age when they have faced it, both strike me as twaddle. It's not a matter of facing it; I don't believe normal people ever think or have thought much about it at all; this life is all any one really bothers about. And as for Tom, if one *can* imagine the whole world suddenly facing this alleged unpalatable truth, then I don't think it would make a ha'porth o' difference."

"The poor we have always with us and always shall," I put in solemnly.

"More or less; and the rich and the idle and the cruel and the beastly; the tyrant and the slave, and all the rest of it."

"The same yesterday, to-day and for ever!" Norrie laughed. "Well, I don't believe it; I think Mr. Frankell's right and—and I thought Crispin horrible."

"Crispin's sick," Michael said.

"Do you mean ill?" Norrie asked. "Has he——?"

"Well, not ill; not as far as I know; not that I know much; we don't see much of Cris these days, any of us, do we? But he's clearly—how shall I put it?"

"Clearly living beyond his strength," Norrie put in quietly.

"I dare say. But that's common enough. Val is, too, to look at him. But I didn't quite mean that. He's in with a racketty set, and so forth, and burning the candle at both ends; but we all do a bit of that—some more, some less—and get washed out and pale about the gills and jaded; used up, drained; but that's nothing. Crispin looks to me not as if his body were a bit temporarily used up and drained, but as if, well, hang it all, his soul were. Sounds fat-headed, especially as I don't believe in souls, but one has to use these old terms for lack of any others."

"Not only the scabbard but the blade tarnished," Norrie said.

Michael grinned. "Sounds like Stanley Weyman," he said; "but that's the idea."

"I don't read Stanley Weyman," Norrie smiled. "It's mine." She yawned openly and laughed. "And now we've settled everything perhaps you'll see me home. I have to be on duty by nine, and it's past two. And we've two major ops in the morning. Sir Harry Sutherland's doing one, a fistula; and Mr. Prestcott the other, a duodenal."

"Then it's to be hoped," Michael said, "they haven't been cutting our capers to-night. Shall we try to get a cab or walk?"

"Walk and hope for a cab!" Norrie laughed.

Chapter Eight

ROLL-AND-COFFEE CONFIDENCES

EARLY that May, about eight o'clock one Saturday evening, I took a taxi to Aldgate and, dismissing it there, went for a walk along the Mile End Road. I went partly because I found that famous East End thoroughfare amusing and exciting to the eye, with its markets and stalls and naphtha flares, its cheery jostling crowds, its garishly-dressed young Jewesses and the slim darting exotic-looking children (as lovely as dark flowers, some of them), and partly for the sake of studying types and, rare chance, of finding inspiration in some passing face or in the swiftly-transient pose of some graceful child. I had indeed more than once found a model in that strange world of rich, warm, vulgar humanity, and I was just then turning over in my mind the details of a picture I had long wanted to paint: the Boy Jesus with his father Joseph in the carpenter's shop; an old subject, but in none of the pictures I had seen of it was either Joseph or, and especially, the Boy Jesus, anything like the vision or image I had of them. There was, then, at the back of my mind the mild hope that perhaps among that drifting swarm of faces under the street lamps and the naphtha flares I might find, like a gift from heaven, one of those I wanted; that mild hope did not venture as far as two.

I am chary in the ordinary way of mingling with a crowd, for sometimes in such circumstances there descends upon me an extraordinary sensation of terror which may pass quickly, or persist until almost in a panic I push my way out. But this was rare with a moving crowd, and I had also come to the conclusion that such a morbid visitation was only to be feared when I was unwell or run-down and, as I was feeling particularly fit just then, I refused to allow the possibility access to my mind.

I came to a street leading out of the main road and, withdrawing myself aside from the bustle of the throng, stood apart for a few minutes at the corner watching the scene. On the opposite corner was a big brightly-lit public house and, looking across at it, I suddenly saw Val standing outside the wide entrance almost immediately beneath the portal lamp. He was very smartly dressed, but not in his usual rather flowing style: sombrero, wide bow-tie, and so on; he was wearing a light grey overcoat with a cap of the same shade well down over his eyes and a pale blue silk scarf. Acquaintances and even friends might well have passed him by unrecognised; but the trained eye is not so easily deceived, and indeed the slightly languid stoop of the tall, slim body and the familiar poise ("insolent cock," was Crispin's chaffing description) of the head was more than sufficient to single him out from a million. It was some weeks since I had seen him, and I was about to cross over when a young and pretty woman, ripe-bosomed, heavily-hipped and flauntingly dressed, accosted him. He turned his face so that the light fell upon it, and I saw it break into a smile. And then with a gay gesture he tucked her arm in his own and, turning quickly with her, went into the tavern.

I crossed the road and walked on towards Bow and suddenly my heart quickened and I stopped short, astonishment outstripping reason so that I exclaimed, "Great Lord! Alison, what on earth——!" And then, as she laughed and said, "Oh, Julian, how nice!" I went on quickly: "But of course!"

I turned with her and she took my arm, and we walked on, slowly threading our way through the shoppers on the pavement. "Do you know, Alison," I said, "I'd never really visualised you as being jostled and buffetted about by a Saturday night crowd of East Enders. Is it, well, exactly——" I broke off and added after a momentary hesitation: "What does Piers think about it?"

"Much the same as you, I expect, or he used to. But it's just rubbish. There are a hundred places in London where it mightn't be rubbish, but not in the Bow Road on a Saturday night. Don't be silly. Besides, the people know me."

"What? All of them? What colossal conceit."

"Lots do. They're all doing their Saturday night's shopping; I know many of the mothers."

"I'm not thinking of the mothers."

"And the fathers are at home minding the little ones or putting them to bed."

"Or in pubs."

"Not till mother gets back and sees if she's a shilling to spare."

"You seem to know all about it," I laughed. "But it was the sons I was thinking about."

K

"Would you like to see them? And the daughters, too, for that matter?"

"Not en masse, Alison."

"No, just a hundred or so enjoying themselves."

"You mean you propose to take me along willy-nilly! Where is it? The Mission?"

She nodded. "Owen Hall. It's not far from here. But not willy-nilly."

"May I see you home afterwards?"

She looked up into my face and smiled, and I thought how little she had changed since childhood. And I thought also other less happy things. "You may see me to the Tube," she said lightly.

"The Tube? Good God! Can't——?"

"No, a bus. That'll be nearer. And I'd prefer a bus; it's a marvellous show from the top of a bus on a Saturday night. It's number 25."

"Couldn't I come too? It's a free show. And I suppose number 25 goes somewhere near civilisation."

"Meaning Clifton Hill?" she laughed. "It goes to Victoria, but I shall get off at Charing Cross, as I've a call to make. And you can get a train there."

"I'll drop into the club," I said gaily. "Is this it?" as she stopped in front of a lamp over the door of a long two-storey building from which came the tinkle of a cheap piano, the wail of a fiddle, and the shuffling-trample of many feet.

She nodded. "We'll just look in at the dance first and then we'll pop upstairs."

I noticed for the first time that she was carrying a magazine with a pale green cover.

"What's that?" I asked.

"It's a new review," she said; "I bought it to read

in the Tube when I was coming." She smiled. "It's really a coincidence we met, Julian. I'll show you something in it presently."

We entered and stood by the piano. There were about eighty young people dancing, their ages ranging from fifteen to twenty. A number of girls were dancing together, but most had a male partner. The quality of the dancing ranged from the expert to the ludicrous; some couples were just hugging rapturously and determinedly and shuffling round with an air of enduring the powder for the sake of the jam; a few of the boys, as if overcome by the intoxicating propinquity of a soft female body, clutched their girl with a sort of desperate intensity, plainly dumbstruck; others proceeded, as it were *à posteriori*, from one collision to another; quite a number were chatting easily and happily as they danced; most were smiling or trying to smile; all were sweating. Many of the girls as they came by the piano smiled at Alison and their partners nodded a little stiffly, their lips moving as if in greeting.

Presently we went upstairs. In one large room fitted up as a gymnasium boys were boxing, wrestling and using the parallel bars; in the second room boys and girls were sitting reading; while in the last one the girls were knitting, sewing and darning and the boys working at a bench.

Alison talked and seemed on the easiest terms with them all, leaving me a good deal to my own devices. I made tentative conversational advances to some of the boys, but so plainly failed to make any contact with them that I finally gave it up and contented myself with the rôle of onlooker.

After nearly an hour we went downstairs again; and as there was now an interval for refreshments I was unable to escape a cup of coffee from a big urn. But at last it was over and we came out.

"Well," Alison asked, "what do you think of it?"

I could think of nothing more original than: "It keeps them out of the streets." At which Alison laughed and said, "Is that all?"

"Well, no," I replied. "My chief impression is that the coffee was the most abominable I've ever tasted. I suppose it was coffee. Can't you give them something that tastes and smells like coffee? If not, why don't you give them tea?"

"Because they prefer coffee; and they like it as it is; when we gave them stronger they wouldn't drink it; and when we suggested tea they said they got plenty of tea at home, and anything for a change. And that's true enough; whatever time of day you call on them there's always the teapot on the hob. And one can't refuse a cup; not that I want to; it's quite nice tea, if a bit strong." She smiled. "You know, Julian, there's an awful lot of humbug about tea. They buy tea dust about here at ninepence a pound and we pay five shillings and had our water tested for a suitable blend; and I really can't taste much difference."

"You've killed your palate with the wretched stuff; mind you don't ruin your digestion. Who was that pretty little golden-haired girl you stopped to talk to as we came out?"

"Oh, that was Ruth. You wouldn't think she was a Jewess, would you? I was asking after the baby; it's only a week old; I go every morning to see the mother; the poor mite's blind and has no roof to its mouth."

"Good God!" I said. "Why didn't the doctor kill it?"

She went on, as if she had not heard me: "Mrs. Mendoza, that's the mother, was very excited this morning; she said the nurse told her there was every hope now it would live."

"I think it's a damnable crime, Alison. I don't think that coffee's going to agree with me."

"That's your pampered stomach. I'm feeling quite hungry. Wouldn't you like a good cup of coffee and a roll? I know where there is a Lyons open They make lovely coffee. Piers says their black coffee is quite as good as any you get at the Ritz or the Savoy; and much better than in many houses he's dined at."

I smiled. "All right, Alison."

Alison had quite a meal: two rolls and four discs of butter and a large white coffee. I contented myself with a small black, which I soon finished.

"Do smoke," she said; "you'll look less uncomfortable."

"Thank you, I will, but I'm quite comfortable; much more than that, in fact. What was it you were going to show me in that review?"

She held up the book; it was called *New Poetry*. She smiled, but I thought it rather forced. "There's a poem in it by—guess."

"Michael."

"Well, there is; but it's not that. Now who?"

"Yourself."

"Idiot. Crispin."

"Crispin! I didn't know he wrote verse."

"Well, he does; he's written one poem, anyhow—if that's what it is. Read it. It's on page 33; I've turned the corner down." I flicked over the leaves till I came to it.

PÆAN
by
Crispin Farne

Down among the rushes
It floats like a bladder.
Three children in the town
Cry for their dadda.

Fishes and beetles
Nibble at its face.
Three children on their knees
Pray God grace.

Weeds twine in its hair;
Its eyes choke with mud.
Pray, pray, children;
God is good.

Hush crying, children;
Dry your eyes;
I hear the hissing
Of big blow-flies.

I put down the review and looked over to Alison, to find her eyes watching my face. "A bit silly, isn't it?" I said vaguely.

"I think it's vile." She stirred her coffee. "Julian, what's the matter with Crispin?"

"I don't know that there's anything the matter with him. Just going the pace a bit, perhaps."

She shook her head. "It's more than that."

I smiled. "Don't look so solemn. That was what Michael said."

"Don't look so solemn?"

"No; about Crispin." And I told her of Michael's remark and of Norrie's.

She nodded her head slowly. "There's a queer poem by Michael here, too. It's on page 40, I think."

"And you've turned the corner down. All right. Is it as daft as Crispin's? Powerful's supposed to be the word." I flipped over the leaves. "Here we are. Chemozzle. What a title! What the devil does it mean?"

"What does any of it mean? But read it."

CHEMOZZLE
by
Michael Conway

Chemozzle lay drinking, nine bottles round him stood,
Nine mandrils were lapping out of cups of gold;
Nine noisome pea-hens lay nine ivory eggs;
And a maid of Ethiopia sang songs of old.

Hast thou seen the fish-face painted on the rafter?
Hast thou heard the patter of the pied pink rat?
Ten green-haired women bore ten still-born infants;
Hast thou heard the wings a-beating of the blood-
    red bat?

Blown and satiate a gross blue-bottle buzzes
On the porphyry lintel, over cups of jade;
A death's head moth expires upon the brazier
Wherein the sickly smoke of sin is hourly made.

Chemozzle stares before him; his eyes are like a torch.
The mandrils pause in lapping, and the pea-hens cease
*   to lay;*
The ten green-haired women refuse to bear more infants:
Hast thou harkened to the shrieking of the blue-
    tailed jay?

I put the paper down and laughed. "Are all the others up to sample?"

"They're all horrid. But what does it mean, Julian? I don't mean the poems; but the whole thing; and this is only the first number. Isn't there something —something, well, degenerate about a body of young men who can write that dreadful stuff?"

I smiled. "I think it's only high spirits, Alison; just having a bit of fun with the public and the critics, especially the critics. There won't be a second number. It's the sort of thing young men, poets and painters, are always getting up to in France; they don't do it often over here; we're too serious about the arts; do us a lot of good to have a grin at them occasionally."

"Well, perhaps it is; but I don't think it's funny; and I'm sure Crispin didn't mean his as a joke."

"Who knows what anybody means? I suppose Piers isn't in this galley, by any chance?"

"Piers!"

"I was only joking. When are you getting married?"

"When are we getting married?" slowly, as if she were considering the question for the first time.

"You are?"

"I suppose so. Oh, of course we are—some time." Her glance searched my face.

"Well?" I said.

"It's not well; if only it were." She looked into her cup. "I think I shall have another cup of coffee. Will you mind?"

I beckoned the waitress. Presently I said, "What isn't well?"

"Lots of things, Julian."

"You love Piers?"

"Yes."

"Of course. What woman wouldn't?"

She regarded me a long while, looking frankly into my eyes as if she were weighing something, or perhaps me, in the balance. And then she said quietly, "That's just the point, Ju. I loved him despite myself. That is in a way how I still love him. I feel that I ought not to love him so much when—when it is not all my self which loves him. Don't you see?" almost impatiently.

"I think so."

"I despise myself sometimes for loving him the way I do."

"Aren't you rather hair-splitting?"

"No. If you think that you don't know what I'm talking about."

"I assure you I do, Alison."

"We ought not to love each other, people like Piers and I; so apart as we are in many things; it's—it's an abominable trick of—of—what, Julian?"

"Of the flesh."

"I hate that word. But it's true. Piers doesn't believe in my work down here; he doesn't believe in the people; they're just a lot of—of, well, necessary animals to do the manual work of the world; he believes in aristocracy; of birth and breeding first and then of the intellect; that's how he would have the world ruled; and the common people just workers and—and breeders; he believes in force and empire; in great fleets and mighty armies controlled by a small proud aristocracy. Democracy to him is just a silly sentimental mistake which the world has tried out and, he says, has found wanting and will soon abolish. I said to him once angrily, ' What you would like, Piers, is a return to the slave state.' And he smiled and said, ' The world has tried all possible forms of rule and has never discovered a more efficient one than the slave state of ancient Greece; and to that the world will sooner or later return.' In the face of all that, Julian, my love for him seems degrading, horrible. But I love him. There's something wrong about love when that can happen. It seems to me as if—if it were, well, all of a piece with this sort of thing." And she made a scornful gesture towards the small green book upon the table. "There are horrible poems in there; many more like Crispin's; a sort of slime smeared over fine decent things. I love Piers, but I'm not happy."

"But don't you think, Alison——?"

"I know what you are going to say. No, I don't. Some people are completely, utterly happy in their love for each other. There's John and Sylvia. Aren't they perfectly, rapturously happy, utterly in love with each other in body and—and spirit; in every way.

It's queer that of all of us they should be the only two really happy."

I smiled. "Piling it on, aren't you!" I said lightly. "I think most of us are pretty contented."

"I said happy."

"All right, happy. But it's a word, or an abstraction, about which the philosophers have disputed since the year one."

"Never mind the philosophers. What do they know about it? Let's keep to plain men and women and plain English."

"Very well; then I say most of us are happy. Look at dear old Humfrey; he's as happy as a sandboy with his book-peddling and his club and his wine cellar."

"We're not discussing that, Julian. Don't be exasperating; if it were just a matter of wine——"

"'I often wonder what the vintners buy,'" I quoted, "'one-half so precious as the goods they sell.' But leaving all that out, I'd say we were as happy a crowd as the average."

"Are Crispin and Val happy? And are——" She broke off and I waited and at last said, "Are who?"

"Crispin and Val."

"What others?"

"Just those two, Julian."

"I dare say; but isn't this all a bit like the old discussion of the schoolmen on how many angels could stand upon the point of a needle? Queer that the old boy who first mooted that silly poser should have been, as well as the acutest, the fattest man of his age; I believe he weighed over twenty-five stone."

"Who did?"

"Duns Scotus. But never mind him; let's keep to

ourselves. Norrie's happy enough and so are Faith and Nan. And Michael, for that matter. And Miles and Aunt—h'm, well no!"

"No," nodding her head and smiling in the grave fashion of her childhood. "Go on."

"Well, Uncle Luke and Aunt Olive and—and Piers." I lit another cigarette. "A pretty good average I should call it."

"You've not mentioned yourself."

"I thought it was too blatantly obvious, Alison."

Chapter Nine

THE CRUCIBLE

I was passing Lord's cricket ground one afternoon early in July. The Eton and Harrow match was being played and outside the main gate was a small group which attracted my attention. Two Eton boys (one looked barely fourteen and the other perhaps a year older), very smartly turned out, complete with button-hole, stood side by side staring straight ahead of them and determinedly oblivious of three nondescriptly-dressed young Cockneys, standing a few paces away from them. The faces of the Eton boys were set, masklike, only their eyes betraying their uneasy awareness of the amused, impish, half-malicious scrutiny of the others, of whom the eldest, a plump, fair-haired youngster, was openly grinning, and whose whole attitude suggested that he was weighing the pros and cons of a sudden attack upon one of the toppers; or was at least allowing his mind the delight of toying with the notion as the next best thing to actual performance. The thought occurred to me with some amusement that a pleasantly-ironical picture might be made of the group and given the title "The Brotherhood of Man." My glance left the group as a whole and wandered to its individual units; and abruptly I forgot my amusement and moving a little to one side I stood where I could watch the young street-boys without attracting their attention. Or rather it was one of them I wanted to watch. He was a slim, well-made boy of, I judged, about thirteen, black-haired and olive-skinned; and as I watched the play of his features (for the three were now talking and smiling) I knew I had found my model for the boy Jesus.

I went up to him and asked him where he lived. He did not reply, but looked up into my face, a little cheekily, but with a touch of fear, of anxiety, in his eyes. "Do you live near here?" I then asked. The two others had drawn a pace away, watching us out of the corners of their eyes, their attention on tiptoe.

"What d'you want to know for?" he said.

"I want to have a talk with your father."

"He's not at home; he's at work."

"Your mother, then."

Again he looked up into my face, clearly weighing this odd business up. I took the bull by the horns. "I'm a painter," I said; "and I'd like to paint you."

The plump blond boy had edged close and he put in an explanatory oar. "He means a nartis', Frank; don't you, sir?" cocking a smiling eye up at me.

I nodded and smiled; and at this my boy laughed and said, "I thought you meant a house-painter." He hesitated, still doubtful, and then went on, "you could come and see Mum."

"Where do you live?"

"Five Benker's Row."

At this the blond boy put in, "*The Elms*," at which all three laughed, as if it were a familiar jest.

"Is it far?" I asked, "and what's your name?"

"Frank May; 'tisn't far; 'bout half a mile, isn't it, Ernie?" to the smallest of the three, a dusty urchin

who, delighted at being brought into it, said eagerly,
"Yerss, that's right, Frank; yerss, that's right; 'bout
'alf a mile."

I meditated a moment upon the dilemma. Clearly
we'd have to walk; to drive off with him in a taxi was
out of the question; but I certainly did not want to
make one of a procession. I fell back upon the only
solution which occurred to me. I pulled out two
half-crowns and offering one to the plump boy and the
other to the dusty little chap, I said, "I want to go
and talk with Mrs. May; now you trot off and treat
yourselves to something." I saw their expression
change, their eyes darken, and for a moment thought
the bribe not enough; and then I realised that it was
so overwhelmingly too much that its lavishness had
aroused their suspicions. I thrust the money at them
impatiently. "Good Lord!" I snapped, and then
laughed and added, "look here, if you think I'm going
to eat your friend you can follow us on the other side
of the road and at the first bite you can call a police-
man." And at that every one laughed, and with a
cheeky sort of perfunctory salute the two went off
and I turned to Frank May and asked him to lead the
way.

Half a mile considerably underestimated the distance
and it took us quite twenty minutes to reach 5 Benker's
Row, one of some twenty or so small houses in a
Kilburn back street.

A knock at the door brought Mrs. May, a fat, dark,
breathy woman carrying, a little alarmingly, a flat-
iron. Her face was red, her arms bare to the elbow.
Her glance went over us quickly. "Gawd! Frankie,"
she said, "what 've you been up to now?"

I explained things, and watched doubt and suspicion slowly spread over her heavy yet comely features. "You'd better come in," she said finally; "m' iron's getting cold." She led the way through into a small room whose temperature must have been in the eighties. Three smallish children were playing on the floor. She flicked a chair with her apron and I sat down and she resumed her ironing, saying, "Well, now then, mister, and what is it?" as if nothing had yet been said. The boy Frank took up a position near the stove and stood there watching me, his expression grave, almost sedate.

I said, "I'm a painter, an artist, and I want to paint your son. I should only need about four or five sittings of about one hour each and I will pay," I hesitated, fearing to offer what might sound too much, and then went on, "ten shillings an hour, or say three pounds for the sittings. The time can be arranged to suit—er—I suppose he goes to school? Yes, well, the sittings can be fitted in and I will send a cab to fetch him and bring him back." I paused. Her expression was not encouraging. The three children on the floor had crawled close to me and had turned upon me the fixed and apparently unblinking stare of inquisitive childhood. The boy's face was now turned to his mother.

I went on hurriedly, "I shall only want him for the face."

"How d' y' mean?" impassively.

"I just want to paint his face, not his figure; I mean it will not be necessary for him to undress."

"I see," her tone now ominous; and reading her thoughts, I said, "You could, of course, Mrs. May, come with him."

"Oh, of course! with my five and the house to do and my husband's dinner to cook. Yes, I don't think, Mister."

"My name's Farne," I said, "Julian Farne." I gave her my card which she put down without looking at it. Thinking it might perhaps serve in her eyes as a credential for at any rate my respectability I added, "I paint pictures for the Academy."

"Ah," she said, beginning to iron a shirt, "the Academy; I see. Well, Mr. Farne, you'll have to ask his dad; he'll be in any minute now, and if he don't object—there he is; Susie, go and open the door for your dad."

A heavy tread announced Mr. May. He was a big burly man in the uniform of a bus driver. He seemed surprised, stared from me to his wife and then to the boy Frank, said, "Afternoon," and stood leaning against the mantelpiece while once more I explained matters.

"A painter," he said, with an engaging grin; "well, so am I, eh, Mum!" and at this the children laughed and Mrs. May said, "That'll do, Ted," and placing her iron on its stand, wiped her face with her apron. Here was obviously some family joke, and welcoming the lighter atmosphere it brought into the discussion I waited without speaking.

Mr. May was clearly determined I should be enlightened. He sat down and I offered him a cigarette, which he took and stuck behind his ear. He smiled at me and said, "Did you notice the name of the house when you came in?"

"Well, I'm afraid I didn't," I replied; "it's number five, isn't it?"

L

He nodded. "Yes, but it's got a name 's well, *The Pines*. It's over the door in a frame; painted it myself." Giggles from the children suggested there was more in it than this. He aimed a light, good-humoured cuff at the elder girl and went on, now thoroughly enjoying himself, "and if you'd called here last week it 'd a' been *The Elms*, an' the week afore that *The Cedars*." He chuckled. "And next week it might be *Victoria Villa*; Frank, get me the names."

"That'll do, Ted," his wife said again, but indulgently, "the gentleman doesn't want to see your nonsense."

"But I do," I smiled; "I'm tremendously interested."

The boy rummaged about in a cupboard under the dresser and presently brought to his father a pile of tin plates about two feet long by four inches wide. Mr. May took them and putting them on the table, after clearing a space with his arm, beckoned me over and began to spread them out as if he were dealing cards. On each one was painted a different name. Besides the three he had already mentioned there were *Westgate Lodge*, *Acacia Villa*, *The Nook*, *Swanee*, *Sunnyside*, *Oak Villa*, *Seaview*, *Restholme* and others I've forgotten. As he displayed them with much chuckling he said, "Bit of invention of my own, nothing like a change, they say, don't they; they all slide into the frame outside and when we get fed-up with one we change it."

I laughed. "Don't the postmen object."

"Not they! we're number five and that's all they care about; 'sides they don't come more 'n about twice in a blue moon. Here's a good 'un," and he tapped one with his finger. It bore the odd name *Umdrum*. "The wife thought o' that one."

"That'll do, Ted," she said; "I didn't do nothing of the sort."

"All right, Mum." He winked at me and went on, in a pretended whisper, "she said one day life 'ere was blinkin' 'umdrum and I said, ' That's a good un, Mum, that is; we'll call the house 'umdrum.'"

"It ought to be humdrum, Dad," the boy Frank said, speaking for the first time.

"Dare say it did, m' boy; but we weren't taught aitches when we went to school, were we, Mum!" He laughed again. "Nobby idea, isn't it?"

I nodded and smiled and he began to shuffle the tins together and, as if struck by a sudden thought said, "Now about this 'ere painting job. No offence, but there's nothing doing."

"But why not?" I asked.

He made a humorous grimace and spread his big strong hands. "Can't help hearing tales, y' know; no offence, but that's all there is to it."

I had an idea. "But if I came here," I said quickly, "and at times to suit you, wouldn't that do?"

"Ah, now you're talking. Can't see any objection to that eh, Mum? When would you want to come?"

"Any time; but of course preferably in the day-light."

He nodded. "I'm on early shift all this month. How about five o'clock in the afternoon, any afternoons you like 'cept Sat'days and Sundays?"

"That will suit me down to the ground," I said; "I forgot to mention payment although I told Mrs. May; I suggested ten shillings an hour or——"

"That's more than you get, Dad," the boy Frank put in with a smile so unaffectedly cheeky that it told much about that small household and its nominal master.

"Blinkin' blimey! it is, my boy," his father laughed; "an' more 'n you'll ever get again if you don't buck up a bit at school. Well, that's all Sir Garnet, sir; when d'you want to make a start?"

"Next Tuesday would suit me best, if that's all right," I said.

"All right for you, Mum?" he asked.

She nodded, and Frank said, "An' for me," at which his father tweaked his ear and said, "you're not being asked, my boy; you're not the organ-grinder, you're on'y the perishin' monkey." Father and son stood regarding each other affectionately for a long moment, both obviously proud of each other; and, I thought to myself as I took leave of them all, not without very good reason; and carried away with me thoughts that gnawed unhappily at my mind for the rest of that day.

I prolonged the number of sittings to a dozen, spreading them over the rest of the month, and made about a score of studies of Frank's head and completed one small oil which I presented to him at the end and which he received without being much impressed. This prolongation of what I had originally intended to be no more than a total period of five or six hours was for various reasons, but chiefly perhaps because I wanted an excuse for giving Frank a fee in excess of our bargain. He appealed to me at first merely as a fine model to a painter; but he began presently to appeal to me in other ways; I liked his sense of fun, his airy independence, his impudence (for he was soon cheeking me as he cheeked his father); I liked his precocious comments upon life; and his chatter about the people of his small and to me unfamiliar world I found extraordinarily illuminating and fascinating. But even apart from the boy I liked going to 5 Benker's Row and was soon on the easiest of terms with all its occupants; and for the last three or four of the sittings I had tea with them and did my painting afterwards. I liked Ted May, his racy Cockney speech, his banter and his exuberant boyish laughter; and I found his wife Alice and the younger children no less agreeable. I never knew what Ted's wages were exactly, but I gathered they were something under three pounds a week; but there was no feeling of poverty, no stint of anything, and the children were plainly well-fed and healthy. It seemed to me a very happy family circle; and in the atmosphere of that small cramped house in a mean street there was a warmth, a rich humanness, which I had never known in my own home; it may have been an animal warmth, a vulgar richness, but its effect on me was as tonic as a wind off the sea. And I saw with considerable regret the approach of the final sitting.

At that tea there was another guest, a young woman in the early twenties, named Kitty Sears. She was short and plump, dark and extremely pretty; she was, it appeared, in service rather vaguely "somewhere off the Tottenham Court Road"; she was very smartly dressed, a little garishly perhaps, but her gay crude colours rather took the eye. She was quickly at her ease with me and before the end of the meal was out-doing Frank in impudence. When Frank and I left the table for that last sitting she said, with a smile and a roll of her eyes, "What about me for a model, Mr. Farne?" and when I said lightly that I should be charmed, she grimaced, made an odd little clicking noise with her tongue, said, not very relevantly I thought, "hold your hand out, naughty boy!" and burst into loud laughter.

Towards the end of August, Michael rang me up one morning, said he was going down for a month or so to Percuil, the tiny place near Falmouth where the Conways had a villa and houseboat, and suggested I should join him, if only for a week. He said we should have the place to ourselves, that there was some quite decent fishing, and that if we got bored we could hop over to Portscatho, where there was during the holiday season always a gay crowd.

I went down a week later and Michael and I spent a very happy ten days pigging along in the old house-boat and doing for ourselves, which we preferred to the more civilised comforts of the villa. But then Piers and Alison arrived, followed a few days later by John and Sylvia; and Michael, feeling bound to do the honours, we took up our quarters at the villa. And with the change the zest somehow went out of things, at least for me. If I say that I found the raptures of John and Sylvia a little trying, and that the association of Piers and Alison did not seem to bear out her description of herself as a reluctant lover, one made captive by the flesh despite the struggles of the spirit, it is merely to say that I felt out of things and that my chagrin vents itself in a wilful distortion of the facts, which were simply that John and Sylvia were a very happy pair of lovers whose contemplation any one but a misanthrope might have found warming and inspiring; and that with regard to Piers and Alison things were precisely as she had stated them; she loved him passionately but with a profound sense that something of great worth was lacking in that love.

But there it was, and the blunt truth is that I was unable to support with equanimity the daily spectacle of these two pairs of lovers; for the time being the ignoble and the mean in me conquered whatever I may possess of decency (it was perhaps no very difficult conquest); and that after enduring it a week I made an excuse for returning to Town and took leave of them with the self-pitying feeling of a snubbed and unwanted urchin creeping away from party revels to hide in some solitary corner and nurse his woes.

And so I came back to London the end of the third week in September, meditated upon and rejected a dozen plans for a holiday on my own, and finally decided to pull up my roots in England, if only for a year, and to travel, first going to America. But with everything packed and my passage booked something happened which postponed my leaving England for the best part of a year.

It was the Thursday before I was sailing on the Saturday, and after having dined at my club I found myself, about half-past eight, strolling rather aimlessly along Oxford Street a few hundred yards from *The Horseshoe Tavern* in the Tottenham Court Road. And suddenly, under one of the lamps, I pulled up short to avoid a collision with a young woman who was looking back over her shoulder, and who turned quickly and disclosed the pretty smiling face of Kitty Sears. We walked along together chattering in a bantering way; and then she took my arm and said something and I realised her profession; and I knew I wanted her; I felt that here would be at least something snatched from life; something rich and warm and animal; and something too of balm and of ease for my hunger; and over and above all I was overwhelmed by the feeling that I was on trial; I was to be weighed in the balance of the flesh; here at last, at that immediate moment, was a crisis in my life which I could boldly face or cravenly evade.

I went with her to her flat.

Fifteen eternal minutes dragged themselves over me; and then I had flung her a five-pound-note and was rushing down the stairs, my ears magnifying a thousand-fold the derisive laughter which followed me.

Chapter Ten

THE SHOW

HAVE YOU ever—but of course you have; we are all built on the same plan; bones and muscles, flesh and nerve ganglia; and all human experience in the main must run along similar lines; the uniqueness of one's pain or pleasure, happiness or wretchedness, is an egotistical bubble life quickly bursts. Let me then ask you to recall to your memory some great mental shock; not at the moment when the blow fell, but some minutes afterwards when the mind is slowly recovering and tries confusedly to piece together the various trivial incidents, to recollect the train of thought, immediately preceding the impact of the bolt. Shortly after noon the following day I was engaged in that odd mental process, a process which is, I imagine, a protective one, giving the mind a breathing space to regain something of its poise.

I had gone into my club, called for a whisky and soda, and while drinking it had picked up the mid-day edition of *The Evening Herald*. It consisted chiefly of racing news, in which I was not interested; but as I put it down my eye was held by a smudged heading in the Stop Press column: WOMAN MURDERED. Beneath were some half a dozen lines of letterpress: A young woman Kitty Sears was found dead in her bedroom at 15 Bear Street, a small throughfare off the Tottenham Court Road, about eight o'clock this morning. Her

throat had been cut and the head was almost completely severed. The discovery was made by the landlady when taking a cup of tea up to the unfortunate
woman's bedroom. The police were immediately
summoned and took charge of the case.

I had a second drink and then a third, and having
dulled the jangle of my nerves was able to consider
what I should do. I was from the first definitely
determined that I was not going to the police; I was
not going to be dragged into the vile affair by any
move on my part; and as I turned things over in my
mind it seemed to me most unlikely that I could be
connected with it. I was quite unknown in the
neighbourhood; while I was with Kitty Sears we had
met no one she knew nor had I encountered anyone in
my flight from that disastrous bedroom. Everything
pointed to the wisdom of doing and saying nothing.
But what of my American trip? Should I go or cancel
my passage? I was considering the pros and cons of
this when my heart missed a beat and then set up a
rapid thumping. There had suddenly slipped up into
my mind the forgotten fact that the previous day I
had gone into a small West End shop where I was not
known and tendered a five-pound-note in payment for
a necktie. The man had, as tradesmen occasionally
will, asked me to sign it and I had scribbled my name on
the back in pencil—an indelible pencil; I had then
remembered that I had before coming out put my
sovereign-purse in my hip pocket and I took back the
note, not wanting to be encumbered with a lot of
change, and gave the man a half-sovereign and a
sixpence. That note, with my name on, was now in
my note-case; or it was the one I had tossed on to the

bed as I fled. And I found that I could not look; not just then; I must wait a few moments to summon all my strength to face things if the note were not there; I watched the minute-hand of the clock move slowly over a small arc of the blank face before I put my hand in my pocket, took out my case, and released the tens and fives from the snap band. I felt that I knew it was not there and perhaps this apparent foreknowledge softened the blow, for presently when the most careful search had failed to find it I found myself feeling calmer and more self-controlled than I had done since I had read those few lines in *The Evening Herald*. It was, I reasoned, a thousand to one against her having changed the note that night; it was therefore in her possession now, or rather in the possession of the police; and that being so I was as good as under arrest. Even then I did not consider for a moment the question of going to the police; that I would not do; my chance of avoiding implication might be small but I was not going to destroy it entirely. The only definite act I decided upon was to cancel my passage on the *Mauretania*; apart from that not very positive activity I would do nothing. There was the chance that the police might lay hands on the murderer within the next few hours; that was indeed my chief comfort; quite unreasonably, for I was still implicated by the five-pound note; still branded as an associate; might still be arrested; or if not that, badgered and questioned and, worst of all, sub-pœnaed; something of that eternity in the sordid little bedroom might be dragged out of me and displayed for the lubricious entertainment of the mob. But I refused to reason; I built up a protective wall of casuistry about myself; and with that and the whisky made a tolerable effect of being quite unperturbed. I am certain that none of the two or three score members of the club who came in for a drink just then, nodded to me, or stayed a moment for a few words, noticed that I was anything but my usual self.

I skulked (that is the apt word) about London for the rest of that afternoon and evening, buying each fresh edition of all the papers as they appeared. But although there was much cry there was little wool; there were columns containing the mainly apochryphal life story of Kitty Sears; there was the inevitable quotation from Tom Hood; and there were gossipy bits and pieces obtained from Mrs. Peachey the landlady of 15 Bear Street and from neighbours, as well as from acquaintances of the dead girl. But of any real and fresh information there was none; the activities of Scotland Yard were veiled in a most uncomforting silence.

I did not know what to do to kill the time. I did not want to meet anyone I knew and have to discuss the case. I was finding it trying enough to hear strangers discussing it; and I found myself somehow resenting such discussions as if they were intrusions into my most private and intimate affairs. I did not want to be alone for then there was nothing to distract my thoughts; but neither did I want to go where it was not possible to buy the latest editions of the papers. And so, as I say, I skulked about London, walking, I suppose, some twenty miles by ten o'clock, when it suddenly came into my mind that if the police were looking for me they certainly could not find me while

I was wandering about the streets. The thought having once taken possession of my mind remained in harassing occupation and would give me no rest. I felt I had got to settle that point at once and hailing a cab gave the man my address; and so on edge were my nerves, so morbidly roused my imagination, that it seemed to me he gave me a queer glance as he nodded and repeated the address after me.

I let myself in and rang for my man Baker, and as soon as he came I knew at once that so far nothing had happened; but I asked him if there had been any callers, personal or telephone. "Only the tailor, sir," he said, "rang up to ask if you would call for a fitting at your convenience."

I told him he need not wait up, and when he asked me if there was anything I wanted I realised that I had not dined and also that I was emptily hungry. I was on the point of asking him to get me something and then changed my mind and told him no; and as soon as he had gone I got myself a scratch meal of biscuits and cheese and sherry. And then I settled myself down to read.

But no book would hold my attention and one after another I picked up and discarded new novels and memoirs, and old favourites which had never before failed me. Finally I got my water-colours and half a dozen boards and managed to distract my mind by covering them with quick impressionistic sketches.

I drank a lot of whisky and about half-past eleven I thought I heard newsboys calling and opened my window to listen; but there was nothing except the low rumble of remote traffic. I came back to my chair and as I did so the thought crossed my mind that I might possibly get some information from one of the newspaper offices. The first name that occurred to me was Tom Frankell; but *The Call* was a weekly and it was most unlikely the office would be open at nearly midnight on a Friday. And then I thought of Squitters Beamish and *The Morning News*. It was true he was only assistant literary editor and the chance of his being there very remote, but it was enough for me, and I rang up the *News* office. Of course he was not there, but a voice said, "I'll put you through to the night news-editor," and without waiting for my reply switched me over and I heard a staccato irritable voice say, "News-editor speaking, what is it?" I was explaining that I'd hoped to find Beamish there when he cut me short and asked me sharply if he could do anything. I said I wanted to know if there was any further news about the Bear Street murder and caught a muttered exclamation of annoyance; there was a long pause and then he said grudgingly, "Well, there's been an arrest; I can't tell you any more; it's only just come through." "Can't you tell me the name?" I asked. "Sorry," he said, "afraid I can't; you'll see it in all the morning's papers; good-night."

I sat for some considerable time casting about in my mind for some method of obtaining this inform-ation; and then caution whispered to me that it might be unwise to pursue the matter any further; this ringing up of people at midnight smacked of a more than normal interest in a sordid business. And so I resigned myself to wait until the morning, drank another stiff whisky, went to bed and, amazingly, fell quickly asleep; and, more amazingly still, did not

wake till Baker brought me my early tea and the
papers just after seven.

And there on the front page of some and on the
middle page of others stared out at me the face of
Val and the headlines: BEAR STREET MURDER—ARREST
OF FAMOUS CARTOONIST. But beyond the headlines,
and the information that Val had been arrested at his
flat at ten-thirty the previous evening, there was
nothing else in the way of news, although there was
a great deal about Val and his career on *The
Peepshow.*

I turned to the Stop Press columns. In each paper
there was the same three-line note: Valentine Grey
arrested in connection with the Bear Street murder,
will be brought before the magistrates at Mine Street
Police Court this morning at eleven o'clock.

I drank three cups of tea and found my mouth still
dry. I smoked several cigarettes in succession without
savouring them, my mind a tumbling wash of chaotic
thoughts.

Baker came in presently to tell me my bath was
ready and I caught his glance and knew he had seen
the papers; and thinking it best to speak of it openly I
said, "This is a terrible business, Baker." He made a
little gesture with his hands and said, "It's a mistake,
sir; must be; Mr. Grey and that little trollop!" And
then he asked me about breakfast and withdrew with
the air of one leaving a death-chamber.

After breakfast I rang up Val's solicitors, who told
me they were not representing Val in Court, on their
own advice to him, and had obtained the services of
Mr. Arthur Royden, a solicitor famous for the part
he had played in several recent cases on the capital

charge. "That means," I said, "that Val will have Hamilton Lane if—if it is necessary." "Possibly," was as far as they would commit themselves; and to my inquiry whether they could possibly get me a seat that morning in Court they said it was quite hopeless, as already there were applications enough to fill the court a dozen times over.

I had barely rung off five minutes when the telephone bell rang and the operator said there was a call for me from Percuil, and a few moments later I heard Michael's voice. After asking me if I knew anything beyond the mere fact of the arrest, their newspapers not carrying the Stop Press news, he listened to the little I was able to tell him and then told me they were all returning to London by the eleven forty-five from Truro and asked me if I would meet them.

But the day had not finished with us. The early afternoon papers contained the bald statement that the proceedings at Mine Street had lasted only ten minutes, that the police had asked for an adjournment until the following Wednesday, that Mr. Arthur Royden had asked for bail, which had been refused with the remark by Sir Henry Morton, the Magistrate, that he was surprised the request had been made. I rang up Mr. Royden and asked if it would be possible for me to see Val and he said he would try to arrange for me to see him in the morning but he could not promise anything and that it was in fact very doubtful. As I drove to Paddington to meet Michael and the others the newsboys were careering down the streets with placards bearing the bewildering statement: BEAR STREET MURDER—TRAGIC DEATH. I stopped the taxi, bought a paper, and found that Sir Hereward

Grey had died from a seizure just before noon at Knocke, in Belgium, where he and Lady Grey were on holiday.

There was more to come. I found Paddington Station charged with an extraordinary atmosphere of mingled tension and secrecy. All I could learn at first, from deprecating officialdom, was that the eleven forty-five from Truro would be late; half an hour went by and the news was allowed to circulate that there had been an accident; finally just before seven o'clock we learned that the express had run into a stationary train just outside Exeter, that a number of people were injured, but none as far as it was known, killed. Further information would be given, said officialdom, as soon as it was known. But I did not wait. I rang up Baker who told me Michael had rung through about three o'clock to say all the party were unhurt, although shaken; that they were staying in Exeter over night and hoped to come on the following day, but that I was not to think of meeting them as it was uncertain which train they would catch and there was the possibility that they might stay in Exeter a day or so as Sylvia had been the most shaken and might not be able to travel.

They did, however, get back to London on Sunday evening.

I was able to see Val on the Sunday morning. Royden took me along with him to Brixton Prison and left us alone for about a quarter of an hour.

Val looked well and entirely unmoved by the events of the last forty-eight hours. He greeted me with a smile and said, "Hello, Ju; don't bother to say you're

M

sure I'm innocent because I shan't believe you; every one's of course convinced I'm guilty." He paused a moment and then went on with a harsher note in his voice, "father included; that's what killed him. I suppose the only person in the world who doesn't believe it is my mother." He had risen from his chair, but he sat down again and added, "and as usual the minority's right. I didn't kill Kitty Sears. If I had I'd have owned up to it; one of my virtues. I knew her and I've slept with her but not that night, although I met her. I've made no statement yet, as you know, but of course I've told Royden everything and it's all in his hands now; he's a clever chap; he says he's quite hopeful it'll go no further than the Police Court proceedings; he's defending me there; if it does go for trial Hamilton Lane's going to accept the brief. I'll tell you what happened."

While he spoke I watched him, wondering if he was aware of my connection with the affair; but as he went on to describe his meeting with Kitty Sears that night I felt certain by his manner that he did not know; and with that awareness came the humiliating realisation that my sole preoccupation up till then had been with my own safety.

"I met Kitty that night," he said, "shortly after nine outside *The Oxford* and we spent the next two hours at three pubs, *The Horseshoe*, *The Star* and *The Plough*. We were at *The Plough* from ten till nearly half-past eleven, when we left together. At each of these pubs she met and had a few words with friends or acquaintances but I knew none of them and did not talk to them. They'll be able to identify me all right but it won't be necessary. That I was with Kitty till eleven-thirty won't be disputed; nor my previous connection with her.

"Earlier in the evening I'd considered going home with her for the night but I changed my mind later, as she was pretty tight, and I can't stomach (it's about the only thing I can't) being in bed with a tipsy woman. She was annoyed when she found I didn't intend to come home with her; she was loud and excited and while we didn't precisely quarrel (since I refused to) she went off in a bad temper refusing to let me put her in a taxi and saying she didn't want any more truck with a half-baked eunuch. By the bye we had a meal of sausage and mashed at *The Plough* about half-past ten. After leaving her I thought of going to the Club. Nine times out of ten I should have done and probably slept there, which would have been a cast-iron alibi and saved me a lot of trouble. But I decided to go to my flat and feeling muzzy and generally thick in the head and congested in the guts I thought I'd walk; a thing I did about once in a blue moon. I reached the flat about a quarter to one, let myself in and went straight to bed, not having met a soul who knew me since I'd left Kitty.

"Not too convincing a yarn, I'll admit; but it happens to be true. Kitty of course picked up someone else, took him home, and he cut her throat. May have been an old client with the usual grudge against her." He smiled. "I'm not sure I hadn't my share of that grievance against her; nearly a year ago (I've known her nearly two) I suspected I'd picked up a dose; but old Barentz of Harley street nipped it in the bud for me; and of course it might have been from someone else; just about then I was, I suppose, averaging five whores a week for months on end, so I'm probably loading the dice against poor little Kitty." He grimaced at me. "If they hang me, well, good luck to Ketch; I've no regrets; I've had a dam' good time, Ju.

"You're wondering why I didn't go to the police? That, of course, is what's worrying Royden. And when I give you one more piece of information, the —er—sort of *clou*, the prize-exhibit, of the whole business, you'll wonder a dam' sight more why I was such an infernal fool as to lie low. The devil of it is, Ju, I can't give any plausible, let alone valid, reason why I didn't go. I can of course say that in view of my position I didn't want my association with prostitutes, pimps and panders to be known, and that will be good enough as far as the case is concerned. But not as far as I'm concerned, old boy. *I* am not ashamed of it. But you don't need me to tell you that. Then why the devil didn't I hop along at once to Scotland Yard and tell them I'd been with Kitty up till nearly midnight? and all I can answer is that I just didn't want to; I just simply wasn't going to. Tell the Police? one of the things that isn't done. Sounds dam' silly and it'll sound a dam' sight sillier in a moment. For I'd every reason to believe I'd left with Kitty a piece of evidence which would shout my name from the house-tops, even to the police, whom we needn't accuse of being art connoisseurs. While we were guzzling in *The Plough* a Salvation Army lassie came in selling copies of *The War Cry* and I bought one, tipping her a shilling and thinking what a waste she was at that game, for she had a ripe little figure. The cover was a photograph of some old codger but there was a lot of blank space; of course there was the grey stipple-effect of the half-tone process; but blank enough. And to amuse Kitty I took out a pencil and drew some five or six caricatures of people in the bar, including the potman, the boss and one of the barmaids. And Kitty took it away with her and for all I knew had pushed it into a drawer in her bedroom. That in fact was what she must have done. Anyhow the police found it; and every line of those damned sketches howling out Val of *The Peepshow*. You'd think so, wouldn't you; even to the Police." He paused and smiled. "We flatter ourselves, Ju; think we're no end of swells and everybody knows our stuff as they do their own faces, when the cold truth is they neither know nor care. However, the police realised it was a clue at any rate, had *The War Cry* cover, or the part of it with the drawings on, photographed and sent prints round to all the papers asking them to publish at once. They were pretty slick about it and the drawings would have been in all the Saturday papers. But about ten o'clock on the Friday evening someone rang them up, someone who refused to say who he was, and informed them that the drawings were obviously done by Val of *The Peepshow* who was Mr. Valentine Grey. And in less than an hour they'd arrived at the flat and I was on my way to chokee. Pretty good going. And so the papers were asked not to publish the drawings; but they'll do so no doubt later, as they're exhibit A, and you'll be able to see for yourself. And that's the tale, Ju; that's the hole Royden's to pull me out of, or failing him dear old Hamilton. Well, good luck to them! By the bye I don't suppose you need me to tell you that none of my jibby friends, my little wantons, knew who or what I was; Kitty knew me just as Dick; to most of the others I was Charley; one or two, with a reputation for wit to sustain, called me Clarence. And that's the lot, old boy, and here comes Royden. Wish I could get you a ticket for the big show if it comes off, but," with his old engaging grin, "my name's mud at the box-office. You'll have to get round Royden."

"But who, Val," I said hastily, as Royden seeing us still talking paused in the corridor, "who was it rang up the police and gave you away?"

"Ah, who!" he laughed. "Not that it matters much; it merely pushed things forward a few hours. Obviously someone in a newspaper office for no one else had then seen the prints." He chuckled. "Probably old Finny of *The Globe*, hoping to get my job with *The Peepshow*."

"Or Squitters Beamish," I said.

He shook his head. "Not very likely," he said slowly; "probably wouldn't have been in the office at that time. But of course he might; and he'd be glad to do it on the quiet; he hates all our crowd."

I nodded. "On principle. Unlikely or not I've a feeling he's the scut." And as Royden coughed outside the door I rose and took both Val's hands in mine. I thought that the faintest flicker of emotion passed swiftly over his face but as I turned away he was smiling with all the old flippant cynical gaiety.

The inquest, which had been opened on the Saturday, was formally adjourned *sine die*. On Monday, Kitty Sears was buried in St. Pancras Churchyard. The case had seized the public imagination and so great were the crowds along the route and the radiating thoroughfares that traffic was wedged into a jam from

Camden Town to Hyde Park Corner. The crowds luckily controlled themselves for the Police, who were unprepared for any such demonstration, were unable to handle them. It was Crispin who said sardonically that it was an illuminating commentary upon our civilization that the two biggest funeral processions of the century should have been those of Victoria the Good, Empress of India, and Kitty Sears, a little East End doxy. But that was a mere mild foretaste of the mass hysteria which was presently to envelop the Bear Street Murder Case.

On Wednesday October the twelfth, at the resumed inquest, the coroner's jury returned a rather strangely-worded verdict: We find that the deceased Elizabeth Katherine Sears met her death by wilful murder, and that the evidence we have received is sufficient to commit the accused for trial.

Meanwhile at the Police Court the magisterial proceedings had been going on directed by the Senior Counsel of the Treasury, Sir George Manners; and in spite of Arthur Royden's defence that there was nothing but circumstantial evidence, and that not of the strongest, to connect the prisoner with the murder, Val was sent forward for trial before the November Sessions of the Central Criminal Court.

On Tuesday, November the eighth the Grand Jury, charged by Sir Ernest Lawson, K.C., had before them the deposition in the case of *Rex v. Grey*; and having considered them they returned a true bill against the accused and the trial opened two days later.

The day before the trial began most of the news-papers in the country published the drawings Val had done on the corner of *The War Cry*, and this is perhaps

as good a place as any to give a reproduction of that
notorious scrap of paper.

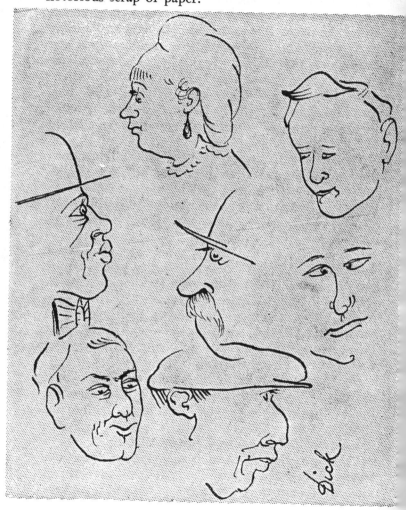

The judge was Mr. Justice Carden. The counsel for
the Crown were Sir George Manners, Mr. E. P. Gates
and Mr. L. R. Needham; they were instructed by Mr.
A. J. Porson of the Treasury. The counsel for the
Defence were Mr. G. Hamilton Lane, K.C., Mr. Charles
Fenway and Mr. F. Dale-Scott. They were instructed
by Mr. Arthur Royden.

Crispin, Michael and I all managed to obtain seats
for the whole of the proceedings. None of the rest of
our people was present, although Lady Grey would
very courageously have had a seat at the solicitor's
table had not Val expressly asked her, through Royden,
not to attend.

The scene in court was not unlike that of a fashionable first night: wealth, society and the arts were
represented as perhaps never before in the criminal
trial of a commoner; and every day and all day long
(and the trial lasted six days) crowds hung about the
precincts of the Old Bailey, while in bars and clubs,
in shops and restaurants and in the foyers of theatres
and music halls, the case was the main topic of conversation. And from the first day of the trial it was
clear that Val in the public estimation was the hero
of the occasion. That vast animal, the public, prone
to the lowest and so strangely incapable of the highest,
which can within the space of one short fickle week
cry *hosanna!* and *crucify him!* took Val to its heart; and
few accused men in the long history of criminal
procedure in this country can have faced their judge
with so tremendous a mass of sentimental hysteria
solidly behind them. There is no accounting for such
things. True, he took the eye with his tall languid
figure, his pale face, fine features and yellow hair;

there was too about his perfect poise, his calm, quiet demeanour that nothing could ruffle or perturb, something almost gallant; he was moreover that romantic figure—an "artist"; and perhaps over and above all there fought for him most potently that immemorial strangely cruel, strangely inexplicable mass hatred of the prostitute. Yet, giving full weight to all this, here was a young man who, for all the public knew to the contrary, had gone home with a young woman, received her caresses (venal as they might be), slept in her arms and then, waking some hours later, had cut her throat with such brutal violence that the head was only held on to the trunk by the few muscles which had escaped the knife. And of this young butcher the public was prepared to make, had indeed made, a hero, without apparently one thought of pity for the wretched little wanton whose young body, so recently a rich enticement for men, was already corrupting in St. Pancras Churchyard.

From the magisterial proceedings the tenor of both prosecution and defence was known; no surprises were expected; no one was believed to have anything dramatic up his sleeve; it was to be a straightforward fight between two great lawyers, the one Sir George Manners, small, dapper, precise, shrewd, imperturbable, cool and subtle; the other Gordon Hamilton Lane, tall, burly, handsome, quick-witted, a brilliant if emotional orator; the one resting his case entirely upon circumstantial evidence, the other upon the inherent dangerousness of such evidence, plus the weakest of alibis. In short, a duel between two skilled opponents; a duel to the death, but not the death of one of the duellists. And so, assured of a grand show,

the public settled itself comfortably for the overture.

It would not serve the purpose of this story of mine
to give the trial in detail, nor could I if I wished
without reference to the verbatim report; all descriptions of such events are bloodless things in comparison
with the vitality of the actual scenes as they unfold
themselves before the eyes. I shall therefore limit
myself to a summary, diversified and coloured, I trust,
by just those small incidents which remain in my
memory because of their very vividness.

I remember very clearly the overture, an overture
in a packed yet almost breathlessly silent court. The
Clerk of Arraigns, a portentous figure, said: "Valentine Arthur Hereward Grey, you are indicted for, and
also stand charged on the coroner's inquisition with,
the wilful murder of Elizabeth Katherine Sears. Are
you guilty or not guilty?"

All eyes went to Val. He had been seated, leaning
forward with his arms on the rail, but had stood up
as the clerk addressed him. His face was calm, almost
expressionless; he seemed completely master of himself. Before he answered his glance went round the
court; and then he said quietly, "I am not guilty."

A jury was empanelled and sworn in; and the clerk
then addressed its members: "Gentlemen of the Jury,
Valentine Arthur Hereward Grey is indicted for, and
also stands charged on the coroner's inquisition with,
the wilful murder of Elizabeth Katherine Sears. To
this indictment and inquisition he has pleaded not
guilty, and it is your duty to inquire whether he is
guilty or not."

Sir George Manners then rose to open the case for

the Crown, and as he did so there was an audible exhalation of breath from the crowded court; it was almost a sigh, a contented sigh, the sigh of a boy at his first play when the curtain goes up.

Sir George's speech gave all the details of the affair as a simple consecutive narrative, and as far as I can recollect ran somewhat as follows: "The charge is that of murder and that some one on the early morning of September the twenty-sixth last, at a house situated at 15 Bear Street, Tottenham Court Road, did commit the crime of murder, you will have no doubt whatever. Who was the guilty person? Upon that morning there was discovered the dead body of a young woman whose full name was Elizabeth Katherine Sears, but who was known to her intimates as Kitty Sears. On examination of the body, which was lying in bed, it was seen that the throat had been cut from ear to ear and that death had been almost instantaneous. It was apparent some very sharp weapon had been employed with great force. The body was naked, and the medical man who was immediately called in was of the opinion, because of the young woman's peaceful and restful attitude—she was lying on her left side, her legs slightly drawn up and her left arm behind her. The medical man for these reasons, as I say, was of the opinion that she had been murdered in her sleep. The deceased young woman belonged to the ' unfortunate ' class, and I do not think it will be unfair if I add almost to the lowest class of unfortunates.

"The accused is a young man of good birth and education; he is a brilliant artist and well known to the public as the cartoonist Val of the weekly periodical *The Peepshow*. He has on his own admission been acquainted with the dead woman for a period of not less than two years, and he has admitted having intimate relations with her on several occasions.

"Let us come to the events of the evening preceding the murder. You will bear in mind that the accused admits the sequence of events up to a certain point. He met Kitty Sears just after nine o'clock outside the Oxford Music Hall and they went together into the saloon bar of *The Horseshoe Hotel*, where they sat drinking for nearly half an hour, during which time Kitty Sears spoke to several friends whose evidence to this effect is unnecessary, since the fact is not contested by the defence. The two left *The Horseshoe*, walked along the Tottenham Court Road and, coming to *The Star Inn*, entered and remained there for half-an-hour. Here also Kitty Sears met and chatted with friends. On leaving, they continued in the direction of Camden Town and entered *The Plough*, where they remained until half-past eleven. While in *The Plough* they had a meal, somewhere about half-past ten, and this fact is of great importance, of sausages and mashed potatoes. But there was something else of equal importance which happened at *The Plough* that evening. A young woman of the Salvation Army entered the saloon bar to offer copies of *The War Cry* for sale. The accused bought a copy and to amuse his companion drew on the blank parts of the cover several caricatures of people in and behind the bar. With those sketches every one is now familiar from their publication in the press.

"The accused and the deceased woman left *The Plough* at half-past eleven. The accused says that he refused to go home with her, as she was tipsy, and after angry words from her she went off alone, having refused his offer of a taxi to take her home; and that was the last he saw of her. According to his story, he then decided to walk home, as he felt the walk would refresh him, and he set off, finally reaching his flat in Hampstead at about a quarter to one, and going straight to bed without meeting anyone either on the way or at the flat. His manservant, John Cooper, did not see him come in.

"Now let us come to the early hours of the next morning. The medical evidence is to the effect, in view of the condition of the stomach and alimentary canal of the dead woman, and bearing in mind that a meal was eaten by her not earlier than half-past ten, that the murder took place at some time between the hours of three o'clock and half-past four. Those are the extreme limits, but it was probably, and I again quote the medical evidence, not much later than half-past three and almost certainly not later than four o'clock. I must here refer to the fact that no weapon has been found, and that while there was so great an effusion of blood that the bed-clothes and mattress were saturated and blood had even dripped through on to the floor, no bloodstains have been discovered on any of the accused's clothing. I do not think any stress should be laid upon this circumstance, as it is fairly obvious that the murderer was naked when he committed the crime. That he afterwards washed in a bowl and had probably used some of his victim's clothing to wipe the weapon on, and probably his hands before washing them, is suggested by the state of the room as given in the police evidence.

"Now living at Number 13 Bear Street, the house

next door, is a young couple, Mr. and Mrs. Henry Adams. Mr. Adams is a railway foreman, and that week he had to be at King's Cross Station at a quarter to six. His alarm clock was set to go off at half-past four, when his wife got up to get him his breakfast, leaving him in bed for another quarter of an hour or so. Mrs. Adams got up within a few minutes of the alarm clock going off, washed and dressed; and then, before going downstairs, woke her husband. As she passed the bedroom window she heard a gate clang and, looking out, saw a man walking away from number fifteen. He was, she says, a youngish man, as far as could be judged from a back view, and was wearing a light-coloured overcoat and a light cap. She particularly noticed a peculiarity in his gait which she has described colloquially as a sort of Weary-Willie slouch. She watched him until he passed beyond the range of the street lamp outside number eleven.

"But that morning there were two other people afoot in Bear Street, or close to Bear Street, at that early hour. One was Mr. Frank Spencer, who was cycling to his work in Leadenhall Market; and the other Mrs. Alice Brown, who was walking to her work, which is that of charwoman in the buffet at Euston Station. Mr. Spencer will say that he overtook a young man, who was walking along on the right-hand pavement which is the same side of the street as number fifteen. This young man was wearing a light overcoat, and Mr. Spencer particularly noticed his lounging gait. He did not see his face. But we have some one who did, or partly so. Mrs. Brown will tell us that she saw a young man coming towards her as she turned into Bear Street. He was on the opposite side of the road, but she crossed over, as that was the way she had to go; but as she drew near this young man turned his head away, but not before Mrs. Brown had noticed his pale complexion. He was, she says, wearing a light overcoat and, she thinks, but is not certain, a bowler hat. She turned a moment to watch him because, as she will tell you, he looked, in her own words, such a toff; and she will also tell you that what struck her chiefly, apart from his pale face and his smart appearance, was a sort of tired slouch, to quote her own words again.

"At various identification parades at Mine Street Police Station yard each of these three witnesses, Mrs. Adams, Mr. Spencer and Mrs. Brown, picked out the accused as the man they saw that morning; and each time the deciding factor was his gait.

"Gentlemen of the jury, that is the case for the Crown against the accused. I will not close without saying this: I hope I have said nothing unfair to the young man who is upon his trial; but it is my duty to press upon you the facts, as the prosecution hopes to prove them. You will be not only wise but just, and you will only be just. You will listen carefully to everything which can be said for as well as against this young man."

Evidence for the prosecution was then called.

Mr. Hamilton Lane's cross-examination was concentrated upon shaking the evidence of the three witnesses who had identified Val as the man seen in Bear Street that morning; and he succeeded to a considerable extent in doing this. Under his cross-examination Mrs. Brown finally agreed that the man she had seen was wearing a bowler hat, and Mr. Spencer also admitted that it was probably a bowler hat, but that he hadn't taken much notice. Only Mrs. Adams could not be moved from her statement that the young man she had seen was wearing a light cap. But this conflict of opinion was definitely a point for the defence, and it was later much strengthened when the defence stated, and offered to bring evidence to support the statement, that Val had never in his life worn a bowler, that he now usually wore a sombrero, and that on the night of his meeting with Kitty Sears he was wearing a dark check cap. A good deal of evidence was called in connection with this cap question, and while there was some conflict of opinion, the evidence tended to show that he was wearing a cap and that it was dark rather than light.

With regard to the identification evidence, the defence brought out the admission that Spencer had at first picked out another man and that it was only when the parade was made to walk that he picked out Val, and then only at the second attempt; further, that Mrs. Brown had failed to pick out Val until he walked. More damaging still was Spencer's admission that before he went on the parade he knew there was some talk of the accused's slouching gait. But the point which told most strongly in Val's favour, by discrediting the three witnesses in Bear Street, was the fact that the electric standard lights in the streets were extinguished that morning at 4.37, as shown by the record chart at the Electric Light Department of the St. Pancras Parish Council. The witnesses were then obviously mistaken about the time, or about what they had noticed "so clearly and particularly," as they had said, for the street after the extinguishing of the lamps would have been in a rather dim twilight.

The evidence for the prosecution was not finished until noon on Monday, the fourth day of the trial. There had occurred on the Saturday afternoon, during the cross-examination of a medical witness, an odd little incident which by its touch of domestic intimacy had relieved the long-drawn-out tension, displaying before the court, that court holding the balance of life or death, so warmly human a little picture that many there smiled, Val among them.

The judge had put a question to the witness concerning the position of the dead woman's left arm as she lay in bed, it having been suggested several times in the evidence that it would not have been naturally behind her and that it had been forced back by the murderer. There was seen to be some whispering among the jury, and the foreman stood up and said, "My lord, one of the jurors has passed me a note." It was handed to the judge, who read it and then said, "Although I do not think the point is an important one, I think I should acquaint the court with the contents of this note which has very properly been handed to me. One of the jurors says that his wife always sleeps on her left side and almost invariably has her left arm stretched down behind her." He folded the note, placed it upon his papers and then added: "It is clear, therefore, that the position is not necessarily an unnatural one."

Hamilton Lane began his speech for the defence shortly after two o'clock that Monday afternoon. Perhaps oddly, I remember but little of it; it was so richly oratorical an affair, so rapidly swept along the emotions, that I imagine its effect upon the mind was, by that very swiftness of emotional appeal, transitory. His first sentence was unforgettable; few in that packed court will not remember it all their days. The immediate result of its impact upon the minds of all those present was to evoke a startled gasp. He stood quite still a moment before beginning to speak, one hand upon his hip, a magnificent figure dwarfing every one else there, and allowed his glance to go round the court, over the jury, thence to Val and finally it rested upon the judge, and he began: "My lord, I submit that there is no case to go to the jury." He paused for quite ten seconds and then went on: "You will find in the evidence that has been put before the court everything absent that ought to be present. The law is well established that the presumption of innocence is in favour of an accused person until his guilt is proved. In the first place there is an absolute and utter want of any evidence that the accused was ever seen upon the premises in 15 Bear Street. Secondly, the evidence of identification is of the weakest description and ought not to be taken into account; it is utterly unreliable; it is tainted by the admission that one of these witnesses already knew what he was to look for. Thirdly, there is not a suggestion of motive attributed to the accused, not one iota of evidence even of a suggestive nature. I ask your lordship to say that the accused ought not to be put in any further peril on evidence such as that which has been put before the court."

He paused here and looked at Mr. Justice Carden, who said quietly, "I cannot say that there is no case to go to the jury. Even putting aside that evidence altogether, I cannot say there is no case."

Hamilton Lane bowed slightly and continued: "Very well, my lord, I will presently call the accused and other witnesses. Grey shall speak for himself in the witness-box, and it will be for you, gentlemen of the jury, to judge his story."

Counsel then went on to outline the case for the defence. There comes back to me but little of that long speech which lasted until the court adjourned for the day. Again and again he referred to the three witnesses of identification, calling them scornfully "these wonderful people who can see in the dark." Three times during the speech he drew attention directly to Val, saying, or using words to this effect, "I want you to look at him. Clear your minds of the admitted fact that he has consorted with prostitutes —never mind that—but look at him and ask yourselves whether he is a man capable of that bloody violence which took away the life of that unfortunate girl; it is unthinkable." Dealing with Val's return to his flat in the early hours of the morning, he said contemptuously, "The prosecution have made great play with the fact that no one saw Grey. No, no one saw him. His manservant John Cooper did not see him. Mr. Arthur Compton, who occupies the flat above, did not see him. But they heard him. Mr. Cooper and Mr. Compton will go into the witness-box and tell you what they heard and what construction they put upon those sounds; those noises which were so clearly just those which a man would make in his own rooms while being careful not to disturb others. The prosecution in another court have already put forward its cock-and-bull story to account for what was heard. It was the accused's dog—a cocker spaniel! Can theorising go to more preposterous lengths? A cocker spaniel turning in its sleep or scratching itself, to awaken a man already asleep and another just dozing off, and to be mistaken for the movements of a man!"

Each time Hamilton Lane called the court's attention to Val, and all eyes were turned upon him, I watched him closely and marvelled at his calm impassivity under that flaying inquisition; once indeed the faintest of smiles flickered over his face.

But the most dramatic moment of the trial, the tit-bit every one was impatiently waiting for, was the calling of Val into the witness-box to give evidence on his own behalf. This facility bestowed upon a prisoner by the Criminal Evidence Act of 1898 was so recent an innovation, was the subject of so much legal controversy, was considered so risky a proceeding, that advantage of it was rarely taken, and only once since the passing of the Act had an accused murderer, availing himself of the facility, successfully maintained his plea of not guilty.

The whole morning of the fifth day was occupied by the evidence of witnesses for the defence and their cross-examination by the Crown. But so eager was the public for Val's calling to the box that it was plain they listened with impatience and boredom even to such evidence as that of Val's manservant, Cooper, who could not be shaken from his statement that he was woken just before one, heard the noise of movement downstairs, listened for a minute or so, and then, being assured by the familiar sound of the movements that it was Val, turned over and went to sleep again.

At half-past two on the Tuesday afternoon, the fifth day of the trial, Val was called to the witness-box. He stood there facing his counsel, his glance for a moment straying over the court; and once again there was that massed exhalation, that sigh of almost unbearable expectation. The two central figures of that tense scene made a dramatic contrast: the defender—tall, dark, burly, magnificently imposing, strikingly handsome; the accused—tall, slim, drooping, pallid, yellow-haired, almost boyishly beautiful.

Counsel's left hand went to his hip; the fingers of his other hand toyed with a gold-cased pencil. His glance held Val's for a long moment, and then he said, "What is your profession?"

"I am an artist; a black-and-white artist."

"You have a permanent post on the periodical *The Peepshow* as cartoonist?"

"Yes."

"When were you arrested?"

"At twenty minutes to eleven on the evening of September the twenty-sixth at my flat in Hampstead."

"You have been in prison since the twenty-sixth?"

"Yes."

"Did you kill Kitty Sears?"

"It is absurd. If I had killed her I would have said so."

"You must answer straight. I will ask you only straight questions. Did you kill her?"

"No."

And so it went on all that afternoon till the court adjourned, counsel taking Val step by step through all the events of the significant hours. Towards the close of his examination Hamilton Lane said, "When you left Kitty Sears that night why did you decide to walk home?"

"I felt unwell, and I thought the walk would be the best thing for me."

"There was no other reason?"

"None whatever."

"What time did you reach your flat?"

"Roughly about a quarter to one. I don't remember looking at my watch, but I had probably done so just previously, as that was the impression I afterwards had of the time. Also the distance is, I should say, about five miles and my usual rate of walking is roughly four miles an hour."

"That would be pretty fast for a slouch?"

"I don't think any one could slouch at four miles an hour." Val smiled and added: "I don't think I slouch."

"And when you let yourself in what did you do?"

"Patted my cocker and went up to bed."

"Where was the spaniel when you entered?"

"On my best arm-chair, where it usually sleeps." (A ripple of laughter went round the court at this reply.)

"Is it a restless dog? I mean is it in the habit of moving about during the night?"

"Not as a habit; but I have heard it."

"How many bedrooms are there in your flat?"

"Five; it is much larger than I need, but I took it because of its situation; there is a beautiful view from my bedroom window."

"Is your man's room near yours?"

"No, it is the farthest away."

"When did you first hear of the death of Kitty Sears?"

"About twelve-thirty the next day, just before I

went out to lunch. I was in my studio and Cooper brought me in the sporting papers."

"Did he say anything?"

"He said, ' There's a murder case in the Stop Press.'"

"Anything else?"

"No. It was not until some five minutes later, after he'd gone out, that I picked up the paper and discovered what had happened."

"You were very distressed?"

"Naturally."

"And frightened?"

"Well, not frightened. I was considerably perturbed."

"When you made those sketches on the cover of *The War Cry* did you sign them?"

"Not as one signs a drawing. I just wrote Dick in the corner."

"That was the name she knew you by?"

"Yes."

"She did not know your real name nor what you were?"

"No. None of the—the women I associated with knew who I was."

"And you gave the paper to her as you left *The Plough*."

"I don't remember giving it to her. I had forgotten about it by then. But obviously she took it with her when we left."

"You left her shortly after half-past eleven. Was that the last time you saw her that night?"

"Yes."

"Do you swear that?"

"I swear it before God."

When the court assembled the next morning, the sixth day of the trial and the last, Sir George Manners rose immediately to cross-examine. He spent nearly an hour cross-examining the witnesses for the defence, and then Val was called. This was, I imagine, for those spectators packed in the court, the tastiest morsel of the case. Sir George had a great reputation as a cross-examiner, and it was realised by all that Val was now to be put upon the rack. There was nothing about Sir George of Hamilton Lane's imposing magnificence, nor of his emotional theatricality. His approach was quiet, almost suave, and his voice so low that only the closest attention rendered it always audible. He made no gestures, had no mannerisms, unless it were the keeping of his left hand in his trousers pocket.

"How long had you known Kitty Sears?"

"About two years."

"That association had been of an intimate nature?"

"Yes."

"When you left her you walked home, a distance of five miles?"

"Yes."

"Because you felt unwell?"

"Yes."

"Would it be an exaggeration to say you were intoxicated?"

"A gross exaggeration. I was not even mildly tipsy. I felt rather sick; it was due to the sausages."

"They were bad?"

"Not at all. They simply had not agreed with me."

"It was not a usual thing for you to walk home from such a distance so late at night?"

"Most unusual."

"What was your usual habit?"

"I should take a taxi."

"To your flat?"

"Not always. I frequently went to my club to play cards or billiards, and often slept there if it was late when the game was over."

"Why did you not go to your club on that night?"

"I felt unwell and wanted to go to bed."

"A taxi would have achieved that object much quicker than walking."

"I thought the walk would settle my stomach."

"You could have gone to your club and slept there. It was nearer than your flat, was it not?"

"Quite a lot. I can't say why I chose to go home rather than to the club, except that I certainly didn't want to play cards or anything else."

"You reached home about a quarter to one?"

"Yes."

"And went straight to bed?"

"Yes."

"You heard nothing?"

"No. I fell asleep almost at once."

"At what time did your man call you in the morning?"

"I couldn't say exactly. He has said a quarter to eight, and that is no doubt correct; it is about the usual time."

"That was the earliest he had seen you?"

"Yes."

"What time would he have got up?"

"About seven."

"You are a fairly fast walker?"

"Pretty fair."

"You could walk from Bear Street to your flat in an hour and a quarter?"

"Comfortably; in an hour if I were really in a hurry."

"Is slouching a correct description of your gait?"

"Quite incorrect."

"How would you describe it yourself?"

Val smiled. "I have heard it called a lope."

"Yes, but yourself."

"If I were deep in thought it might probably be described as a lounging gait."

"Yes, but as a general rule."

"I really couldn't say; I am not aware that it differs from anyone else's."

"You are something of an athlete?"

"Not at all. I do the usual things: swim, play golf, fish and ride."

"You are a good swimmer?"

"Well, yes."

"Quite a powerful swimmer?"

"I suppose so."

"You are, in fact, quite a powerful man? A muscular man?"

"I'm a fair average. I'm probably stronger than I look."

"When you learned of the death of Kitty Sears why did you not go to the police?"

"It's obvious."

"Never mind its being obvious. Why didn't you?"

"Any average man would appreciate——"

"Grey, I'm asking you a straightforward question. Please answer me directly and without equivocation. Why did you not go to the police?"

"I did not want to be involved in so unsavoury an affair."

"You are an intelligent man. You must have realised that you could not escape being involved."

"I don't follow you."

"There was *The War Cry*. As a noted artist you must have realised that those drawings sooner or later must implicate you."

"She might have destroyed the paper."

"Why take it home merely to destroy it?"

"Why do people do all sorts of unaccountable things?"

"You are not to ask me questions."

"It was rather a rhetorical question, wasn't it?"

"Never mind that; answer my question."

"It is impossible to answer it."

"Try."

Val looked over to the judge and said quietly, "My lord, I appeal to you. It is an impossible question to answer."

Mr. Justice Carden said, "I do not see that it is of any importance, Sir George."

"Very well, my lord," Manners said, and continued to Val: "You wished to avoid implication in an unsavoury affair. That was your sole reason for not going to the police?"

"Yes."

"You were afraid?"

"It was not fear; it was merely a desire to keep clear of an unpleasant affair."

"Did you sleep with Kitty Sears on the night of September the twenty-fifth?"

"No. I slept in my own flat."

That ended Val's cross-examination and almost immediately after the court reassembled after lunch Hamilton. Lane rose to make his closing speech for the defence. It lasted till nearly half-past three and, compared with his opening speech, it was a quiet and unemotional affair. I was watching Val during the speech and noticed he was calmly engaged in making sketches, not only of his counsel but of the judge, and apparently of some of the well-known men and women among that fashionable crowd which had been so avidly watching the show for nearly a week and which was now settling itself comfortably to enjoy to the last squeezed-out drop the final scenes of what the next morning's papers were to describe as "the classic British crime of the last hundred years," whatever that might mean.

I have said that speech was a comparatively unemotional affair, but it closed on a note of feeling which, despite its theatrical touch, was obviously sincere. Lane had begun: "Gentlemen of the jury, I should like to remind you that you must return your verdict, the responsibility of which is yours and yours alone, not on speeches of counsel or the summing-up of the learned judge, but on the evidence and on nothing else but that evidence. And on that evidence I am entitled to a verdict of not guilty."

He ended: "If you are satisfied beyond all reasonable doubt that the man standing there, on the night of September the twenty-fifth murdered Kitty Sears, then, although it breaks your hearts to do so, find him guilty and send him to the scaffold. But if under the guidance of a greater Power than any earthly power you feel on the evidence laid before you that you could not honestly and conscientiously say beyond all reasonable doubt that the prosecution have proved their case, then I say it will be your duty as well as your pleasure to say, as you are bound to say, that Valentine Grey is not guilty of the murder of Kitty Sears."

Five minutes later Sir George Manners rose to make the closing speech for the Crown. It was short and precise and notable chiefly for its personal reference to Val. Sir George began: "I wish to impress upon you, gentlemen of the jury, no less sincerely than my learned friend, that if you have any reasonable doubt it is your duty to bring in a verdict of not guilty." He ended, speaking very slowly and for the first time during the whole trial raising his voice, "I ask you to act not upon suspicion, but only upon evidence; and upon the evidence as it has been put before you I submit that the only possible verdict is one of guilty." Of Val he had said, giving one quick glance in his direction, "You have in the accused a man who is a peculiar man, a man cool and collected, a man whose nerve is so extraordinary that nothing can move him. You have seen him day by day throughout this long trial; but more than that, you have his own words. When he heard that the girl in whose company he had been that night had been found murdered he was, he has told us calmly, perturbed. That is all. But even that is more emotion than he has displayed throughout this trial. Doubtless that is self-control; a commendable attribute; but such control is only possible to a man of quite extraordinary insensitiveness; a cold-blooded man. And I would remind you that the murder was one of the most cold-blooded in the annals of crime in this country."

Shortly after five o'clock the judge began his charge to the jury, the summing-up. By now all the thoroughfares outside the Old Bailey were congested with tremendous crowds waiting for the end. Within a circle whose radius was half a mile and whose centre was the court there was not from five o'clock onwards a single turning wheel. Again and again that crowd could be heard from inside the court as a vast low ululation; but it impressed itself upon more than our ears; its surge and press seemed close about us; we felt its presence like that of some tremendous animal; it had, to me at least, the quality of a beast in ambush.

As Mr. Justice Carden began to speak, Crispin, who was beside me, whispered, "Look at Val. By God! he's a man." And indeed he was facing the last stage of that long and eroding ordeal as he had faced all the others. Possibly he was a shade paler; but the court was stuffy and malodorous and most of us were, I imagine, white-faced. His expression was calm, impassive, almost serene; there was not one visible nervous movement of any part of his body; he seemed a mildly-interested auditor, but no more than mildly; and after a while even that mild interest he seemed to lose and allowed his glance to wander about the Court. And before the end he was drawing on a pad in front of him; not those meaningless sketches and scribbles which so often betray extreme nervous tension, but carefully-drawn little portraits, and most of them of the man whose words then being so slowly and deliberately spoken meant life or death to him.

His utter, almost incredible, sang-froid was the

more remarkable because, to the amazement and, I think it is fair to say the consternation, of the great majority of those present, the summing-up was dead against Val. The judge's voice, low-toned, deliberate and with something of the effect of an accumulation of hammer-strokes, went on and on in its merciless indictment: ". . . His defence has been conducted in the most able and masterly manner and in a way worthy of the best traditions of the English Bar. That defence maintains that the accused is not only entitled to a verdict of not guilty, but that there is no evidence at all against him. Counsel for the defence apparently holds there was no evidence for anyone to have committed the crime. But it is clear that the woman must have been murdered by a man who was leading a double life, by a man whom nobody would believe to have been guilty of a shocking murder, but would pass in decent society as a highly-respectable citizen. It has been said during the present case that there was nothing in the accused's character to suggest that he has been guilty of such a crime. You have been asked to look at him and then to ask yourselves if he could possibly have committed that brutal and violent murder. I am sorry to say that the whole of the evidence shows that the accused has been leading a double life. You have two pictures of him; in the one he is a man of birth and education, of brilliant gifts, whose work has made his name known to many thousands of his fellow-countrymen, who numbers among his friends and acquaintances many people of distinction, and who has doubtless been a welcome guest in their homes; in the other picture you have a man known variously by the name of Dick or

Charley or Clarence, who spends much of his time in public houses, who consorts with harlots of the lowest class, spending his substance and degrading his body and soul in disgusting intimacy with them; a man who with every advantage that life can offer, with the best, the finest and the highest open to him, chooses the lecherous, the sordid, the base and the infamous. Am I not therefore justified in saying that the accused has been living a double life, a double life without precedent in my experience, and it is a long one, of life and humanity. Am I not justified in saying, are you not justified in thinking, that such a man is capable of the brutal crime with which he is charged? We have heard much of the degradation of the dead woman. Is that degradation at all comparable to the degradation of this young man?"

There was now in all the court a breathless, an almost unendurably painful, attention to the words so slowly and deliberately being spoken by the judge. Never, surely, had there been a charge to a jury more damning, more clear. The doom seemed already to have been spoken. I glanced swiftly across to Val and could not withhold my wonder nor indeed a stirring of admiration in my heart. The serenity of his pale face was untroubled; he alone of all those present seemed utterly unmoved, calm, remote, unperturbed.

The slow, deliberate voice went on in those cool accents of denunciation, reviewing item by item the evidence of the Crown and for the defence, telling yet once again briefly, yet omitting nothing of significance, the story of the crime.

And then at a few minutes to six o'clock, and so abruptly, so startlingly, that once more there was a

o

gasp of amazement, there came a change: "In this case there is not an atom of direct evidence against the prisoner; the case depends entirely upon circumstantial or presumptive evidence. Although undoubtedly there is the gravest possible suspicion against the accused; although undoubtedly it is my duty to do all I can to further the interests of justice so that criminals are brought to justice and convicted, it is also my duty to inform you—to inform any jury—that however strong your feelings may be against him, you must not find a verdict of guilty against the accused unless no loophole is left by which he can escape." He paused a long moment and his glance went from the jury to Val, rested upon him gravely and deliberately for a while and then was raised, and the slow voice went on: "In my judgment, strong as the suspicion in the case undoubtedly is, I do not think that the prosecution has brought the case home near enough to the accused ——" There crashed out (no other word is apt) at this, interrupting the judge's voice, a storm of applause which for nearly a minute could not be quelled. It was heard by the vast crowd without and was taken up and went roaring tumultuously along the packed thoroughfares. It died away in court as suddenly as it had begun and Mr. Justice Carden continued, as if there had been no break in his words: "You are not bound to act on my views at all; but it behoves us to be most careful before we find a man guilty of such a charge. It is, of course, a matter for you and for you alone, gentlemen. I think I have spoken plainly. You are free to please yourselves and you need not act on my view at all.

"I am now going to ask you to retire to consider

your verdict. Weigh carefully the evidence heard from both sides. If you think the prosecution have proved the case against the accused, your verdict will be one of guilty; if, on the other hand, they have not done so, if there is any loophole, however small, your verdict will be one of not guilty."

The jury then retired. It was exactly fourteen minutes past six.

An hour passed.

A second went by.

Another half-hour and then there was a stir, a noise of movement, a great whispering. It was coming now. I felt Crispin's hand upon my arm, heard Michael's rapid breathing beside me. My heart began a suffocating quick throbbing. Val was brought into court; the judge slowly entered and took his seat; the jury filed in. The Clerk of Arraigns stood up. The utter stillness and silence in the court was unbearable. Somewhere a woman uttered an hysterical sobbing cry. I looked over to Val. He stood with his hands clasped lightly behind his back, his head a little raised, his expression calm, unmoved.

The Clerk of Arraigns said in a husky voice, clearing his throat after the first word, "Gentlemen of the jury, have you agreed upon your verdict?"

The foreman, a short, spare, grizzled man with something of the look of a shaggy terrier, said loudly, "We have."

The Clerk of Arraigns then asked, "Do you find the prisoner at the bar guilty or not guilty of the wilful murder of Elizabeth Katherine Sears?"

"We find him not guilty."

And at this a woman's voice screamed, "Oh, thank

God!" And there broke out so tremendous a clamour of cheering that nothing more could be done, despite the efforts of the ushers, for some three or four minutes.

And then the Clerk of Arraigns said, "You say that he is not guilty. Is that the verdict of you all?"

"It is."

Mr. Hamilton Lane then rose and said quietly, "I have to ask your lordship that the accused may be discharged." And Mr. Justice Carden, looking from Counsel to Val, nodded his head and said, "Yes, certainly."

Of the renewed uproar within the court and of the unprecedented scenes without I shall say nothing. Let one scene, enacted twenty minutes later at the Regent Theatre in the Strand, stand for and typify them all. The curtain was rung down in the middle of the second act of *Caste* and was raised again at once, revealing Mrs. Delabre, the famous actress and the lessee of the theatre, standing alone in the centre of the stage. She had no part in the play and was wearing her outdoor clothes. She was panting for breath and had one hand upon her breast. "I have just arrived from the court," she gasped, "the court where young Valentine Grey stood in peril of his life. I am glad to be able to tell you that the jury found him not guilty." After waiting a full minute while the cheering echoed round the auditorium she held up a hand and went on: "I am pleased to hear the reception of the tidings I have brought. While the jury were out we seemed to hold our breath, and we hoped, but we feared perhaps the jury would after all—after all——" She paused as if overcome by emotion and then continued:

"I was one of those who burst into tears, others burst into cheers, which were taken up and echoed and re-echoed by the myriads in the streets."

She did not mention the dead girl. That would have smacked too much of anti-climax and would, in any case, have been gravely indecorous.

So, in a wave of emotional hysteria, of almost maudlin sentimentality, ended Val's ordeal.

But there yet remained some moments of ordeal for me.

The telephone beside my bed rang soon after seven the next morning and I heard Val's voice. "Sorry to disturb you," he said, "but I'm off for a holiday; Egypt, probably; I'm leaving London this morning, but I'd like to see you before I go. Could I come along and have breakfast with you?"

While we ate, both of us kept steering the talk away from the trial; but it seemed to return of itself. I asked Val about *The Peepshow* and his work there. He grimaced and said, "I resigned, quitted, as soon as the row started; they wouldn't have kept me on, anyway; it's a respectable rag at bottom and, from their point of view my name's mud, whatever happened. Thank the Lord I don't need anybody's brass. And I was getting a bit fed-up with it; the job had lost its savour." He lit a cigarette and went on: "Talking of savour, so has tobacco. I hadn't had a smoke since my arrest and had been looking forward to my first cigarette; and it tasted like hay; so does this one. Wonder how long it takes to get the old palate acclimatised to the poison again." He smiled. "I spent a jolly half an hour this morning with the newspapers. They'd make you sick. My marvellous sang-froid and all the rest of it."

"Well, it was pretty colossal, Val," I said.

He looked at me and smiled. "My dear Ju, I appeared unmoved for the simple reason that I was unmoved. Don't misunderstand me. I wasn't exactly looking forward to being throttled to death; but I'd faced that part of it and got it under; for the rest I didn't care twopence. I hadn't killed the poor little bitch, but if twelve respectable tradesmen, pretending to themselves to be outraged by my way of living, said I had, well, good luck to them. And my way of living is the only one that appeals to me, and if you come down to rock bottom truth, which most people refuse to do, it's not much different from anyone else's. Carden's degradation clap-trap was just silly. But that's part of his job to talk a lot of lying rubbish about life. For the satisfaction of my sexual desires I prefer prostitutes; other men other preferences; that's all it is. The trouble about sex is that it's got all mixed up with procreation and paternity and dear old mother and home sweet home; to say nothing of parsons and God and the life eternal. Get rid of those excrescences, which are mostly humbug, and what remains? Appetite; hunger. I am hungry—fill my belly; I am thirsty—give me a pint; I desire to couple—bring me a woman."

I laughed and shook my head. "You don't carry me there, Val; there's more in it than that; or there is for most men."

"I don't want to carry you or anyone else," he smiled. "I'm no proselytiser; merely a plain and straightforward fornicator." He lit another cigarette and said after inhaling, "Glory! I believe the taste's coming back." And then he put his hand into his pocket and, taking out something, tossed it over to me, saying, "Thought you might like to have that as a keepsake."

It was a folded five-pound note. I had picked it up and begun to unfold it, so slow sometimes is thought, before I realised what it was and almost immediately I heard Val's voice saying distressfully, "By God! I'm sorry, Ju; I didn't mean——" and found his voice trailing away into inaudibility as I struggled to get a grip on myself while there hammered in my mind, repeated endlessly: *What does he know?*

And then Val leaned across the table, put a hand upon my arm and said, "I *am* damned sorry, Ju; no intention of bowling you over like that. Kitty Sears asked me to change it for her; said if she proffered a fiver in a shop they took it with only half-concealed sneers; all she told me was that a swell had chucked it at her; she said he was either sozzled or barmy; that was her description of him; and that was all."

I was watching his face as he spoke, watching it as closely as I have ever scrutinised anything in my life, and bringing to the aid of my scrutiny all the knowledge taught me by my trade of what the expression reveals of the thoughts behind it. And so sure was I that Val spoke the truth, that my shame and my degradation (far deeper than his own) were unknown to him, that in my sudden relief I lost control of my emotions and broke into a foolish laugh.

At this he smiled. "I just stuffed it into my coat pocket when she gave it to me, and it was not till the next morning that I came on it, and then I noticed your signature." He chuckled. "The old phrase: Could have knocked me down with a feather! Be damned if that wasn't the bare truth for once in its long and honourable career." He screwed up his eyes in the old familiar mocking fashion and went on: "Never dreamt your tastes wandered in those directions, Ju."

"They don't," I said as lightly as I was able. "There was never anything between me and Kitty Sears or—or any other——"

"Whore," he interrupted with his gay laugh; "whore's the word; and find me a better!" He clapped me on the shoulder and added: "I never for a moment thought there was, old boy."

Chapter Eleven

ABOVE THE BATTLE

I DID not leave England myself until nearly the end of the following July. Crispin had a queer little play running at the St. Martin's Theatre; I say little because the performance, apart from a curtain-raiser which took nearly thirty minutes, only lasted just over two hours. It was called *The Cormorant* and had been running since January, but somehow or other I had not seen it. I had in fact seen Crispin but twice since Val's trial. Val had returned from Egypt and was that July in Orkney with his mother and Sylvia. I had an appointment one Friday evening, I think it must have been somewhere about the twentieth, with Collinson the sculptor but he had to cry off at the last minute, and being at a loose end for a few hours I decided to drop in and see Crispin's play. Owing I suppose to the shortness of the play there was a fifteen-minutes interval between the second and third acts and I immediately went into the bar for a drink and the first man I saw there was Piers Rowland, looking very handsome and imposing and the picture of health and prosperousness.

" Alison with you?" I asked.

He nodded. "She doesn't like bars; she has no vices."

" You're her only vice," I said.

He gave me a swift quizzical look. "Are you any one's?"

"I don't think so," I replied. "Pretty stifling in here, isn't it? What do you think of the play?"

"Just about that," he rejoined; "stifling's the word; I can't stand Crispin's mephitic erotics; but it's certainly hot in here; let's stroll down the Lane and get a breath of air."

We walked out into St. Martin's Lane, which was almost deserted and seemed very quiet and peaceful after the theatre. Presently Piers said abruptly, with the effect of unburdening himself, "Do you know, Julian, this archduke business is going to spring the mine."

"Do you mean there's going to be trouble?" I said; "I'm afraid I've not been following things very closely."

"We'll all be following them, willy-nilly, before the month's out," he said; "Germany means business this time and we know it; and as far as I'm concerned I'm glad of it; Europe's been cringing and truckling to the Teuton for the last five years and it's beginning to turn my stomach. It's coming now and it's a pity it didn't come three years ago when the Agadir trouble was on; we should have taken up the challenge then and trounced them."

"I thought that was France's grievance, not ours," I said.

"They're one and the same," he said, lighting another cigarette, the flare of his match lighting up for an instant the dark strong beauty of his face. He blew out a cloud of smoke and added, "We're in with France to the last man."

"Look here, Piers," I said, "do you seriously mean that we're in for war this time and will be fighting with the French against Germany?"

"I mean just that, Julian; and before we're a month older; Asquith knows it; Grey knows it; and so do Poincaré and Bethmann-Hollweg."

"And simply because some crack-brain murders an Austrian Grand Duke," I said.

"An Austrian tom-cat would have served," he rejoined; "it was merely the needed pretext. It's daylight clear if you've followed the European situation as I have." He stopped at the end of the Lane and we turned back under the street-lamp and I saw that his face was alight with enthusiasm. "Political intrigue is breath and blood to me," he went on; "the play and interplay of brains with war in the balance and the fate of nations at stake fascinates me, intoxicates me. One plays it like chess; one makes a move not for any immediate advantage but for the sake of a dozen moves ahead."

"Provided the other side sticks to the rules."

"They can't help it; all the gambits are known. One can prophecy with such accuracy that to the lay-man it has a thaumaturgic touch."

"For example?" I smiled.

"Austria will make impossible demands to Servia; there will be an ultimatum; Russia will become uneasy; so will France; Germany will pretend alarm; general distrust, some diplomatic lyings, all-round secret and not-so-secret mobilisations; and then anything will serve as the spark, some little frontier incident for example, and the magazine explodes."

We were nearing the side-door of the theatre.

"Sounds incredible to me, Piers; saving your presence I don't believe it."

"Of course not; few would over here; that's why I told you; it's the plausible which is indiscreet to talk about not the preposterous. Shall we be seeing you after the show? We're going to the Savoy; care to join us?"

"I'd like nothing better but I've an engagement at the club just after eleven; I only dropped in here to fill in the time."

By breakfast-time the next morning Piers's prophecy had lost much of its fantasticalness. I spent the day at the Club, which I had always found a sort of clearing-house of current intelligent opinion; its members were about as catholic a crowd as could be found anywhere and included the services, the professions, the arts and politics. An hour or two in its big bar gave one a pretty fair notion of what was being thought and said by those members of the community who are, in the last resort, responsible for the country's well-being and who, in the event of war, must shoulder the largest burdens whether naval, military or financial. And by the evening, when I went to my flat for dinner, I had come to the conclusion that while Piers's certitude would have found few supporters there was a strong body of opinion that things were beginning to look ominous. I slept on that conclusion and by the morning had come to another and a much more personal one: if there were going to be a war then very definitely I was not going to play any part in it. Fear had nothing to do with that decision; I could, I knew, muster up as much courage as the average man when it was demanded of me. It was a more disturbing matter than mere physical danger; any service in the armed forces inevitably meant a medical examination and I was determined at all costs to avoid such a pawing. The only course open to me was to leave England; if war did not after all come, well, I'd make it a holiday jaunt of a few months; I had long been planning a holiday in America and should in any case probably go before Christmas. It merely meant putting things forward a trifle. Before I had finished my breakfast I had made up my mind to go and not to wait too meticulously upon the order of my going.

I sailed from Southampton that day week, Saturday, July the twenty-fifth.

I did not return till the War was over.

Most of that period I spent in the United States, but when it became clear that America was about to enter the War I skipped out to the Argentine.

For what was happening to the people of my circle at home during my absence I had to depend for information upon correspondents. About what was happening to the country, its allies and its enemies, I was much better informed than any one living in Europe, and was occasionally able to tell Alison or Norrie of events in the fighting zone or even under their very noses in England about which they, in common with the rest of the nation, knew nothing. For some considerable time (probably nearly two years) after it had become apparent that I had no intention of returning to England my letters from home (except business ones) became very infrequent. Certainly during the whole of 1915 few of the men I knew wrote to me; I don't think there was any deliberate dropping of me because of my supposed recreancy; they simply didn't bother to write, and understandingly enough, for they had much else to think of. Val wrote to me in May, 1915; why he did not write again that letter will explain. The two correspondents who did not fail me during those years I was absent were Alison and Norrie. Alison's letters to me must have numbered several dozen, while Norrie kept up a regular monthly exchange. Towards the end of the War I began to pick up again my broken correspondence with the men of my circle. Of those letters (and I kept all of Alison's) there are only six which have any bearing upon my story: Val's, two each of Alison's and Norrie's, and one written by Crispin a few weeks after the signing of the Treaty of Versailles.

Alison's first letter was dated January 10, 1915, and ran: Dear Julian, I was most disappointed not to hear from you at Christmas. It is a long while since a Christmas Day has gone by without a line from you. It must be nearly twenty years. Even when we were children and you would be seeing me the next day at a party you used to put in a letter with your Christmas card. And now that you are thousands of miles away and we may not see each other again for many months, perhaps years, if this terrible war goes on, as people are now beginning to say it will, you don't even send me a greeting—why? Did you treat all your old friends that way? But I won't ask you any more questions, but do write and let me know what you are doing.

Are you thinking of returning to England soon? But perhaps I ought not to ask this. I think perhaps I hope you won't, for then there will be some one out of all of us who is not fighting (I mean the men, we're not fighting although I suppose we are "doing our bit" as every one says, rather smugly, some of us, these days). I oughtn't perhaps to have put a full stop there but punctuation always bothers me and once I begin putting in brackets I get dreadfully confused as I'm sure you must be by this time. What I was going to say was we'd have some one out of all of us not mixed up in the war. Although Humfrey isn't either.

Do you get much war news out there? Perhaps you know a lot more than we do and if so you must forgive me if some of my letter reads like a last week's newspaper. I'll have to write about the War because it's quite impossible to think of anything at all without thinking of the War as well. I feel sure it need never have started and I am sure the ordinary people didn't want it and now want nothing else so much as for it to stop. Even the soldiers would be glad to stop now if they were allowed to. Did you read about the truce and the fraternising on Christmas Day between our men and the Germans? If only there had been some one big enough and wise enough and strong enough to say, "We won't start all this bloodshed again," there might now have been peace, a peace honourable to everyone. But I'm afraid there aren't many people who think as I do. Piers says that the truce was a foolish piece of sentimentality only possible with such sentimental people as the Germans and the English. The French, he says, allowed none of that nonsense, but then, they are realists. And it won't be allowed to happen again. Piers is an intelligence officer attached to general headquarters in France and has already been mentioned in despatches and cited in the order of the day of the French army. I was very surprised at this as I thought only the soldiers in the trenches were mentioned in despatches and Piers says he has not yet been in the trenches although he's going at the first opportunity, and I'm sure this is true enough for he joined up with the fighting soldiers and tried to get out to France in September but they wouldn't let him go and then attached him to the G.H.Q. But of course nobody who knows Piers could doubt his physical courage for a moment. Not that physical courage isn't common enough now; all the men are heroes.

Michael is with the London Rifle Brigade in France. He is a sergeant. Doesn't that sound funny? But he is coming home soon to take a commission. He is one of the war poets and has had several poems in *The Pall Mall*, *The Westminster* and other periodicals and just before Christmas had a strange one (I mean strange compared with the others) in the *Saxon Review*. I don't suppose you will have seen it and so I've copied it out here for you. It is called "Ultra Credem" which also seems strange. Beyond creeds, isn't that what it means? Or is it part of a quotation? But it doesn't matter. Here is the poem:

> Out of the dark where lie the uncaring dead
> I heard a voice that whispered: "Dream no more;
> All these have stood astare upon the shore
> For their dream-argosies that now are sped.
>
> "These knew the Hag desire, and her elf-child
> That men call Hope; this dust cried to the dust
> Of all the gods we frame of fear and lust,
> And with their suppliant echoes were beguiled.

"Thou fool, be comforted! This thing is sure:
The grave must hold you, and the afterdark
Knows no resurgence of the living spark
That ran like flame, and shall not more endure.

"Bewitched by creed, and lured by Paradise;
Blinded by lies, priest-led to godlihood;
What have they made of all your human good
But bloody altars and young sacrifice?

"Seed as the seed of flowers. Wherefore weep
For life on life or everlasting bliss;
Drink deep of beauty, answer kiss with kiss;
The nothing all things end in yet is sleep."

That doesn't sound like Michael, does it? But I
think it is significant (is that the right word?) of the
change of feeling which is taking place among the
soldiers. The soldier poets are not writing as they did
in the first days of the war when it all seemed fine and
gallant. Those first days when Rupert Brooke wrote
his brave sonnets and Julian Grenfell his beautiful
"Into Battle" which I love, if for nothing else, for that
lovely verse:

The blackbird sings to him, Brother, brother,
If this be the last song you shall sing
Sing well, for you may not sing another;
Brother, sing.

Miles is out with the Guards and is already a captain
although he is so young. But then, promotion is very
quick because of the dreadful casualties and Miles went

out of course with the Expeditionary Force in August and fought at Mons. Piers says twenty-four-year-old captains are as common in France now as blackberries in September and that there are plenty of majors under thirty and more than one colonel. But I suppose they are only temporary ranks, brevet isn't it? Piers is a staff-captain.

Val went out with the Artists' Rifles; he went out as part of a draft just before Christmas; he joined up as a private. Sylvia says he wouldn't even try for a commission; he said they wouldn't give a commission to a man with his record but he was perhaps only joking; he was always flippant and cynical and hard to understand. Sylvia is doing V.A.D. work in a military hospital in London. I don't suppose I'm allowed to say which one; there are so many things one mustn't say or do these days. Piers says all the trains and even the trams and buses in France have notices in them: "Attention! les oreilles ennemies vous écoutent." It's all perfectly dreadful. Ordinary nice warm-hearted human beings seem all suddenly changed into angry beasts. Sylvia spends a lot of her time with us at Baker Street. She took up V.A.D. work because she said she *had* to have work and hard, unpleasant work just to keep her thoughts off John who is in command of one of our submarines. He got a five-day leave over Christmas and spent three of them here with Syliva and then both went for the other two days to Aunt Olive's. It was heartrending when John went back, they're so terribly in love and for days Sylvia looked so haggard and ill. Oh, Julian, sometimes I feel that it is all too wicked and cruel to be endured, that surely God will not allow it to go on. The young men who are being killed and maimed all over Europe and some of them just boys. And old men too. Uncle Luke is nearly sixty but of course being a doctor he was needed and he's serving out somewhere in the east; I think it is Egypt.

Humfrey is still at the business and is not going into the army. He has an exemption as he is in control of the business now and if he went it would have to close down, for daddy, although he is only sixty-two, has aged a great deal lately and is quite feeble. His heart is very bad.

I forgot to mention that Michael in one of his letters said he'd run across Crispin in France. Crispin is in the H.A.C. He is also coming home for a commission.

And now what am I doing? You'd never guess. I'm a chauffeur. Or should it be chauffeuse? Well, anyhow, I drive a car. I wanted to join one of the women's units, the W.A.A.C. or W.R.E.N. but neither mummy nor daddy wanted me to and mummy actually wrote to Piers to persuade me not to. And Piers came prancing home on a special thirty-six-hour leave and was very cross and vehement about it and wanted me to marry him there and then. But I couldn't get married, Julian; I felt I just couldn't; it seemed somehow so appallingly callous with thousands of people being bereaved. Of course Piers said that was all the more reason why we should get married at once. But I wouldn't although I half-promised I would in the spring. And so he "arranged things"—that was his phrase. He wouldn't hear of my joining any of the regularly-recruited organisations but went along to the War Office and arranged for me to be on duty there every morning at nine-thirty with my car. I wear a uniform of sorts, a kind of feminine version of an officer's uniform even to an imitation Sam Browne belt. What I am really is a private taxi to drive any staff officer anywhere from just round the corner for a cup of coffee to the other side of England, but so far the shorter jaunts have been the chief and the only journey of any length I've been was to Colchester.

I finish, or am supposed to, at four each day but it's often later. Still, I've plenty of leisure to carry on with my work at the Mission and this enables me to see the war from two points of view, that of the big-wig brass-hats who are very chatty and tell me lots of things as we go along, and that of the people in the east end who of course know me so well that they talk to me like one of themselves. And you can guess there's no small difference in the points of view!

Do you remember Ruth, the pretty fair-haired little Jewess you saw when you were at the Mission? And her mother with the blind baby? (It died by the way). Well, I called on the mother a few weeks ago. I was on my way back from driving a Colonel Beckworth to Romford and leaving him there. So I was in my uniform. And it seems Mrs. Mendoza had seen me as we were going. They think down there I'm just a W.A.A.C. or at least a sort of N.C.O. of the W.A.A.C.'s. She said, "I saw you this afternoon, miss, with Old Red-Tabs sitting beside you. There's too many of that sort knocking about. A bit of the trenches would do them good." Now as it happened, Colonel Beckworth went out at the beginning with his regiment, has been wounded three times and has still a lot of shrapnel in his body; that's why he has a staff-appointment. I told Mrs. Mendoza this and she said, "Ah, well, if you

say so, miss, perhaps he has done his bit but there's
thousands haven't and don't mean to.   All they want
to do is to dress up like chocolate-box soldiers and have
a good time with the girls.   I hope you don't let them
be saucy with you, miss.   Our Ruth's in the W.A.A.C.'s
too, and the things she tells us 'd fair make you sick.
Disgusting.   Lot of nasty old men taking advantage
of young girls being under them and having to obey
orders or having things made rotten for them.   I don't
mean it's only the old men;   the young uns are worse
but then, you expect a young man to have his fling
and of course I don't say the girls don't encourage them.
Still, it's not right or decent and Ruth says the number
of girls who've got in the family way is something
chronic."   And so she went on and on, Julian;   just as
I am, you're thinking.   And so I'll go on no further.
Now do write and tell me all your news.   Always
affectionately, Alison.

Val's letter was written from a base-hospital in
France and dated May 15, 1915.   He wrote: My dear
Julian, I'm writing this to you because if it had not
been written to you it wouldn't have been written at
all and I want to write it: sort of testament of Valentine
Grey.   As we say out here I " caught a packet" about
six weeks ago at a little place which was once the
village of Pilkem.   Like poor old Admiral Kempen-
feldt's packet in the poem we learnt at St. Benet's, " it
was not in the battle."   In fact I was out with a working
party engaged just behind the line in the unheroic
task of grave-digging.   It was a whizz-bang, a nasty
little shell of about fifteen pounds   It exploded almost
at the feet of three of us;   two were killed and I caught
my share of the iron full in the cods.   I'm not going

to dwell on the pain; that's mostly over now and anyhow there are too many chaps here taking their gruel without whining for me to whimper about my ration. I was sent here and when the surgeons had finished with me I was nothing, Ju. Or just something that a eunuch would be fully justified in grinning at. They told me, with what I thought was a lack of humour, that I'd be all right in time as far as the excretory process goes; just now I'm rigged up with so much rubber tubing and what-nots that I'm a bit like the old Laocoon. I shan't be sent to England for a few weeks yet but I'm being allowed out in a day or so for an airing and as soon as I can arrange things I shall shoot myself. Life has never been more than one thing to me and now that is beyond my reach for ever I don't propose to go on with what is left. For to be quite frank, nothing is left. My work? But I don't imagine your asking that. My work, like the work of all men doing our sort of jobs, derived entirely from what the whizz-bang and the knife have taken from me. All I am left with are the old hungers and these may torture me for years. That, Ju, is all that remains of what used to be a man.

I said to one of the surgeons, a decent sort of young cock-sparrow, a Canadian, "Why the hell did you patch me up like this when you might have let me shuffle off peacefully under the anæsthetic?" He said, "Keep your tail up, buddy; you won't feel that way in a year's time. —— isn't everything." And I told him maybe it wasn't but that nothing was anything without it, to me anyhow, and asked him to slip me a phial of morphia. But he only played the same tune again with the optimism stop full out.

Well, old boy, that's that. You're the only man I wanted to write this to. You'll get it all right. I've seen to that; money will do a lot in the army although it's not yet succeeded in getting me morphia; one has to be so darned cautious and I don't want to find myself landed in a mental hospital, a way they have with those who clamour too openly for Euthanasia. The easy death, Ju, eh? Any death 'll be easy after the last six weeks. I've been doing a lot of thinking the last week (couldn't even think before then) and I've been turning over in my mind the lives of our little crowd and I've come to see things pretty clearly I imagine, more clearly than I've ever done before, and that is why I've written to you, old boy, because I feel pretty certain that you're about the one man in the world (better say one of the few) who will be able to read this letter and then put it aside without comment, because you know that there is nothing to be said—nothing is here for words, to misquote old Milton. And in fact, old lad, to quote him this time, "nothing for tears." I've enjoyed my life; I've taken what I wanted. And now the taking's over. Good-bye, Ju. I'll remember you to God and ask him why. Affectionately, Val.

I did not receive that letter until two days after I had seen Val's name in the casualty list under the military euphemism: Died of wounds.

The first of Norrie's two letters was dated June 12, 1916. My dear Julian, You will of course have heard of Kitchener's death and probably know more about it than we do but you cannot at that distance realise with what a shock we over here received the news. We were just stunned and that is not exaggerating; we couldn't believe it; and now a week afterwards people still don't believe it; it doesn't seem possible Kitchener is dead; it is almost as difficult to think of him as dead as to think of one's self as dead. I think perhaps the *first* reaction of the public's mind to the news (I know it was of mine) was, as the Tommies in our hospital say, "that's done it"; it seemed the final disaster. And yet everything is going on as if nothing had happened and the papers have already ceased to comment upon his tragic end. But it was a great end and a fitting end for a great man; somehow Kitchener has always seemed several sizes larger than life; a Gulliver among the Lilliputians. There was a magnificent poem signed "X" in the *Times* the day after the news came out. I cut it out intending to send it but it got lost somehow as so many oddments seem to get lost in my hustling bustling life these days. But I'll get a copy and send it along next time. Father says "X" is T. W. H. Crosland, the man who wrote "The Unspeakable Scot" and of whom father strongly disapproves because of his dissolute habits. Well, if a dissolute man can write lovely poetry like that it's a pity dissolution (but that can't be the word, can it? should it be dissoluteness?) isn't more common. But it's probably not true; you know what father is. He's very well, by the way, and so is mother but he's very trying about the war. He says we must go on till Berlin is reached and the Huns (he still calls them that) taught a lesson they'll never forget. A week in our wards would enlighten him— but no, it wouldn't! nothing would. And he browbeats mother into agreeing with him as he's always done. And didn't we know it as children!

John's death nearly killed Sylvia. That is really the literal truth. I've always been a little sceptical about grief killing but I've altered my opinion now. The war's made us alter a lot of opinions. I think what wore Sylvia down was the long wait and the uncertainty after we knew the L20 was missing. And of course what his end was will probably never be known. And so when at last she had to face the truth she had nothing left to face it with. She just went down, not wanting to live any more, willing herself to die. Death had to be fought for her; she would not fight herself. And then when she was getting about again and she looked dreadful, it was heartrending to see her, she took herself off to Orkney and shut herself up for nearly six months. She's now found some comfort. If it is comfort; I suppose it is for literally hundreds of thousands are turning to it now for consolation. I mean spiritualism. She's back in London now and we see her occasionally. She looks better in her physical health but so much older and somehow stricken. And you remember how lovely she was and how bright and laughing and vivacious. She has of course got into touch with both John and Val. The mediums have seen to that. I can't help thinking they're a pack of mercenary rascals preying upon people's grief. Still, I suppose if they get comfort from it—but there I don't know what to think. She is also writing a lot of religious and mystical verse which is being published in the spiritualist press and also in some of the newspapers. She still writes under the name of Hazel Fayre.

I think I told you Nan was in America at Hollywood. I wonder if you'll ever run across her. But that's

rather like the old countryman asking the vicar to
keep an eye open for his boy next time he was in
London. We were all pleased and proud to hear of the
success of your one-man show in New York. Here it's
mostly war pictures although it's said that the government won't allow any shows by the official artists like
Orpen and Nevinson; or at any rate will only allow a few
pictures to be exhibited. That is of course on all fours
with everything else; we're spoon-fed and know little
of what is really going on. I get to know more than
the average person because my work brings me into
daily contact with the men direct from the trenches.
And many of them are eager to talk about their experiences, especially those who've lost a leg or an arm and
are now out of it. People will tell you that the soldiers
won't talk of their experiences at the front. That is
like all general statements—true and false. Some will
and in fact will go on and on like Tennyson's Brook;
while others just lie mum, not talking about anything,
some of them not even answering when they're spoken
to. But those that will talk, well, they'll talk a donkey's
hind leg off and never tire of telling how they "stopped
their packet." I'm learning a lot of soldiers' slang;
it's very fascinating and they like telling me; giving
me a lesson in the bat they call it; and the younger ones
are not above slipping out some rather indecorous
examples now and then. I think a philologist would
find it tremendously interesting. I jotted down quite
a lot at first and meant to go on but let it slide like so
many other things. I expect you know most of it
but here's some which may be new to you and
alphabetically arranged—see how methodical I was!
Bags means plenty, e.g. There's bags of room. Band-

hook is a rifle. Billjim is an Australian. Bonce is the head, e.g. he copped a packet in the bonce. Bumf is toilet paper (a cheeky red-headed boy who'd lost a leg told me that; he's only eighteen). Canteen medals are beer-stains on the breast of a tunic. Char is tea and a chat is a louse. Clobber is clothing. Clock is one's face and crumby is itching (because of lice). Dicky-dirt is a shirt, dippy and doolally both mean insane and drum-up is to make tea. Flog is to sell part of your kit (usually in order to buy beer) and fug is a hot stifling atmosphere. Jippo is hot bacon-grease, joanna is a piano and jug is the guard-room. Kip is to sleep or a place to sleep and knock-off means to steal—but there! I expect you've had enough. But if you're really interested I'll send some more the next time I write. I must get on with my news or I'll never be finished.

Crispin is home, wounded. He is in hospital at Bournemouth; shrapnel in the shoulder. You knew he had a commission. He is in the Essex regiment, a captain. He won the M.C. when he was wounded; it was, I think, near Ypres. He has a play running in London. *Form Fours*. It is something new for him, a farce, and really very funny. It's very popular with men on leave. Perhaps it will come to New York and then you'll see it. But then of course you're not in New York now; are you still considering that Mexican ranch?

We see Avis occasionally; it was she who gave us the news about Crispin. You remember what a gipsy-like little thing she used to be with her frightened eyes? There's nothing frightened about her now or much gipsy-like. She seems to have found herself or the war's found her, like Piers. She's a very important personage these days, a Commandant (I've altered that to a capital as I'm sure it demands one) in the W.R.A.F. and in her uniform she looks quite capable of leading a fleet of bombers to Berlin and ending the war. She has just had published (but anonymously so tell it not in Gath) a book of sketches or stories or whatever they're called describing something of her life in the W.R.A.F. Its title is *Wings and Tales* and it's had a fine press and is selling like the proverbial hot-cakes.

By the way, talking of Piers (and you'll be angry at me not telling you this earlier in the letter but I honestly forgot) well, Piers is a staff major now and at the War Office and tremendoulsy important. But that wasn't what I was going to tell you. Alison broke off her engagement to him only a week ago. I think she's wise. In many ways you couldn't find two people farther apart than they are. His gods are not her gods. Quite the contrary. But it's an odd sort of breaking-off. Piers apparently merely smiles blandly and says he still considers himself engaged and ascribes Alison's change of heart to war-hysteria, according to Avis, and predicts its quick passing. And Alison although she cut the knot herself is plainly very much in love with Piers and very miserable. This also according to Avis. Now why on earth can't Avis and Piers make a match of it? If it would not be a marriage made in heaven it would certainly be one worthy of every worldly encomium—on both sides brains, looks, money, and that supreme Britishness which makes the word " foreigner" the most depreciatory substantive in the language. Avis would of course jump at him.

But then so many women would. And poor Alison loves him despite herself. He's terribly attractive to women, there's no doubt about that. We were all in love with him that summer at Stromness. Alison, by the bye, has also taken to authorship; queer how many women do this when their love affairs go askew. She's writing quite regularly for that woman's weekly which you and Crispin used to call "Fuss and Bother." It fusses and bothers now like a hen with a duckling, as you can imagine; I must try to remember to send you a copy; it's become very superior but is still as funny (unconsciously) as ever.

Faith is still with her concert-party at Le Havre. She was home for a week at the beginning of May. She's a very popular turn with the troops and inclined to be, I think, a little spoilt by her popularity. As poor Sylvia said rather bitterly (if a little cattishly) she's *loving* the war. Well, she's enjoying her share in it but it's not all a bed of roses, four shows a day sometimes. And she's really awfully good. She brought a young fellow from the party along one evening when she was over here and they did several of their turns. We were helpless with laughter. Even father's arctic circle was melted. She told us that the most popular songs are still "Tipperary," "A Long, Long Trail" and "Pack Up Your Troubles" as far as the concerts are concerned, but that the songs the soldiers sing on the march are never these but much older things, ballad sort of things as old as the army probably and of an indecorousness perfectly hair-raising some of them. She and her partner (he's a young second-lieutenant named Roberts—a nice boy with three wound stripes. But perhaps you don't know what wound stripes are.

They were only introduced this year. They are thin
gold strips worn longitudinally on the left sleeve, one
for each time wounded. Miles by the bye has four and
also the D.S.O., the M.C., and is a major into the bargain
—little sparrow-legged Miles!) But I was telling you
about the soldier-songs. Faith and her partner sang
some of them—very expurgated. I jotted down bits
of some of them. Faith did tell me a few of the
improper ones but I simply couldn't write them down.
The intimacies of conjugal and extra-conjugal love
expressed so crudely, so anatomically and so crapulously
can't be put to paper. But terribly comic some of it,
naïvely, schoolboyishly comic. Here are one or two
of the proper ones. And remember they are the soldiers'
own marching songs:

> At the halt on the left, form platoon!
> At the halt on the left, form platoon!
> If the odd numbers don't mark time two paces
> How the hell can the rest form platoon?

That is sung to the air, " Three Cheers for the Red,
White and Blue."

A very popular one is this variant of "John Brown's
Body" and sung of course to that air:

> John Brown's baby's got a pimple on his—shush!
> John Brown's baby's got a pimple on his—shush!
> John Brown's baby's got a pimple on his—shush!
> The poor kid can't sit down.

I love this next one, which is sung to the air, " My
Love is like a Red, Red Rose":

I have no pain, dear mother, now,
But oh! I am so dry.
Connect me to a brewery
And leave me there to die.

And so I do this one (Air: "Here's to the Maiden of Bashful Fifteen"):

What did you join the army for?
What did you join the army for?
What did you join the army for?
You must have been bloodywell barmy.

But the most popular (so my Tommies tell me) is Skibboo. I fancy this version, which was copied out for me by a V.A.D. who got it from her boy, is somewhat expurgated. And what a libel on women!

Oh landlord have you a daughter fair!
        Skibboo! Skibboo! } *bis*
Oh landlord have you a daughter fair
With lily-white breasts and golden hair
        Skibboo! Skibboo!
      Ski-bumpity-bump skibboo!

Oh yes I have a daughter fair!
        Skibboo! Skibboo! } *bis*
Oh yes I have a daughter fair
With lily-white breasts and golden hair
        Skibboo! Skibboo!
      Ski-bumpity-bump skibboo!

But my fair young daughter is far too young $\left.\right\}$ *bis*
　　　　　　Skibboo! Skibboo!
But my fair young daughter is far too young
To be messed about by a son of a gun.
　　　　　　　　Skibboo! Skibboo!
　　　　　Ski-bumpity-bump skibboo!

Oh father, oh father, I'm not too young $\left.\right\}$ *bis*
　　　　　　Skibboo! Skibboo!
Oh father, oh father, I'm not too young,
I've been to bed with the parson's son.
　　　　　　　　Skibboo! Skibboo!
　　　　　Ski-bumpity-bump, skibboo!

I think that's enough! And that's what our soldiers sing on the march and if only history books told us what our soldiers used to sing say in the Hundred Years War or in the Wars of the Roses how much more interesting it would be and how much more human it would make the people of history, who never have seemed real to me.

At present there's nothing but rumours of the coming big offensive in France. Every one is talking about it and of course every one has met someone who knows somebody "in the know" who says so-and-so. What a time it is for rumours. They're a part of our daily bread. But ours are apparently bloodless things compared with the fine crop grown at the front. At least according to my Tommies. Am I boring you? I think sometimes I'm like the proud father telling the latest sayings of his horribly precocious little brat of a son. I'm afraid I'm always talking about my wounded soldiers and repeating the things they tell me. I'll have to begin to watch to see if people sidle out of the room as soon as I enter! But I must, before I close, tell you just one or two of the front-line rumours. They call them latrine-rumours. I think that's delightfully apt. I'm afraid I'm becoming a vulgar woman. But anything's better than our dreadful national hypocrisy and keep the blinds down and let's pretend we've no bodies and no physical functions. A doctor ought to love vulgarity; how can he be really human and understanding if he doesn't. Now Piers is never vulgar. If he read this letter he'd be quite sincerely shocked I'm sure. And poor Val was never anything else. And I suppose he'd use that (Piers I mean) as a text.

But perhaps you're not interested. If you are I can always tell you some next time. I'll just give you one as a sample! A very celebrated and eminent person (his identity varying with the politics of the rumour-monger) paid a visit to the front line to see Tommy cooking his steak and chips (a pet joke of the soldiers, by the bye). He was a very pompous and plump personage and during his brief peep at the trenches the Germans unluckily made a raid and captured him. They returned him unhurt half an hour later, via No-Man's-land, without his trousers and with the Union Jack painted upon one side of his posterior and the French tricolour upon the other.

And I hope when you've read this long letter you'll remember the two-page scrap you wrote last time and be suitably ashamed. With much love, Norrie.

P.S. Don't forget to let us know about the Mexican venture.

The second letter of Alison's was dated February 17,

1917, almost exactly two years later than her previous one, but it must be remembered that during that period I had received over twenty other letters from her. This particular letter did not reach me till the end of March, it having followed me down into the Argentine where I had gone in some haste as soon as it became clear that America's entry into the war could not be long delayed.

If for no other reason this letter would be memorable because of its beginning, an abrupt breaking of news without any formal address. I have had only one other letter in my life which began in similar startling fashion:

Miles is blinded. And he is only twenty-eight. Oh Julian, it is too cruel and wicked. It happened early in November somewhere on the Somme, Givenchy I think, and we only knew a week ago. I mean that he was blind. We knew he was wounded—you of course knew that—but he had not told any one what it was beyond saying it was a wound in the head. It was a bullet and sheared both eyes away, utterly destroying them. He had been at a base-hospital till just before Christmas and had been sent to Dorchester. But he would not let any of us come to see him. He said he was getting on all right but his face was a bit damaged and he didn't want any visitors till he was more presentable. Of course we all thought horrible things but none so bad as the reality. We ought to have guessed because his letters were not in his own hand but somehow we didn't. Mummy had written to the sister several times but her replies were just formal and said Miles was getting on nicely and we could come down soon to see him. And then we had a message saying we could come down. That was not a week ago. We went, Mummy and Humfrey and I (Norrie was coming but she couldn't get away at the last moment)—daddy of course couldn't come; he doesn't often go out now, especially this time of the year.

We went prepared for something dreadful but for nothing so heartrending as we saw. His eyes were just two scarred pits and nothing can ever be done in the way of artificial eyes for the lids are gone. We didn't see this at first because he wore dark glasses. He put a brave front on it and was smiling and joking but his face was drawn and lined, almost unrecognisable as Miles, and it was so obvious he was playing a part for our benefit. He kept turning his head from one to the other of us as we spoke until presently I couldn't bear to look at him and felt that if I stayed another moment I should break down. And then mummy leant forward to help him to do something and with her eagerness and his anxiety not to let her bother and being blind and I suppose not yet used to the darkness he knocked his head against her arm and his glasses fell off. And he said, Sorry, sorry, Aunt Aggie, and began to grope for them and none of us could move for seconds—we couldn't move, we just sat there horror-stricken. And then it all passed and I no longer feared I should break down; I just wanted to do something, anything to help him (although I knew there was nothing anybody could do) and I got up and put his glasses on for him and said something jocular. And I'm sure it affected mummy and Humfrey in the same way for after that somehow we lost all our constraint and nervousness and the four of us were presently talking away easily and all really laughing. Later he talked of his future but in the rather flat tone of a child repeating a lesson. He is inclined to go to live in the small cottage at Walberswick which is now his but I don't think that would be wise in some ways although it is true as he said that he could wander about the village without help after a time and without danger whereas in town he would need an attendant and it's the feeling of utter dependence which at present appears to be one of the things hardest to bear. Already that pathetic phrase, "I can do it," seems the one most frequently on his lips.

To write about other things seems rather futile and unfeeling and callous and indeed for some days after we got back from Dorchester I found myself not doing all sorts of things because any enjoyment seemed wrong with Miles down there blind and broken and so pitiful. Of course that doesn't help and is foolish and life couldn't go on at all if we did not shut our eyes and ears and hearts to so much that is happening and so I'll tell you a few other bits of news which you may not have heard. But before I do that I'll answer your question (although it wasn't put as a question and perhaps you didn't mean it to be so) about Piers and myself. We are going to be married this year, perhaps this summer. Our engagement has not been renewed because Piers says it was never broken off and of course it never was publicly. I want the marriage to take place now. I shall be glad when it is all over. I am tired of not knowing what to do and I feel I can't fight any more against it and against Piers. That sounds disloyal and unfair to him and I couldn't write it to any one else but I feel I can say this to you and you will understand. I love him and that will have to be enough and if I don't believe in the things he believes in, and I don't and I can't, well, I must do without that side of marriage. If I could fall in love with someone else—but what nonsense I'm writing. But it's so difficult to put down on paper; I can't put it down because whatever words I used would leave out the truth; or any words that I know would. It's all vague and intangible; so much a matter of shades of meaning. To say we're incompatible wouldn't be quite true any more than it would be quite false. I enjoy being with him; he's stimulating to listen to and entertaining and, well, what's called tremendously good company even though I disagree with much that he says. And presently, when I'm with him, I no longer want to argue; I just want to agree and pretend it doesn't matter and to let myself be surrounded, wrapped about, by the comfort of his physical attraction and his fineness (for he is fine) and his brilliance and that magnificent masterfulness which is one of his chief attributes and which is somehow so attractive and so, well, comforting in times like these when everything and everybody seems confused and doubtful and apprehensive. And so we're going to be married.

Did I tell you last time I wrote that Michael is in Italy? A lot of British troops have been sent there to reinforce the Italians as many German divisions are being taken from their eastern front and sent to Austria and a German-Austrian offensive is feared against the Italians. Piers says the Russians can no longer pull their weight in the war and that revolution is likely to break out there at any moment and the Russians will then probably make a separate peace.

And then the Germans and Austrians would smash Italy or try to. That's why we're sending so many troops there. But Piers says that even if all that happened it will make no difference in the end; we are bound to win whether America comes in or not. We're the only country who can stay the distance, he says; and he says it with such complete confidence and assurance and with such cheeriness that it's like a tonic with all the gloom and long faces in London and the rumours of defeats and the sinkings of ships by the U-boats.

We've had a good many letters from Michael and he's apparently enjoying life there; he says it's a paradise of peace and plenty after the western front but his poems haven't undergone any change of heart if he has. But all the war poets are writing in the same strain now. Humfrey says the notable thing about the verse being written now is not so much the spirit of war-weariness and disillusion which pervades it but the complete breakdown of form—free verse or *vers libre* taking the place of the old regular rhyme-patterns. He says it's symptomatic of the times; everything breaking down. He hates all this new verse; says it's perhaps because he's a publisher and therefore conservative and in love with *les temps passés* but you can see he doesn't really think that but that it is the poets who are all wrong. I often think that Humfrey is more of daddy's generation than of ours. Perhaps he grew up too quickly and his fighting out in S. Africa when he was really only a boy stole his young manhood away from him so that he jumped from boyhood to full maturity. Perhaps that's nonsense but if it's true, what of our generation and all these boys going straight from school into the worst war the world has ever known. Michael says our generation is doomed and will never come to maturity. He'd a poem in *The Fortnightly* a few weeks back called "*Ici repose un soldat inconnu*" which is the inscription put on the crosses of unknown French soldiers. I don't know whether it's good or bad. Humfrey says it's not poetry at all but just rhetoric. But I thought you'd like to read it and so I've copied it out:

> Hereunder lies,
> Broken and stilled,
> Dirt in his mouth and eyes,
> The beginning and end
> Of twice ten million years;
> Sunlight that spilled
> Out of the sky in the dawn of the world;
> A thousand empires and ten thousand kings;
> The inarticulate wrong
> Of beast and slave;
> Each cradle and each grave;
> All triumph and defeat;
> The bitter and the sweet.
> All these have come
> To break themselves and spend
> Their pain and splendour
> In this surrender
> To the dirt in his mouth and his eyes.
> He is the sum.

Now I've written it down perhaps Humfrey is right. But it read better in print. But so do most things, I think. I'm sure my own little things do in *Time and*

Tide. And I remember Crispin saying that he never has the faintest notion whether a play of his is good or bad until it's actually staged. That farce of his which he pretends to despise is still running here and for all his pretence Norrie says he was obviously pleased when she gave him your letter to read with the account of its reception in New York. You knew of course about his being gassed. He is at present convalescing in Wales and pretends it was nothing; but Humfrey, who saw him just before Christmas, says he looked like a ghost. He said he would be writing to you. Perhaps he has by now. Good-bye for the present, Julian. Write and wish me happiness. Ever affectionately, Alison.

Norrie's second letter was dated April 30, 1918. My dear Julian, we're still all alive although the foe is at the gates—or very near them, some sixty miles or so nearer than he was a month ago. But of course we know nothing or next to nothing. We're not getting very many fresh cases in the wards (probably that's all a part of the hide-the-truth plan) and what new cases we have are about as hazy as to what's happening "over there" as we are and beyond saying that "Jerry's got us on the run" are quite unable to lighten our darkness. This darkness is a foolish policy and its psychology is all wrong; we simply assume that things are even worse than they are. But perhaps the military view is that this is not possible! Even then why not let us know? We're not likely to panic now after four years of it.

Instead of sending us new cases they seem to be clearing out the base-hospitals and sending their cases here. And thereby hangs a tale.

As I was going through Ward 4 the other morning a voice hailed me. Not a familiar voice but one I knew I'd heard before somewhere. Guess. It was Tom Frankell, Sergeant Tom Frankell of the 3rd Suffolks, minus his left arm but very jolly and pleased with himself and with a tale to tell which for coincidence deserves all the medals. The affair happened early in March ("so I missed the Big Push" as he said with his nice grin). He was in the trenches at Monchy which is in front of Arras. In an attack on the German trenches Tom was bowled over and remembers nothing more for over forty-eight hours. What happened was that he got shrapnel in the arm, splintering the humerus into a pulp, a crack on the head and several superficial wounds in the scalp. While he was lying unconscious in a shell-hole the Suffolks were relieved by the Gloucesters and apparently shortly afterwards Tom began to make some movements or noises. Two of the Gloucesters who tried to get him in were wounded and then that night a sergeant of the Gloucesters went out and rescued him. I won't ask you to guess this time. It's really too much even to ask you to believe it. But it's true. Tom's rescuer was his old friend (or is it enemy?) Beamish, that boy with the queer nickname who was with you at Selborne and after Oxford went into Fleet Street as Tom did. Isn't that really extraordinary. Sergeant Beamish got the Military Medal and would have had ten days leave but the German break-through came just in time to prevent it. And no one of course knows where he is now.

But then no one knows where anyone is at the moment and so I can't give you any fresh news. Not about the men anyhow. Crispin is somewhere on the

French front, Michael on the Italian and that's all. Tom, by the bye, had gas-gangrene in his arm and it couldn't be saved.

Faith is going to marry her Roberts young man. Or so they both say. But I hope she won't. He's very charming and delightful but weedy and unfit and with no prospects of anything of the kind which might be called marriageable ones. He's quite a good comedy actor; good but no better than dozens of others. Of course Faith has her own money but—oh, well, I suppose it's none of our business. Still, I hope she won't.

Alison and Piers you know all about. Or as much as we do. To put it in the Victorian style—a happy event is not yet expected.

Mother is very well. Father not very well lately and he looks very old at times. I am always well. Much love, Norrie.

P.S. Tom Frankell is of course returning to *The Call* as soon as he's well, but as editor-in-chief. He's bursting with plans for a new world and says the war's made the coming of world-wide Socialism certain within the next ten years. Well, it couldn't make a worse mess of things. But I don't think socialism is a remedy for the world's ills—not that I know much about it or feel very interested. But a good doctor humours his patients' fads—up to a point. N.

Crispin's letter dated July 28, 1919, ran: My dear Julian, a notice of your S. American pictures in the *N. Y. Herald Tribune* reminded me that I'd not seen my distinguished cousin for five years nor written to him (not that he's written to me!) and I was amused to see that old Jacob Hauptmann had bought one of your pictures of the savage dancers of Tierra del Fuego (what do they call themselves, Fuegovians?) for eight thousand dollars. Now what can Jacob want with savage dancers (unless it's the wild calling to the wild). I also gathered your show was something of a sensation and brought additional blushes to the incarnadined cheeks of the dames of the Four Hundred. Are you bringing them over here? In short, are you ever coming home or are you—God forbid—becoming a naturalised American citizen?

London isn't too bad now, believe me. Every one's kicking up his and her heels and spending the blood money at a great pace. Those of us who've got out with our skins are finding life pretty good and are making the most of it while the sensation lasts. News, I understand, you have been kept *au courant* with all along. I have an item you won't have heard probably— Uncle Luke died a few days ago. You'll remember he was wounded just before the armistice—he never really pulled round and pneumonia finished him. That wipes out the Kendalls. Barring Nan, of course— Charmian Claire, by God! Have you met her out there? I've seen her in two pictures but be damned if I recognised little Nan. Sylvia has become an R.C. and is, I believe, seriously thinking of entering a French convent. There's nothing else that you won't already know. Carson is putting a new play of mine on at The Royalty in October. The public will probably howl it down thus joining the critics who have never spared me their kicks. I occasionally wonder if the work we've done, my plays (such as they are) and your pictures would have been different had it been necessary for us to get our bread-and-butter by them. Would they have been done at all? I doubt it, anyhow with regard to myself. I was twenty-five before I made anything above small change and what were you when you sold your first picture? Val of course was different; his stuff was saleable from the beginning; and probably Michael's having brass has made no difference to his poetry; no one expects to live by poetry; it's always done *con amore* to the extent in fact that if a poet happens to sell his wares he is considered *ipso facto* a dud poet.

Being back in ordinary life hasn't yet lost its air of unreality. One still feels merely on leave; even the fingers haven't lost the habit of going to where the old Sam Browne used to be to give it an occasional hitch. But it will pass. But lots of things won't—not while the remnants of our generation cumber the earth. But let us not be gloomy. I assure you I don't feel so. All the sweets of life combine etc.—and I'm glad I came back for another helping. A rivederla, as Michael says these days. You knew he was at Caporetto? It was a toss-up for three months afterwards whether the Italians would chuck in the towel. They were slammed all round the ring and almost out on their feet. Gold kept them in, as it brought in Greece and Rumania, kept out Holland, finished Turkey and Bulgaria and won the Arab campaign. It was Money-Bags won the war, Ju, and not agony and bloody sweat. A great and inspiring thought. Chin-chin! Crispin.

Chapter Twelve

I RETURNED to England early in April, 1920. Norrie had written about the middle of March saying that father was very unwell; that he had had bronchitis and was not pulling round as he should; and in talking with her he had expressed the hope that I would soon be returning to England. I wrote saying I would come as soon as I could settle up my affairs, no small task after a five years' residence in a country, and then went about the matter somewhat leisurely. I did not particularly want to see my father again; it was not that during my absence he had never written to me, for I had been equally negligent, and he was not alone in that. The thing went far deeper; it is a harsh and saddening admission to make but of all the adults of my childish and boyish circle he alone had never shown me any affection, nor had I felt any for him. He was an austere, aloof, unlovable man. I suppose my mother loved him, or had at one time, but I do not remember as a child ever seeing him kiss her or use to her any term of endearment; and that unnatural lack of human warmth was the worst of all possible atmospheres for a family of children. Anything is, I am convinced, better than that, with the possible exception of violence and cruelty, and even they are human. And so my father meant less to me in terms of emotion than any other being I had known. If I had hated him it would

253

have been something; and I think I should then have hastened back to England. And then Norrie cabled me saying he was very ill and no further delay being decent I left the settling-up of the rest of my affairs to my solicitor and sailed for Europe, hoping that death would relieve me of the ordeal of a last interview with him. A wire awaited me at Southampton telling me he was dead.

Relieved of an immediate ordeal I had no hope of escaping another and more prolonged one: my reception by the people I had known. I was afraid of the cold shoulder, the lukewarm greeting, the limp hand, the indifferent, when not contemptuous, glance. How little I understood the temper of this new world which had survived the slaughter of the war, the slaughter of more than bodies. I did not realise how war-sick everybody was at home, sick with a nausea which wanted to forget everything. And I found myself warmly welcomed and within a few weeks had slipped back into my old life as if I had never been away.

But I quickly realised that it was only on the surface, as it were, that I had slipped back; and that between me and all these people I had known and all those others I was now meeting for the first time there was an unbridgeable gulf. Frequently in those early days of my renewal of old friendships and acquaintanceships I heard these people who had been through the war, I mean those who had fought and survived, refer to themselves lightly, flippantly, rather than bitterly or cynically, as the lost generation. But it was I and my kind, the dodgers, the unfit, the too old and perhaps also the too young, who were the lost generation, and not those who had endured and come through and with whom we could not establish now or ever any real contact.

It was a new and unknown, unreal world to me and I was as intellectually and emotionally bewildered and lost in it as if I had been Rip van Winkle. Intellectually I was, in time, to find my bearings in this new world, but emotionally I have never quite been able to.

But at first I was, as I say, all at sea. I found, for example (and I choose the example as being perhaps more obviously significant than others I might have used) such poems as these (they are both Michael's) being written and accepted as the obvious and normal expressions of the poetic urge—if that is the way to put it. With the first I did not feel so entirely lost; here was at least something I could feel in touch with, however hard and seemingly crude the workmanship; but with the chaotic formlessness of *Danse Macabre*, with its apparently deliberate violation of every canon of the art of writing verse and indeed of the elementary rules of composition, I was utterly lost. I naturally jumped to the conclusion that it was a joke, if perhaps a pointless and childish one; but I could not long hug that easy comfort in face of the fact that all over Europe and in America young men were gravely writing such bewildering things and the critics (if perhaps not the public at large) as gravely assessing them. But enough! Here is the first poem:

LEICESTER SQUARE
Preen strumpets, trip lecherously, proffer your fruit
Stale and mildewed.
In the gutter displaying his matches and his medals
(NO PENSION TWICE WOUNDED)
He watches the flesh parade.

He had flesh to sell
At a shilling a day.
How much for a night?
Who'll buy?

And this the second:

> *DANSE MACABRE.*
> *here's a bluebottle on the floor, i*
> *wonder wintery comatose*
> *i (in the bath hot steaming)*
> *wondering watching but*
> *it moves, gyrates,*
> *(buzzes).,*
> *one*
> *wing*
> *is OFF*
> *buzz faintly buzz faintly gy-*
> *rate fast, fast, fast, lie*
> *still.*
> *?*
> *moribund emaciate*
> *a bunch*
> *of legs, legs wispy, comes crawling*
> *dragging, a*
> *spi*
> *der*
> *gyrate*
> *gyrate*
> *buzz*
> *. ? .*
> *creep wispy legs*
> *crawl hunger*

legs emaciate moribund
nearer
stumble stum B L E
further
gyrate, creep, near, far,
near, buzz gy R A T E
hunger
gyrate buzz creep
close
is (death)
the blood is the
LIFE.
, still,

But probably my judgment is at fault in my estimate of that new world which confronted me, because I chiefly, indeed entirely, had under close observation only an almost infinitesimal section of the community and that one whose members could scarcely be reckoned as completely normal or average human beings. What then of the great mass of the country, the men-in-the-street and their wives and children; the labourers, the mechanics, the black-coated workers, the small business men and the minor professional men who make up ninety per cent of any country, who *are*, so it is claimed, that country, and who in the long run must make it or destroy it. What did I know of them, of their thoughts and feelings and their reactions to the war that was over and the peace and the new world which was come? As far as they were concerned I was, as I had always been, a mere looker-on; and I have never believed that it is the looker-on who sees most of the game; certainly it is not true of the game of life where one must mix and rub shoulders, eat and sleep and work, especially work, if one is to understand what is happening and why.

In my rôle of looker-on I watched the passing scene and from my view-point I could note no great changes. The people seemed to be doing as they had always done; nothing on the surface was changed; the daily round of work, play and sleep went on as ever. Whether beneath the surface there were changes I did not know. I wondered if Alison knew with her years of at least partial contact with the somewhat lower strata. Even if she did and gave me the benefit of her knowledge it would be but second-hand and as such about as valuable as the copy of an old master compared with the original. And in any case I did not want to ask her. She had moved, it seemed to me, outside my orbit. Piers at the Hang-the-Kaiser election at the end of 1918 had been returned by a big majority for his old seat, Eastwich, and was now, at thirty-six, Under Secretary of State for Foreign Affairs, a minor public figure, one of whose activities the press took note; one in fact of those notable outstanding personages whose careers are destined to be part of the history of his country.

And then suddenly I remembered the only friends I had ever made outside my own class: Ted and Alice May and their lively youngsters and especially the boy Frank. For some time I played with the notion of paying a visit to Benker's Row, Kilburn, and renewing that friendship; and for long the balance of pro and con remained level. The heaviest weight against the project was my disinclination, my deep aversion indeed, to revive any of the ghosts of Kitty Sears and the Bear Street murder.

But at last I went. It was a hot, brassily hot, June day. The street looked dirtier and dingier than my recollection of it and many grimy children swarmed in its gutters, two of them I noticed were mulattos. Benker's Row itself looked tumbledown and patched and its houses incredibly small. As I approached Number Five disappointment stirred in me as I saw that the frame invented by Ted May as the vehicle for his great joke was gone; and I was ready for the additional blow when the door opened to disclose a stranger. He was an old man, a dirty old man, and he stared at me suspiciously and truculently. But when I asked about Ted May, and said I was a friend of his, his expression changed as if wiped off with a sponge. He smiled a little vacantly I thought but it was probably the effect of his almost toothless gums. "Ah, Ted May," he said, "you won't find him here now, mister."

"Moved?" I asked.

He drew down his lips. "In a manner o' speaking he has. Yerrs. Moved as you might say." And he appeared to be enjoying some secret grim joke. And then he said, "Friend o' yours Ted was, eh?"

I nodded.

"Ted were killed in nineteen-fourteen," he said; "right at the beginning; he took out his old bus like a lot of other London drivers and he were one of the first to stop one. Blown to bits, bus an' all."

"And Mrs. May and the children," I asked.

"Don't know, mister; they lef' soon afterwards; I used to live opposite. Don' know where they went.

Down in the country somewhere. Friend o' Ted's, eh?"

"Yes," I said.

He nodded and sucked a tooth. "One o' the first to be killed, Ted were," he said; "and his name's on the war memorial," with a vague wave of his hand over the roofs opposite. "Ought t' be on top Ted's name ought but it's near the bottom, him being a nem. He were one o' the first to go and his name's near the bottom and a lot o' those above him were artful dodgers who didn't go till they was made to. And he's below them just because he's a nem. It just shows you. War memorial's over there," making the same vague gesture, "if you'd like to see Ted's name. First on the right and then at the bottom o' Cooper Street you'll see the park gates and if you go along there you can't miss it."

I thanked him, hesitated and then offered him a pound note.

He took it, held it dangling, and said with a grin, "Luvaduck! what's this for, mister?"

I felt a fool and stammered something about being much obliged at which he smiled broadly and said, "You're welcome, mister; any friend o' Ted's." He pocketed the note and as I turned away repeated his directions for finding the war memorial.

But I did not want to see, on what was probably a distorted replica of the Cenotaph, those few letters, that brief unmeaning superscription which was all that remained of the burly, jovial soul whose exuberant vitality had so humorously expressed itself in his whimsical invention, and not least in that masterpiece of nonsense, *Umdrum*.

Despite the ease with which I had slipped back into
my old life there was to me at first something of that
feeling of instability, of strangeness, almost of unreality, which one has when returning to normal
ways after an illness and long convalescence (for I
had had a protracted bout of typhoid in the summer
of 1917 in the Argentine). So much had to be renewed,
picked up again; new contacts had to be made. Even
in so minor a matter as the small change of conversation I was at a disadvantage, for mine was in an out-
of-date currency as far as my more intimate friendships
were concerned; with mere acquaintances, either old
or new, I could keep the ball spinning on the surface
as well as the next man.

After childhood a period of six years brings no great
changes in one's appearance. That is the common
opinion and one to which I should have subscribed
whole-heartedly before I left England. I realised on
my return how untrue it was and that it was based
upon the fact that such separating gaps are exceptional.
I found quite startling changes in the people of my
circle, startling I suppose because, naturally enough,
in my own eyes I had not changed at all. Moreover
the reality of their assured positions (and in some
instances notable positions) in contemporary life was
not without its element of surprise. This is of course
trite and perhaps rather naïve but it seems to me of
sufficient human interest to record the vast difference,
in its arresting power over the mind, between the
reading in, for example, Crispin's letter that Piers was
Under-Secretary for Foreign Affairs, and being confronted by the physical Piers in all the (metaphorical)
panoply of that important office.

And much the same was true of the others of my circle. When I first got back there was a play of Crispin's *St. Martin's Summer* having a very successful run at the Haymarket Theatre and his name on the side of a bus as it swept by me one morning in Piccadilly seemed suddenly, and for the first time, to show me (shout at me would be nearer) his very notable position in the English Theatre. And yet I had seen his farce *Form Fours!* acted in New York and even more spectacularly advertised; but the revelation had not come then; some touchstone was, I imagine, lacking. That Tom Frankell, now a very burly fellow, was editor of *The Call* had barely meant enough, when I read it in Norrie's letter, for me to remember it. Yet how striking was the reality of Tom's position in this world where it was difficult for me not to feel a stranger. Socialism was in the air; *The Call* was a force and Tom as its editor, whether penning his denunciatory leaders or declaiming from a hundred platforms about the country, was a personage. Were they not indeed all personages? Norrie now with her plate in Wimpole Street and her large and expensive nursing-home in Portland Crescent, to make no mention of her obvious liking for ex-Sergeant Tom Frankell; Michael the soldier-poet now back with the firm and conducting the educational side; Squitters Beamish with his literary editorship of *The Morning News*, his medals and honours—a hero, but no more likeable than before; Alison, Mrs. Piers Rowland of 2, Cadogan Square, political hostess and social worker; Faith, my little sister Faith, now Faith Darblay starring at the Duke of York's with her picture in all the illustrateds and the young man Roberts a trifle in the background but for all that, or perhaps because of it, an uxorious husband; Charmian Claire enchanting her millions on a thousand screens; Sylvia, a sad figure perhaps, but as Hazel Fayre uplifting countless hearts by her daily poetic message in a score of syndicalised newspapers. Among all these, with their busy paragraphed public lives and their private loves, what was I with my handful of pictures and my craven record but a diffident shadow treading delicately to escape the attention they seemed to court.

Chapter Thirteen

PEAKS

THE HALF-DOZEN or so years immediately following my return to England wear something in recollection of the aspect of a flat plain diversified here and there by a few not very spectacular mountains. Of these peaks but one intimately concerned myself, and as I call its incidents back to my mind something of my harassment and anger at the time return with them; and it is only because its significance (not altogether fully realised by me then) demands its place in my story that I record it, although it must wait a while till I have dealt with the affairs of others.

My father's death, as I have said, left me quite unmoved and I was in this, I imagine, more fortunate than Piers, who must have wished his father dead often enough before the event relieved him of an embarrassment peculiarly hurtful to him in his political career, hurtful, that is, in the eyes of the mob-element among his political opponents, an element which may be contemned as insignificant but can no more be ignored than an urchin in ambush with a snowball—to that grotesquely-outrageous threat to dignity the most eminent are the most vulnerable. Quintin Rowland, Piers's shiftless parasitic father, with his artistic quiver full of blunt, broken or wingless arrows, had during the war taken up his residence in Germany (unaccompanied by his wife) and there he had busied himself in the production of anti-British propaganda far more virulent than the German article and the more damaging and irritating because of his knowledge of the mental attitudes of his countrymen. He was probably supremely happy in this work for he had at last found his métier; he was no longer the writer of scorned and rejected stories, poems and plays; no longer the painter of pictures no one would buy; he was the author, the creator (how the knowledge must have fed his starved little soul) of pamphlets, of booklets, of single sheets, to be dropped from planes, which would not only be read by millions ("and how many" he may be imagined saying with a savage sneer, "of the successful swine with their pompous collected editions speak to such a vast audience?") but would inflict wounds (and even pin-pricks if frequent and numerous cannot be ignored) upon the country which had so blindly failed to perceive his worth, or if perceiving it, had wilfully and enviously ignored it.

Philosophy and metaphysics hold little mental nourishment and few attractions for me but I imagine that happiness of old Father Rowland (as Michael once nicknamed him in our school-days and wrote on him an Old Father William imitation) that happiness of his must count for something in the scale of things (in the absolute—isn't that the jargon?) but it would be heavily outweighed in that same scale by the annoyance and the embarrassment caused to his brilliant son by activities which by reason of that son's political ambitions were peculiarly adapted to injure him. And so when, after the war, Quintin Rowland quarrelled with his perhaps now reluctant hosts and finding few places in the world likely to welcome him left it in the summer of 1923 by a spectacular leap from an aeroplane over the Caspian Sea, his only son must have regarded that incident as probably one of the luckiest and most timely of his career. It is more than possible that the father would have been ironically appreciative of the fact that on the day following his death an account of his career appeared in most English newspapers almost side by side with the report of a speech on foreign policy by his son; and he would have enjoyed an additional relish in noting that the story of his career was given more space than his offspring's eloquence.

That same year, within a few days of Christmas, my mother died. We Farnes are a short-lived race and we seem to marry short-lived women; during the few generations we can trace back no Farne man or wife, except Crispin's grandmother, reached even the allotted span; the early sixties (a traditionally dangerous period) carrying them off. Had I during my father's lifetime or afterwards been asked about my feelings towards him I should probably have replied either that I disliked him or was completely indifferent to him; the truth, I imagine, is that as a child I disliked and feared him and that later I simply pushed him out of my life as one of the things with which I had no concern, nor wanted to have. Had I during my mother's lifetime been asked a similar question with regard to our emotional relationship I should undoubtedly have replied that I was very fond of her. Looking back now upon her death I am sure that my feeling for her cannot be truthfully described as fondness; her dying occasioned me no grief; did not move me at all beyond the mild impersonal sadness that one feels in connection with all death. And in realising this I am led, forced indeed, to ask myself the question whether filial love exists at all outside the triple realms of romance, hypocrisy and the imagination. I mean as a general thing; as a natural human thing such as the love of the sexes or maternal love; and these are instincts rather than attributes. Filial love is not an instinct; does it exist at all normally? Is not a son who loves his mother an unnatural rather than a natural son? In some moods (and I write this in such a mood) it seems to me that nothing else in life is worth much when weighed in the scales against truth. The truth at any price. The truth if the heavens fall. What then is the truth about the normal relationship between mother and son? Mutual love? Or love on the mother's part and complete indifference on the son's (with a small leaven of cupboard-love in the early years)? The only probes I have for truth are my knowledge of myself and my experience of life, i.e. my observation of my fellow human beings; those probes dig out for me the same answer.

The following September Norrie married Tom Frankell at Marylebone Registry Office. It had been clear enough, I suppose, for some time that this was going to happen; but it came to me with something of a mild shock. And when I came to analyse that shock I found, dodging about in my mind and hiding away from the light like a bug in the wainscoting— an apt simile—an incredible bit of snobbery: I didn't think Tom Frankell good enough for Norrie because his father had been a postman; that he had been a postman in the east end was an aggravation, absurdly, of course; but then, the whole thing was absurd. Norrie's great-grandfather had been an illiterate Liverpool dockside labourer. Crispin's remark when he heard of the wedding, which he did not attend, was: "So Norrie's going back to her origins," a remark which it seems to me has the same snobbish implications as my first feeling of antagonism to the match. I could defend my position by pointing out that three generations are by tradition reckoned to make a gentleman or (I suppose) a lady and certainly Norrie was no exception to the traditional rule, while Tom Frankell still carried (however slightly) traces of the mean streets of his upbringing in such matters as accent and his attitude to servants, both domestic and public. I could, I say, thus have defended my position, but I did no such thing; it was, in the light of reason and common sense, untenable, and I abandoned it. Tom and Norrie were plainly very much in love; equally plainly they had the greatest respect and admiration for each other's achievements; both had jobs whose performance so filled their days that their leisure together was doubly delightful. I could imagine no more promising basis for a happy marriage, nor one more likely to last.

Tom and Norrie dined with me at my studio the evening before; and after dinner we sat talking (I mostly listening); and I was a little amused to find Norrie's former indifference to politics replaced by a fervour for reformation, for revolution indeed if that were the only road. Whether she really felt that way I of course did not know; if she did not she acted her part well and thereby showed her good sense, for politics, socialism, was Tom's job (apart from it being, as it was, his only hobby and the very breath of his nostrils) and she was marrying the job as well as the man. Indeed both are, or ought to be, one and the same. But perhaps she was already a convert and whether it was love or study which had converted her is of no moment.

Tom's ambitions were entirely political. *The Call* was merely a stepping-stone and he had in fact already been promised a safe seat at the next general election. Norrie intended carrying on with her practice and her nursing-home, at least for a time; but from the small straws which from time to time blew across the conversation I gathered that her ambitions included for Tom a seat in the cabinet and for herself a political salon which should also attract the brightest brains in the creative professions as she termed them. It seemed to me that those ambitions were certainly not immoderate considering her own and Tom's abilities and her ample private fortune.

Tom had no doubts about the coming of world-wide socialism and he was a most genial expositor of his views. There was nothing of the glib-tongued demagogue about him, no trace of bitterness or acrimony. " You see," he said, while Norrie filled his pipe for him, "the eventual victory of socialism is a matter of pure deduction; it must come. Reason, the mind, is the one thing, and the only one, in human beings still capable of almost infinite expansion, improvement. Physically mankind has probably reached its limits; there will of course be slight changes, the disappearance for example of the appendix, the little toe and possibly hair, although I think that hair on the head will remain because of its æsthetic appeal; but hair on the body will go, certainly on women, even, I should say, the pubic hair. And that is about all. We shall not increase our stature although doubtless we shall increase the length of our lives. But the mind; there lies the hope of the human race; its possibilities are tremendous. And that means simply this: that eventually truth will prevail."

"I'm with you so far," I smiled; "truth at any price; but is socialism truth?"

"It stands for the propagation of truth anyhow. Let me give a small example of what I mean. In 1872 there was published Winwood Reade's famous book, *The Martyrdom of Man*. It was recognised almost at once as a great contribution to thought, to truth. It presented in plain straightforward language the facts about religion, history and biology. I was born in 1887, fifteen years after that book's publication and acceptance by the best minds of the country as one of the most valuable and enlightening books ever written. My years of attending school were between 1893 and 1905, first at an elementary school and afterwards at Selborne; that is to say during a period nearly a generation subsequent to the publication of that book of truth. Did I hear of it at school? Did I even hear of it at Oxford? You know the answer to that. Was there a school in the country using *The Martyrdom of Man* as a text-book? Is there even one to-day doing so? Again you know the answer. And what is the reason? Why this conspiracy of silence about this fine book? There is only one answer and that is that truth is so hated and feared by governments (lay or ecclesiastical) that whenever it shows its head it is either chopped off or, if that be impossible or inexpedient, covered over with a dark pall of silence." He smiled.   "Do you know, Julian," he went on, pulling at his pipe with great enjoyment, "when a socialist government takes office and I'm offered a post in the cabinet I shall ask for the job of Minister of Education and I shall then issue to all the elementary schools the following books as text-books and see that not only the youngsters are examined in them but the teachers as well: *The Martyrdom of Man*; Bellamy's *Looking Backward*; Paine's *Age of Reason*; Blatchford's *Merrie England* and *God and my Neighbour*; the Hammonds' *The Town Labourer*; Carpenter's *Civilisation*; Darwin's *Origin*; several of Wells's things and Whitman's and, well." with a wave of his pipe, "that'll do to be going on with."

"You'll have a tough fight on your hands," I said.

"I'll probably be crucified," he laughed; "but that's the programme."

"Is it socialism's programme?" I asked.

"In particulars, no; but in the general matter of the propagation of truth, yes."

"So socialism's solved the great enigma; what is truth?"

"It's never been an enigma; truth is as far and as deep as human thought can reach at any given period in humanity's long journey."

"In other words," said Norrie, who was watching his animated face with smiling eyes, "it's not the same yesterday to-day and for ever."

"Not in the least, and obviously so if the human mind progresses; as it does and must continue to do.

But there are fundamental truths which can never change in a human world."

"Never's a long time," I laughed; "even two and two may not always make four; or so I'd be prepared to argue if I were mathematician enough."

He waved that away with a smile. "So far," he went on, "the history of humanity has been a long record of the suppression of truth by every force, by every subterfuge, by every cruelty the wit of man could devise. Ever and again in history truth escapes from the pit she has been kept in; and that escape is labelled revolution; and incontinently all the powers and principalities band together to smash that revolution and put back truth where they want her."

"And the Russian Revolution is an escape of truth into the world?" I asked.

"Precisely; just as the French Revolution was. That was choked to death; but the Russian is proving a more difficult job, in fact an impossible one."

"I think," I said, "you load the dice too heavily against the rulers, the governments, and the churches of the world. I think you give them credit for more intelligence, more Machiavellianism than they possess or ever possessed."

"All history disproves that," he replied. "Why, for example, did Rome over six hundred years ago warn Roger Bacon to abandon his experiments in chemistry and optics on pain of excommunication and death? You know——"

"I know," I interrupted him, "that I've to get you to Marylebone by nine o'clock in the morning and it's now eleven; and we've all been smoking without a break for the last two hours. One ought to be in training for a wedding as much as for a prize-fight. It's reckoned to be an equal ordeal. I suggest as your trainer a twenty minutes' stroll and then I'll take you both to your homes and pack you off to bed."

I remember later that night sitting in my studio smoking and lazily thinking of the wedding and of Tom's exposition of socialism, which I fear I had failed to find original or illuminating or even particularly interesting. But then I find all political issues rather boring. But it did occur to me as I knocked out my pipe that Tom's Golden Age, or Age of Reason, or whatever it was, seemed to rest upon the fallacy that people wanted to know the truth, or as he would write it Truth. My experience of life suggests that the great majority of people want nothing of the sort; they just want to be left alone to paddle their own little canoes over the surface of life with as much enjoyment and as little pain (and thought) as possible. Perhaps my judgment is at fault, my estimate belittling, and the passion for truth is as ardent and as universal as the sexual passion. But I don't think so.

It was during this period (roughly the first post-war decade) that Crispin reached his highest achievement as a playwright; or perhaps it would be safer to say his highest material achievement. He wrote six plays during those years and at one time had three running simultaneously in London and two in New York. I saw them all at some time or another but I received no invitation to any of the first-nights; nor, I think, was anyone else of our former circle more favoured. We rarely met and then only by chance and he spent a good deal of his time abroad. He had, to my eyes, aged the most of us all and at forty the sweeping black hair over the marble-white face and blazing blue eyes was freely streaked with grey. He had, of course, matured early and at sixteen looked twenty, which may possibly account for his rapid ageing. Of his plays he said that the public hated them but couldn't keep away from them; and in that hyperbole there was a touch of truth. With one exception, his war-time farce, his plays were unpleasant. Cynical was the epithet most often used to describe them; but this was not very apt; his themes dealt with the worst sides of human nature; but they were presented with an almost scientific impartiality, much as a surgeon might cut out a tumour and pass it round for the instruction of the students present at the operation. He used to say that only his large private means enabled him to write what and how he liked; but again there is only a touch of truth in this, for while I believe he did finance the production of his first two plays it was certainly never necessary for him to do so afterwards, and all his plays, especially his later ones, were great box-office successes.

But enough of Crispin. He had, as I say, drifted (or moved of intent) from our circle; and he was to move even further. Towards the end of that time it was only through Avis that we knew anything at all, apart from what was public, about Crispin. She had come to live quite near me in St. John's Wood. She had written since the war some half-dozen or so novels, light in theme and popular in treatment, which Conways had published for her with considerable profit. There was still at times something of the gipsy about her appearance and while pretty would have been a foolishly inept word to apply to her she was very attractive and distinguished-looking. I often wondered that she had not married or, as far as I knew, had a lover; but then, how far did I know! perhaps she had had many lovers.

She looked in at my studio quite often and would sometimes make tea for us both. One summery afternoon she was sitting sipping her tea and watching me at my easel. Suddenly she said, "Do you know, Julian, I'm going to write a novel."

"I thought you'd done so," I rejoined casually; "quite a lot in fact, and very successful ones."

"Oh, those!" she said and lit a cigarette.

I did not reply and presently she said, "Have you read any of my novels?"

"Why, of course."

"Don't lie," she laughed; "you do it so badly."

"I read two, really."

"Which two?"

"I've forgotten the titles; I never can remember titles; but one——"

"Thank you," she interrupted, "never mind the story; what did you think of them, honestly?"

"Very pleasant little yarns."

"Your tea's getting cold; come and drink it and pay me the compliment of giving me something more than a tenth of your attention."

Presently when I had drunk my tea she lit my cigarette from her own and said, "I've written eight novels, Julian, and the only excuse for writing them would have been as a means of livelihood, that I wanted the money. Since I can't plead that they're just damnable."

"Are they?" I said; "they've provided entertainment

for thousands. Don't let's take ourselves too seriously, Avis. That's my besetting sin; I didn't know it was yours."

"It's everybody's at times. Don't be flippant. You know as well as I do that if people didn't take themselves seriously at times, didn't whole-heartedly believe that something they were doing was the most important thing in the world and of tremendous value to humanity, nothing worth while would ever have been done at all from Michelangelo's David to a Beethoven sonata."

"Were they so portentously serious about it," I said. "I doubt it. But supposing they were, and you tell me I know it as well as you do. I also know that the difference between a monkey scratching in the sand with a stick and Michaelangelo working on David is, in the cosmic scale, precisely nil; or a gorilla drumming on its chest and, say, Paderewski playing one of Beethoven's sonatas."

"Shades of Crispin!" she smiled.

"Shades of Truth," I said.

"Well, it isn't true. But I don't want to argue about that sort of nonsense. I want to write a great novel."

"Wanting's no use. It's like your stature; not by taking thought may you add one——"

"Rubbish; a proper course of exercises will give anybody a couple of inches. All saws are platitudinous lies or half-truths. I believe I can write a big novel; all the others were just apprenticeship, learning how to use my tools; I know now; I can do with words what you can do with a brush. It's the theme I've been waiting for and I have it now; I've had it for months. I'm certain I can make a big book of it."

"Sometimes," I said smiling, "I feel quite certain I can paint a big picture, a masterpiece; I have the theme and, in my eye, I see the finished painting; it's great; but between the eye and the canvas the greatness drips off the brush, on to the floor perhaps, and the completed picture is just one more competent bit of painting, an admirable bit of craftsmanship and that's all."

"Will that always be all? You don't believe that, Ju, or you wouldn't go on painting."

"I should," I said; "if I could not go on with my painting I should go mad." I must have been off my guard for the moment and have spoken with unusual vehemence, for she looked at me swiftly, startled, and then, glancing away, said quietly, "Yes, I know that feeling."

How little, how ludicrously little, she did know; she or any of them.

That conversation was in the early summer of, I think it would be, 1925, and I had entirely forgotten about this great book of Avis's when the following May she rang me up and said she proposed to take me out to lunch. "Of course I want something. How did you like *Prelude*?" "*Prelude*," I said, dredging my wits, but before I could continue I heard her laugh and she said, "Never mind *Prelude*; call for me at one and we'll go to Pascagni's."

As soon as we met, Avis said to me, "Don't you ever open your parcels?" But I had put two and two together on the way and I said, "You've just published a novel, *Prelude*, and sent me a signed copy which I've not yet seen; I'm really awfully sorry but I've been so

wrapped up in a picture the last two or three weeks that
I've let everything slide. And why haven't you told
me about it before? I know I ought to have seen
reviews of it but the extent of my reading the last
month has been to glance at the headlines in the *Times*.
Apart from——"

"That will do!" she laughed; "you've rehearsed
your piece very well; but unfortunately you don't
know much about it."

"Whose fault is that? You've apparently been writing a novel in secret; it is a novel, I suppose? But
why you've said nothing——"

"Do you remember about a year ago when you were
just starting ' The Pool ' and I dropped in for a cup——"

"Of course," I interrupted, recollection having just
come to me; "and you told me of a big book you were
planning. I believe——"

"Be quiet," she laughed; "I don't expect you to
remember all my affairs. As a matter of fact," she
went on with a malicious little smile which lopped
twenty years from her and changed her back into the
dark pig-tailed schoolgirl of that Walberswick holiday,
"I only remember the name of your picture because I've
just been reading Otway's slating of it in his review
of the Royal Academy show. Shall I quote you some
of it?"

"Thanks, I've seen it. Nudity for nudity's sake and
so forth. What does he know about it? But about
your book. When is it—when was it published?"

"It was to be published next Monday. Now don't
pretend any more but do listen. It took me six months
of the hardest work I've ever done to write it and it's
the best book I've written and perhaps ever shall write.

The day before yesterday Humfrey rang me up and said he was withdrawing the book and had asked for all review copies and copies already with the booksellers to be sent back and would I call and see him. I went round; went is putting it mildly; I tore round. He'd received a letter from the solicitors representing Seegars the chain-store people saying they were bringing an action for libel. They'd seen an advance copy; how I don't know and it doesn't matter. Humfrey had seen his own solicitor who had said Seegars seemed to have a case and Humfrey surrendered without firing a shot, abandoned me, agreed to pay a preposterous sum of three thousand pounds and their costs and to withdraw the book. I told him I wouldn't have it; that he must fight the case and I'd foot the bill; but he simply shook his head and drew down his lips, you know that grimace of his, and said it couldn't be done; I insisted; I cajoled him and then bullied him and I'm sure swore at him; but it was useless. I want you to come round with me after lunch and back me up. No, don't say anything now; keep it for Master Humfrey."

Humfrey attempted to burke everything by assuming his most facetious mood. He rubbed his hands as we sat down, and said, "Come to tell me you're going to get married; that's splendid; I've always thought you two were made for each other. Now what shall we say for a present? The Conway Thackeray in blue half-morocco with——"

"That'll do, Humfrey," Avis said, "Grimaldi parts don't suit your appearance; you know what we've come for."

"Ha! then assume I don't," he smiled; "tell me."

"*Prelude* is being published on Monday," Avis said bluntly.

He slowly shook his head with a smile, looking in that moment the personification of bland compromising prosperity. "I'm afraid not, my dear Avis," he said; "*Prelude* won't be published on Monday or at all."

Avis glanced over at me and feeling by no means comfortable I said, "Why not, Humfrey? Why not fight Seegars? Be a grand advertisement for the book, I should have thought."

"It's not an advertisement which commends itself to me, Julian," he said; "and when I say me I mean Conways from old Joshua down to myself. Conways have never fought such an action and they never will."

"But surely, Humfrey," I said, "you don't mean that; why, any Tom, Dick——"

"I mean," he interrupted, tapping on the desk with a gold pencil, "that in my opinion Seegars have a case; but even if it were considerably weaker than it is I would not let the matter go to the courts. It's a matter of principle, reputation, prestige, what you will; but there it is. I'm sorry, as I think *Prelude* a fine book; far and away the best thing Avis has done; but if it were the greatest masterpiece in the world I would not allow it to appear under the Conway imprint if it meant defending an action in the courts."

"Your prestige! Your reputation!" Avis said sharply; "and what of mine? You'll kill a fine book at its birth because for no adequate reason you refuse to fight for it. What is all your talk of prestige and the reputation of your house but the merest clap-trap in the face of that? Is that your great services to literature about which you're so proud? Let me fight it."

Again the bland, easy smile. "Now you're being silly, if you'll allow me to say so, my dear Avis. You can't fight it. In these cases the author, doubtless quite wrongly, is of very little importance in the law's eyes. It is we as publishers, and Thornton as the printer, with whom the law is chiefly concerned. You would have to pay something, of course, although some authors manage to avoid even that necessity; so many, my dear Avis, are financially men of straw."

"Which publishers never are," Avis smiled, despite her anger.

Humfrey nodded genially and went on, "Whatever the right or wrong of the case, my dear Avis, I refuse to allow Conways to be branded; I would sooner close our doors."

"Couldn't you get it published elsewhere?" I said to Avis; "all publishers are not so—er—saving your presence, Humfrey, so thin-skinned."

Before she could reply Humfrey said, "I doubt very much if anyone else would risk it now. I'm sorry, but our settling——"

"Has not only killed but buried it," Avis interrupted. "I'll publish it myself."

"Will you print it yourself?"

"I'll find a printer. It will only be a question of guaranteeing him against all legal costs."

"I'm sorry to disillusion you," Humfrey said; "but even if you managed to find a printer you couldn't get the book distributed, for the court would order its destruction." He shook his head slowly and smiled gravely. It seemed incredible that this bland, prosperous-looking old gentleman could be Humfrey Conway, the gallant young City Imperial Volunteer of little more than thirty years ago; inconceivable that he was of our, of Val's and Avis's, of Norrie's and Alison's generation. "Money won't do everything, my dear Avis," he said slowly, tapping lightly on his desk with the gold pencil which seemed so perfectly suited to his plump white fingers; "and I'm glad to know that it won't."

I tried a last suggestion (out of my ignorance of the book), glancing from Avis to Humfrey. "Couldn't the—er—the offending passages be omitted and the book then issued?" I asked.

He made no reply, looking towards Avis, as if she could best answer that. "No," she said emphatically; "and if you'd read the book you'd know it; it's not a case of passages or even chapters; it's the whole setting and treatment. But it's preposterous rubbish to say it's 'libellous.'" She picked up her gloves and smiled at Humfrey and then at me. "But you must read it, Julian; you have the copy I sent you."

"I think," Humfrey said, with almost ponderous gravity, "you should return that copy to me unread, Julian; and you, Avis, what copies you have."

Avis laughed and snapped her fingers. "Bah!" she said, "don't be a humbug; we'll do nothing of the sort. And, my dear Humfrey, you'll never publish another book for *me*." That malicious little smile tucked in the corners of her mouth. "I'll go to Holroyd and Mason's in future. A fine firm, I think you'll admit, Humfrey."

"Estimable, estimable," Humfrey smiled blandly, as he bowed over her hand.

The following autumn I held an exhibition of my pictures at the Topham Galleries. There were some fifty-odd paintings, including most of those I had exhibited in New York; and among these were six of the savage dancers of Tierra del Fuego; there were also ten never before exhibited.

It was a one-man show, was to open to the public on Monday, September 26; and on the previous Saturday there was a private view for my friends to which the press was invited. In Monday's *Morning News* there appeared a column article by Herbert Felsse, the art critic, headed FARNE'S FLESHINGS AT THE TOPHAM. It was not art criticism at all but a ferocious attack upon the pictures on the grounds of obscenity, and singling out in particular the six paintings of the savage dancers and five of those I had not previously exhibited. There were only two other notices in the papers that morning (one in the *Gazette* and the other in the *Tribune*) and these while favourable and indeed friendly in tone, were, I thought, very guarded.

At four o'clock that afternoon, while the Topham was crowded, an inspector and a sergeant from Scotland Yard drove up in a car and after going round the exhibition ordered the six dancer pictures and eight of the others to be taken down; and took them away with them. I was not at the galleries at the time, but at my studio, where just before five o'clock Mr. Branding, the lessee of the Topham, rang me up to tell me what had happened and adding that they were temporarily closing the exhibition as it was possible there would be police court proceedings. And the following morning when I called on my solicitor he told me the case was coming before Sir Henry Gilderson at the Lime Street Police Court on Thursday morning.

I bolted.

I put it as bluntly as that because I have no reasonable defence to offer for what I did, no defence acceptable to plain common sense. I went over to Paris, leaving the case in the hands of my solicitors, who would pull all the possible wires for me.

But if I cannot appeal to reason, to common sense, perhaps there are other sentiments capable of being moved to some understanding of my attitude and my action. First and foremost I knew I could no more endure the police-court proceedings with their whisperings and mutterings and dirty derisive starings than I could endure the thought, years before, of being handled and pawed by an army doctor; the one was as unendurable to me as the other; so frighteningly so that in both cases I fled before their threat. Moreover I knew I could not defend my pictures; I had been tremendously happy while painting them; their creation had in some strange way brought me a peace of mind, a contentment, a spiritual release, I had not known for years. I saw them as something quite beyond the probe of what is or is not moral; in my own thoughts about them indecency and obscenity were words impossible of application to them. How can I put it? For me to have regarded them as indecent would have been as a woman considering her naked babe indecent.

But the humiliating, the shameful, the horrifying truth was that once they had been publicly labelled indecent, once "obscene!" had been shouted from the house-tops, they were, it seemed to me, smirched and dirtied beyond any defence of mine. I could not have defended them; virtue had gone out of me and with it courage. And so, as I have recorded, I bolted.

Wires were pulled however to some purpose; the police-court proceedings fizzled out on the payment of costs (a technical verdict for Scotland Yard), the pictures were returned to The Topham, and Branding was informed that he would be well-advised not to replace them in the exhibition. But he had already received instructions from me to close my show and return all my pictures to my agent.

One tiny side-light I feel should be chronicled. Piers was one of those approached during the wire-pulling. He refused to move and said, "I've seen the paintings and I think them pretty rank."

Chapter Fourteen

OLD TRAIL

I DID not return to England until the following May; and about a month later I opened my morning paper to find Miles in the news and, because of him, Walberswick. The papers made a great deal of his feat; partly no doubt because of his fine war record and his disability, but indeed at first glance the affair seemed sufficiently incredible to warrant all that was said about it. If I seem to discount something of its extraordinary nature it is no belittling of mine but because Miles later on pooh-poohed it as the merest commonplace for a blind man who had learned to make four senses fulfil the functions of five. What had happened was, briefly, that two venturesome youngsters of twelve had put out in a small sailing-dinghy from Southwold harbour; and when about half a mile south of Walberswick and a hundred yards from the shore their boat had been upset by a gust, but instead of sinking had floated bottom up, and they had been able to hang on and keep themselves afloat. Neither could swim and their shouts for help attracted the attention of the only two people on the beach, an elderly woman who was painting, and Miles, who was dozing on the sand with his collie, Ruff, beside him. He asked the woman what was the matter, removing his dark glasses to obviate explanations; and getting his bearing from her plunged in and swam towards the boys, hailing them as he did so for direction. He brought the boys ashore one at a time, the second return journey being rendered a hazardous one, not so much because the boat had by then drifted out almost as far again, but because the youngster fainted from fright on the way and Miles had to be guided solely by the shouts from the shore.

On the picture page of the paper there were two photographs of Walberswick, one showing Miles's small cottage, and the other the inn; and as I sat looking at them there slipped into my mind one of those ideas which, because of their sentimental associations, are so apt to be regarded as of the heaven-sent variety; and one is therefore strongly tempted to act upon them accordingly, usually with results which fall far short of anticipation. Why not, suggested this bright idea with its crafty nostalgic ally, why not a pleasant little party for a month or so at our villa (it was mine now) at Walberswick in August or September? Just as many of the old crowd as would come, if only for a fortnight. Why not indeed? It seemed a great scheme and I acted upon it at once by ringing up Norrie and saying I proposed to invite myself to dinner unless they were engaged.

And after dinner that evening I revealed my plan with all the pride of a clucking hen with its chick; and its reception was so warm that I became more than ever delighted with the prospect and was not at all damped when Tom said that a fortnight was all he could spare as a general election was expected in October and he wanted to spend as much time as he could in the constituency (it was Limehouse North), where he would be fighting his first election. He might possibly, he said, squeeze out a few days more but three weeks would be the outside; and as Norrie wanted to help him that would be, she said, her limit too.

We were discussing who else would be likely to come when Norrie said, "Do you think Miles would care about us invading his sanctuary? Might it not remind him too poignantly——" and left her sentence unfinished.

I thought that on the contrary he might welcome it, and Tom agreeing that it was in any case as likely as not, we decided to go ahead, with the proviso that Miles should be sounded.

"You'll ask everybody, I suppose?" Norrie said.

I nodded. "Everybody available."

"There's only Nan in America," Norrie said; "otherwise it's a full roll. But I doubt if Crispin will come."

"Pretty sure he won't," I said; "if he's not out of England now he probably will be by then; I'll give him a ring in the morning. I've approached no one so far. If you'd not approved I'd have dropped it."

"Piers," began Norrie doubtfully, when I interrupted, saying, "I'm hardly counting on him; and in any case he was not of the old party."

"That leaves Alison out, too."

"I don't see why; even if she only came down for a week. There's Faith?"

She shook her head. "The Roberts boy isn't well; tubercular trouble; I thought it all along; they were talking the other evening about Davos for him for six months, and Faith will go with him." Norrie smiled and added, "I think theirs is the most extraordinary affair; I mean considering Faith and her good looks and her celebrity as an actress and the Roberts boy is a weedy little runt and very second-rate. And she's more in love with him than she ever was."

"He's probably never once said an unkind word to her or made her feel small," I said; "that counts, doesn't it, as much with a woman as a man."

Norrie glanced at me quickly and then away. "Even more, I should think," she said. "Well, who's left? Michael and Sylvia. It wouldn't do to ask Sylvia; she doesn't want the past revived."

"She probably lives on it and in it," Tom said, blowing out a cloud of smoke. "Hence the stuff she writes, which is just an escape through nostalgic dreaming. Might probably do her good. But perhaps you know best."

"Look here," I laughed, "enough of this whittling down. I'm going to ask everybody, barring Nan, and I'm half inclined to send *her* a cable. I would if I thought there was the ghost of a chance of her coming. But apart from Nan, everybody."

And during the next two or three days I asked everybody, with results much as Norrie had forecasted. Miles was quite agreeable and indeed sounded pleased over the telephone. Crispin was going with Lord Calchott and a party (a gang he called them) for a three months Mediterranean cruise on the young peer's steam yacht *Campaspe*. Faith and her husband were already packing for Davos, and Piers said he was spending any leisure he had that summer in his constituency or in Paris and Geneva on political business, but he'd try to run down for a week-end; Avis and Michael both agreed to come, Michael, I thought, without much enthusiasm; while Alison said she'd manage a few

T

days or perhaps a week before Piers left England. Sylvia was the only surprise; she not only said she would be glad to come but wrote me a long letter, mostly concerned with our holidays as youngsters.

I went down myself the first week in August to the villa, a small staff having gone down three weeks earlier, as *Ardvaar* for the last four years had been unoccupied and looked after by a caretaker.

I shall not dwell on that holiday which was, for some elusive reason, a quite desolating failure. Piers did not come for the promised week-end and while Alison stayed ten days she was quiet and preoccupied, spending much of her time rambling about the beach alone or with Avis, who was also, or so it seemed to me, strangely unlike her usual gay, vital self. Michael, who had had an offer to go to Hollywood and had accepted, was, I thought, grudging the time spent with us and—but enough; the whole thing was a dismal failure, without even the mitigation of fine weather; for there were more cold and cloudy days than sunny.

The second Friday in September saw the end of it. Norrie and Tom had remained till the last; but with all their cheeriness they could not conceal their air of staying by a sinking ship. I saw them off from Southwold Station at half-past two. A leaden sky, a cold wind, and a thin driving rain, lent a last and perhaps a ludicrous touch of depression to our farewells.

Miles alone remained; and that evening after dinner I went over to his cottage, taking my sheep-dog Bess with me. It was dark and still raining, and as I stumbled on my way across the soaked meadow, where hidden tree-roots crawled like malignant snakes to trip the feet, I was in the black mood of Job which would curse God and die, although lacking a God even that relief was denied me.

Miles sat in a big worn arm-chair before a bright log fire, his legs stretched out to the blaze; and I noticed that his flannel trousers were soaked to the knee. Beside him lay the collie Ruff. He seemed glad I had come and would have switched on the light, but I told him I preferred the firelight and sat down opposite him. The collie had got up to greet Bess, but after a few sniffs and much tail-wagging from Ruff (a manifestation denied to Bess, who is an old English blue bob and has to wriggle her entire rump to display her affection) the two settled themselves down, stretched, sighed deeply and drowsed off to sleep. As we talked, and we talked long that evening, now and again Ruff would raise his head, rest his muzzle a moment upon Miles's knee, and then stretch out once more; and Bess would half-lift her head, open slow pale-blue eyes, regard me steadfastly for a while and then, blinking quickly, let fall her head, emit her deep sigh, and doze off again.

Much of what we talked about as we sat smoking has gone from my memory; but something remains; and if as I record it here it seems to be a sort of disjointed monologue, almost a soliloquy, on Miles's part, it is not that my rôle was entirely that of listener, but because as I write there comes slipping back into my mind, fragmentarily rather than connectedly, the things he spoke of rather than anything I contributed to the conversation. And if those things of which he spoke tend to give the impression that the general atmosphere was one of gloom and depression, that is far from the truth; his manner was quiet, his voice touched with that strange flatness of the blind, but there was an undertone of warmth, even geniality, and no trace at all of complaint or bitterness. He seemed, in speaking of himself, to have achieved so complete an objectivity that he might have been discussing some third and absent friend. He had taken off his dark glasses, evidently before I came in, and he did not resume them; so that throughout our talk the dancing flames from the logs played grotesquely in the scarred pits beneath his brows.

"No," he said in answer to some remark of mine, "I don't eat much. It's not a matter of lack of appetite, but I have to be careful. I don't get enough exercise —not enough to make me sweat—and in consequence, unless I keep to a pretty strict regimen, I get indigestion. I don't drink much, either." He smiled. "Beer, I've discovered, is only wholesome when one is doing hard physical work or taking heavy exercise. I smoke a good deal. For the first few months after I was blind I couldn't enjoy a pipe at all; it didn't taste, and I thought I might as well give it up. But the desire to light a pipe after a meal, especially breakfast, persisted; and so I went on with it, and gradually the taste came back. It's a big thing in my life—tobacco—now. So is the wireless. They both mean a lot. Old Vesey told me I wasn't getting enough exercise, which I knew as well as he did. He suggested gardening, and I do a fair amount; but it's rather a sort of digging for digging's sake than cultivation. And I walk a lot, but it's slow motion rather than the real thing. And I'm not sure Ruff isn't a liability rather than an asset, eh, old boy!" stroking the muzzle resting now for a moment on his knee, "for I'm scared to death a car'll run over him in these narrow roads; there's a lot of traffic about here during the summer. I tried riding —I used to get a man over from the livery stables in Southwold—but I gave it up; it was too much like being tied to some one's apron strings." He paused as if the phrase had given his thoughts a new direction, and then went on: "Mrs. Benson and the maid and Hayter look after me well, but sometimes when I get a bit sorry for myself and hanker after a woman beside me—well, just at those times, Ju, they're less than nothing. I'm weak enough then to feel sorry I wasn't married before it happened; but in the main I'm glad; I wouldn't have any woman tied to what I am. Old Vesey told me I ought to get married; it was during one of my hankering moods, and I had to treat the thing flippantly to get out of it without making a fool of myself. I said to him, ' Right. I'll marry one of the village girls.' And he replied, ' Well, you might do worse.' ' Go ahead and parade them,' I told him, ' and we'll play blind man's buff, and I'll marry the one I nail, if she'll have me.' I was once sweet on Avis."

The abrupt revelation startled me into an exclamation; and he laughed and went on: "It was just after I'd left Sandhurst, and she told me not to be silly and to think of my career. So I thought of it. Surprised you, did I? I thought you'd have known."

"Good Lord, no," I said. "I'd not the faintest notion."

"No," he said, turning his head towards me, so that for a moment the scarred orbits held a fleeting semblance to shadowed eyes. "No. I always thought." He stopped short and smiled. "Physical jerks was one of old Vesey's suggestions which I followed; I'm an obedient sort of bloke now. I fitted up my bedroom with all kinds of contraptions, rowing-machines, expanders, a punching-ball and the rest." He laughed. "A punching-ball's no joke when you can't see the damned thing. I came down to breakfast several mornings with the claret tap on, much to dear old Mrs. Benson's alarm. But I chucked it all. I reasoned it out: What was I getting myself fit for? Just so I could eat and drink heartily without getting a tummy and a liver. It didn't seem worth it. Better put a bridle on the old appetites, I thought; the ascetic instead of the athletic. So now I just eat a couple of small meals a day, one at ten and the other about five; have a glass of beer in the inn about one and another (sometimes a couple if the blues are in the offing) in the evening. And that's the sum total of my indulgences.

"I wonder how long it's going on for. Another thirty years if I'm unlucky. I don't pretend now, Ju. It's a dull life. The colour's gone out of it in every way. One hankers like hell. Just hankers. I'm tempted sometimes to take one of those little wenches about here and marry her. Buy her. Say to her, ' My dear, I've got nearly ten thousand pounds a year; enough to buy you all the pretty things you've ever wanted. I'll give you the lot if you're a good enough actress to make me believe you like me and that's why you're marrying me.'" He laughed rather flatly. "But I'm not always so high-stomached. Sometimes I crawl to them on my belly, in these imaginary negotiations, and say, ' Come at your own price, my dear; come on any terms; even if you carry on half a dozen illicit

Chapter Fifteen

OF CRISPIN AND SOME OTHERS

CRISPIN had a new play, *Son of Woman*, produced at *The Royalty* in the following March. It was over a year since I had seen Crispin for more than a few moments, and for several years our one-time footing of friendly association (slowly breaking up since even before the War) had ended; nor was he on any better terms with any of his old circle, and indeed Avis was now the sole connecting link. I had not seen the preliminary notices of the production, and when Avis rang me up on the afternoon of the first night saying she had two stalls and would I like to accompany her, I had to confess that I knew nothing about it. But I was glad to accept, although both of us were sorry we'd gone before the evening was over.

It was Crispin's first real failure, and it was a crushing one, the more so perhaps because his name had by now come to be associated with success; and furthermore there were two other plays of his just then in the middle of long London runs.

It was clear before the second act was over that the play was going to fail badly unless the third act pulled out something extraordinarily brilliant; and during the interval Avis suggested I should go to the bar and try to hear what the vultures were saying, these being the dramatic critics and the epithet hers. I returned just before the curtain rose for the last act and told her that from what I could gather their notices would be obituary ones; that Porson was reiterating openly and loudly, not to say vinously, that it was cold porridge and mud; Hawkes was saying someone had forgotten to put the cat out; Roper had already seen more than he wanted to see and was going; while little Perseval, leaden-faced, crook-backed, hare-lipped and brilliantly venomous, was drawling out between teeth clenched on one of the long Indian cheroots he affected that Farne was now writing in the vein of the *cabinet particulier* school but had omitted the wit which alone made it palatable.

The last twenty minutes of the third act were played to an accompaniment of restive movements and coughs from the stalls and louder and more menacing noises from the gallery. When the curtain came down there was a momentary silence; and then an uproar of booing, hissing, whistling and cat-calls broke out varied with ironical shouts of "author."

The curtain rose slowly upon Crispin alone in the centre of the stage. He bowed, smiled and the din redoubled. Under the spotlight his face was that of a marble statue. With one hand in his trousers pocket and the other playing with the seals dangling from his fob he stood there allowing his glance to sweep slowly over the crowded house. The noise became deafening, rising and falling, dying away, and then breaking out again with additional fury. A group on the balcony in one of the pauses of comparative calm began to chant "Speech speech speech" in the monotonous staccato of a college cry; and presently Crispin advanced a step, smiled again and held up his hand. The noise became a shattering uproar and for a full minute beat towards the stage in waves of swelling sound, each of which seemed the uttermost limit of pandemonium, only to give way to a more tremendous bellowing. And suddenly there was silence as if a sound-proof door had been shut down.

"You have paid for your seats," Crispin said, "and if the play has displeased you, as it seems to have done, you are entitled to get your money's worth of enjoyment in the only way open to you. But will you allow me to say that this right and proper way is proving unbearably distressing to the actors and actresses, who are not responsible for the badness of the play. I do not ask you to forego your enjoyment without offering you compensation for your magnanimity, and if you will apply at the box-office on your way out the money so hopefully expended upon this lamentable production will be returned to you."

He bowed, smiled faintly, and stood as if waiting for a renewal of the uproar; but none came; the orchestra played the national anthem; and the audience moved in a slow but orderly mass to the exits.

Avis and I went to supper at The Red Cockerel, a small restaurant off Piccadilly; and she said, as we took our seats in one of its quiet, softly-lit corners, "I wonder how many went for their money?" A week or so later she told me that fewer than a hundred took advantage of Crispin's offer.

It was very peaceful and calming in the restaurant; there were only a stray couple or two besides ourselves and we sat till after midnight talking and smoking over our coffee.

"What's the matter with Crispin?" Avis said, abruptly changing the topic as she lit a fresh cigarette.

"Alison asked me that same question a long while ago," I said.

"I dare say. And I'm his sister and I don't know. You are his friend; do you?"

"None of us are his friends now, are we?" I said. "And I don't know either, Avis."

She glanced at me swiftly and then at the glowing tip of her cigarette. "I thought you would."

"No more than you. He looks ill. Or doesn't he? You should know better than I?"

She stubbed out her cigarette which was barely a third smoked and took another from my case on the table. "Oh, yes," she said impatiently; "he looks ill; but I don't think he is." She lit her cigarette and watched the smoke for some time. "Rather odd, isn't it," she said, "his intense pallor and my swarthiness?"

"There are other and greater contrasts," I replied, at which she smiled and said, "You knew Piers was in Paris."

"Sir Piers," I said, and we both laughed.

"Have you seen the evening paper?"

"No; I'll see them before I turn in."

"But I want to show you something. Perhaps the waiter has one or can get one; it's the *Standard* I want."

The waiter obtained the paper for us and Avis handed it to me indicating the front page where there was a report (headed: SIR PIERS ROWLAND HITS OUT) of his speech at a political luncheon in Paris.

"You're not asking me to wade through all that, are you?" I said; "I'm a great admirer of Piers's brilliance but not of his politics or of anyone else's— his jingoism and Tom's internationalism both bore me equally. I suppose it's much as usual, the loud drum, the sharp sword, and the big gun, with Britannia over all."

Avis smiled and nodded. "Not forgetting the swift long-range bomber. No, I didn't expect you to read it. Now turn to the stop press."

I did so and read, "There were strong rumours in the City this afternoon that the Secretary for Foreign Affairs, Sir George Lowndes, Bart., is tendering his resignation on health grounds and may be succeeded by Sir Piers Rowland, the brilliant young Under-Secretary at present in Paris." I looked up at Avis and smiled. "Pretty good if it's true; what is Piers? About forty-four? He'll be the youngest Foreign Secretary since——" I paused and Avis said, "Yes, go on."

I laughed. "Oh, I don't know; Fox or Pitt would it be?"

"I've not the ghost of a notion. Now turn to page nine I think; anyhow it's opposite Low's cartoon. That's right. Well, at the bottom of the last column, not quite the bottom, just above a gruesome advertisement for stomach powder, you'll see a four—or five-line oddment."

"I have it," I said, and read: *The World Peace Society held its first meeting of the year at the Queen's Hall this afternoon. There was a large attendance. Lady Rowland was chairman and the speakers included Mr. Bernard Still, K.C. and Lady (Eleanor) Dunston.* "You seem to have had your pennyworth," I laughed; "anything more?"

She shook her head. "Well?" she asked.

"Is it necessary husband and wife should see

eye to eye politically to make a happy marriage?"
I said.

"Probably.   Differences so fundamental as, say,
toryism and socialism must surely make people hopelessly incompatible."

"Alison isn't a socialist; she's just a—well—what?"

"Yes, what?" with her little malicious smile.

"Oh, humanitarian.   And their marriage doesn't
support your hypothesis.   It seems to be quite successful.   And they weren't married yesterday.   Eleven
years ought to be——"

"Don't talk rubbish," Avis said sharply; "it's as
plain as doom they're drifting apart and have been for
years."

"It's a pretty slow drift," I said, "like the drift of the
continents, perceptible only to the eye of science.   But
let's talk of something else.   It doesn't seem quite
decent to be discussing Alison like this."

"And Piers?"

"Yes, Piers, of course."

"Sylvia entered the Convent of the Poor Clares as a
novice last Wednesday."

"What!" I said.

"Must I repeat it?"

"Well, no, but you startled me."

"You're easily startled or else the painter's eye we
hear so much about is less observing than the average.
It's been plain for years where Sylvia was drifting.
She has only been waiting for her mother to
die."

"And the Grey fortune goes with her?"

Avis nodded.

"Well, it's a nice little windfall for Rome."

"To say nothing of her income as Hazell Fayre," Avis said.

"Won't she drop that now?"

"Not a bit. And in addition she'll probably write books of devotional verses and small primers of Roman Catholic doctrine. As you say, a nice little windfall for Rome. Shall we go? I'm suddenly sleepy."

It was a quarter to one when I reached my studio and Baker said, "Mrs. Frankell rang up just after eleven and again just before midnight. She asked if you'd ring her if you were in before one." I nodded and asked him to get her for me and presently after I was through and had told Norrie something of the *Son of Woman* fiasco she said, "Nan has died suddenly in Hollywood. Tom was in *The Call* office when it came over the tape-machine just before eleven. It was apparently an emergency operation of some sort but there'll probably be more about it in the morning papers."

Before I bade her good-night I asked if Tom knew anything about the illness of the Foreign Secretary and she told me that the rumour was true, that Sir George had already tendered his resignation, that Piers was succeeding him and was returning to London immediately to receive his seal of office from the King.

The next morning's newspapers, apart from their peculiar interest to the dwindling members of our circle, would, I imagine, have been found not unworthy of notice by a future historian as a commentary on our age. The picture papers and the three popular dailies with their tremendous sales figures splashed the death

of Charmian Claire, with Piers's appointment not even
in the second place, which was taken by the result of a
heavyweight contest for the British championship.
The rest of the press made the new Foreign Secretary
the news personage of the day and devoted many
columns to his career and some of his outstanding
dicta; while the dead film star received a mere half-
column and a small picture.

Little was added to what Norrie had told me, except
that Nan had been taken ill during a party, was hurried
to hospital where the operation was performed, and
that the famous film comedian George Rennett was at
her bedside when she died.

It was not until six weeks later that I heard what had
actually occurred.

Norrie's baby was born early in April and christened
a week later. At my age one ought not to regard anything that human beings do as odd, yet somehow
Norrie and Tom desiring the performance of this
fantastic rite of baptism, especially as both of them
had been emphatically against a church ceremony for
their wedding, struck me as excessively odd, as almost
grotesque. But perhaps it was merely a sort of
celebration to welcome the mite's advent with a small
convivial gathering. I was the godfather and they
named the child Jocelyn. This was Tom's choice and
his reason was perhaps as odd as the ceremony, for he
said that when he was a boy he had read a book which
had so captivated him that he had never forgotten it.
It was called *A Champion of the Faith* and was a tale of
the Lollards but he could not remember its author.
The rascal of the story was a boy of noble birth named

Jocelyn. "And so," I said to him chaffingly, "when you have a girl babe you christen her Jocelyn; for a future Minister of Education your mind works along quaint lines."

"Rot!" he laughed; "it's a sloppy name for a boy but lovely for a girl. Jocelyn Frankell. Miss Jocelyn Frankell—how fine that sounds!"

"It'll look well among the débutantes presented at court," I said.

"There'll be no court by then," Tom smiled.

"There will," I said, "and for her grandchildren."

But it was not because of that christening that I remember the day. It was notable for other reasons.

That morning I had received a letter from Michael, who had been at Hollywood now for several months. I did not keep it but I recollect a good deal of it. After enquiries about friends and references to one or two small business matters he went on, "——why, during a six years' sojourn in the Americas, you never went to Hollywood passes my comprehension. It's a grand spot for a painter. Also its lunacy is incredible. The Wolfe Meyerstein Company are paying me five hundred dollars a week and so far I've done nothing to earn it except read a few scripts which were afterwards scrapped. I've an office and a secretary-stenographer and about once a week somebody or other smoking a fat cigar will drift in, say, 'I'm Meyerstein' or Collinson or Stoltz or somebody else whose name is good for several millions, pick up a script, read a page or two, say 'lousy' or 'cute' or 'nertz,' toss it aside, give me a cigar, comment on anything under the sun except films, invite me to a party and then drift out

U

again. It was infuriating at first, then amusing, and is now boring. I'll probably clear out soon. Money is chucked about in cart-loads. The most awful punk is put into production, a few shots taken, and then the whole thing dropped. The full moon is the ruling planet. And side by side with all this preposterous squandering is more poverty and sheer wretchedness than could be matched anywhere else in the world I should say. Cohorts of the damned touting for crowd work, for anything to earn them a few dollars; legions of girls with nothing but vapidly pretty faces to commend them and young men with moustaches cut to imitate some star and with nothing behind it but a set of teeth watering for a meal they haven't the money to pay for.

"But it is Nan's affair I want to tell you about. It was pretty foul. There was a studio party at which every one was a good deal more than half-cut. Nan and George Rennett were missed after a time but no one bothered; lots of other couples were missing temporarily and turning up again. And then Rennett reappeared dishevelled and white about the gills and bawling for a doctor. Nan was taken to hospital and an operation performed at once but failed to save her. Rennett only escaped a prosecution for manslaughter by the skin of his great horse-teeth. I only discovered a day or so after the funeral that Nan had been married twice. That will be news to you as it was to me——"

There was nothing else in the letter that I can now recollect.

I suppose the fog that came down upon London late that April afternoon must have made the day unpleasantly memorable to thousands; and certainly, according to the press next day, it was unprecedented for the time of year as far back as the weather records went. I left Norrie's about six, intending to dine at my club and possibly go to a show afterwards. But I was soon in a jam of crawling traffic. We crept and jerked along at the rate of fifty yards or so a minute, amid a confusion of wan side-lamps and the dancing faint nimbi of pedestrians' torches. During a halt by the kerb a very small man, wearing a grey overcoat and a bowler, had said to me with a grimace, "I'm about fair lost and London born and bred too; bit of all right, isn't it? Any idea if this is right for Tottenham Court Road?" giving a jerk with his thumb ahead.

"I hope so," I said, "or I'm lost; but I don't think I am. I'm going nearly to the end of Oxford Street and I'll give you a lift if that's any help."

He thanked me and as I indicated the seat next to me, the back seats being littered as usual with impedimenta, he went round and got in. He was rather shy at first but presently he found his tongue. "They say a blind man's all right in a fog but I don't know; not a London fog, I lay. Old woman's yarn, I reckon. Don't know which is worst, being blind or deaf and dumb. They've a deaf and dumb little 'un in the flat above ours and it fair gives you the creeps."

"Any physical disability is the very devil," I said, not paying any great attention to his chatter.

"You're right, sir," he said; "you want to be like everybody else in this world if you want to be happy; and I know what I'm talking about."

A vehement touch in his tone made me glance at

him and he said with a faint grin, "Being a Tich now is no joke; it's a proper handicap."

"I shouldn't have thought there was much in it," I said, more for the sake of saying something than for any interest, my mind being so busily occupied with the job in hand that I did not fully realise the peculiar significance of his phrase "being a Tich." But his response to my casual comment, spoken with something of acerbity, but with more of the familiar Cockney philosophic resignation left me in no doubt at all of what he was referring to—his insignificant stature; and he began to enlarge on what was clearly an abiding grievance. "Don't you believe it, sir," he said, "being little 's all right for a woman but it's no use to a man; other way about. I've always been small; small as a kid and never grew like I ought. And don't you believe it's no handicap. Not half it isn't and I ought to know. Who do the women like? Don't need answering, does it? Not that it worries me now; I've a wife and five kids; but it used to when I was a young feller. At a dance you felt a fool and got shoved aside and the girls gave you the once over and on'y took you on if there was nothing else. And in a crowd where are you? Looking at somebody's dirty neck. Go after a job and do you get it if there's an ordinary-sized chap after it? Not on your life you don't. You're handicapped all ways. Bit of a sort of joke you are; a butt. People having to look down on you because you're short get into the habit o' looking down on you all ways; think you're half-baked sort o' thing."

"Exaggerating, aren't you?" I said, my interest captured by his vehemence. "Some of the greatest men in the world have been small."

"Don't you believe it, sir. When a little man does anything at all people take notice not because he's done much but because they're surprised he's done anything at all; it's like performing animals. I know that yarn about little men being some of the greatest in the world; my old mother tried to spruce me with that when I was about eighteen and used to come home riled at the chaps pulling my leg or some girl giving me the go-by for a bigger chap. But it's all my eye really; I've studied it; it's a sort of hobby of mine; and I've read history and you can take it from me, sir, that for every little bloke that's done something in the world there've been a thousand big 'uns. It's a fairy tale that yarn is. Being a sort of butt and a joke the only sensible thing they can do is to make a living out of it like Charlie Chaplin and Dan Leno and the rest of 'em. No, I've got five kids an' three of 'em's boys and if a fairy godmother had come to their christenings and said, ' Now what about a gift for 'em?' I'd say every time, if it was a boy, "give him five-feet nine inches and a thirty-eight chest and you can keep all the rest, ma'am, and thank you.' No, it don't matter what it is, work or play or what not, the difference between five-feet four and five-feet nine is five inches; don't look much on a ruler, does it? Draw it on a bit o' paper and it's next to nothing; but on a man it's the longest five inches in creation and I ought t' know."

I nodded and said rather inanely and a little flatly, "We all have our troubles."

"Oh, betcherlife!" he nodded back at me with a smile, "things might be worse as the saying is; but," he went on, refusing to relinquish his bee, "it's true what I'm telling you. Take my job for example. I'm a stage carpenter at The Royalty." And at this my relaxing attention tightened, for at The Royalty a play by Crispin, put into rehearsal as soon as *Son of Woman* had been taken off after four nights, was within a week of its first performance. "Oh, yes," I said, "very interesting work I should say."

"Well, it's bread-and-butter," he replied; "but what I was going to point out was that it's a harder and more tiring job for a short man 'n a tall. Always an extra bit o' stretching up to do here or standing on something there; and in lifting you don't get the *purchase* a tall man does, if you know what I mean. Takes it out of you more." Suddenly his cheery expression and chirpy manner left him and he went on, with a sort of wan inconsequence, "But we've all struck a packet o' trouble at The Royalty, if rumours are true." He shook his head slowly and drew down his lips. "And my experience o' life is that rumours al'ays *are* true when they're bad and perishin' stoomers when they're good."

"What's the trouble?" I asked.

"They say the play's going to be dropped," he replied; "they're not going to put it on; something's gone wrong somewhere and Mr. Farne, that's the author, has gone away and—and well, they're not going on with it. We'll know t'morrow, so they say. Nice little treat for everybody, I don't think. Gone bust, that's about what's happened."

"I don't think that's very likely," I said; and he stared at me and asked, "How d'you mean, sir?" "Well," I went on, "I used to know Mr. Farne and I'm sure it's no financial difficulty; he's a very wealthy man indeed. You'll probably find in the morning that for once an ill rumour is false. It's clearer here; can you see anywhere you recognise on your side?"

"Oh, absolutely!" he exclaimed and grinned; "'mind stopping here, sir. It's the old Ri-alto. Ought to know it; take the missis there every Saturday night. Five minutes and I'll be home and thank you very much." When he got out he stood a moment looking into the car and peering up anxiously into my face; and I realised then what a mite of a chap he was; in his attitude at that moment there was something pathetic, appealing, childlike, but rendered ludicrous almost grotesque, by his bowler hat, his wispy moustache and the pale staring eyes behind steel-rimmed glasses. "You think it'll be all right, sir, then? at The Royalty I mean," he said hopefully.

"Sure of it," I said confidently: "don't let that worry you. Good-night."

But as soon as I reached my club I rang up The Royalty. The stage-manager was there but he said he'd no information one way or the other. I rang up Crispin at his flat and his man told me his master had left England hurriedly, crossing to Boulogne late the previous night. Beyond that he knew nothing. I rang up Avis, but she was out of London and would not be back for several days.

But in the morning papers there was a paragraph announcing the discontinuance of the rehearsals for the new Crispin Farne play at The Royalty. Mr. Farne, the notice ended, is believed to have left England suddenly for an indefinite period.

The next morning, just after noon, I was walking along the Strand when I ran across Squitters Beamish,

now the literary editor of the *Morning News*, the author
of several volumes of biography and belles lettres,
and altogether a vastly important person. I rarely
encountered him and the utmost our association went
to was a cursory nod. As I saw him pacing towards me,
cadaverous, pinched, head raised a little sideways,
pointed nose cocked, eyes darting behind huge horn-
rimmed glasses, Val's phrase for him, "pompous
corpse," slipped into my memory. But this morning
he stopped, smiled faintly, and held out a limp hand.
"Come and have a drink," he said; and I knew something was afoot, for our association had never in the
past moved even sufficiently close for a casual drink
together.

We went into the nearest saloon bar and sat down.
He was evidently in a hurry for he glanced from his
wrist-watch to the bar clock, frowned and then opened
fire at once. "Bit of an eye-opener, isn't it, about
Crispin," he said, his pale eyes on my face, his lips
writhing in what looked more like a grin of agony
than a smile.

"Is it?" I said indifferently.

"Cousinly," he remarked; "cousinly, very admirable; but, well, my dear Farne, isn't it?"

"I'm sure I don't know, Beamish," I replied. "I
know no more than I've seen in the papers."

"Oh, come," he said; and it was so plain he did not
believe me that I said, "I assure you I don't," drained
my glass and beckoned the waiter.

"Not for me," he said; "not for me, I've work to
do. But d'you mean that, Farne?"

"Certainly."

His pale eyes lit up faintly and I am tempted to add

unholily if not hellishly; both epithets doubtless untrue and absurdly maligning him; but I loathe
Beamish. "My dear fellow," he said, "it's already being
chewed over and savoured in half the clubs in London.
Crispin got a nod from Scotland Yard that it would be
healthier for him if he cleared out, did not wait upon
the order of his going, and stayed out."

"Rubbish!" I said unpleasantly.

Again that agonised writhing of his lips; but this
time the pale eyes almost twinkled. "It's true." He
nodded his head slowly. "I rarely bet and then merely
on Derby Day, but I'll wager you an even ten pounds
that Crispin doesn't put his nose back in England under
five years."

I shook my head and glanced at the clock. "I must
be going."

He put a restraining hand upon my arm. His smile
was ugly, his voice corroding. "Wagering apart," he
said slowly, "I'll agree that it's rubbish if by this time
next week Essenhigh, Carruthers and Poulenny haven't
also skedaddled."

I said nothing, but rose to go; and as he got up also
he slipped a sideways glance at me and said blandly,
"The authorities have at last decided on a clean-up."

Chapter Sixteen

THE HAND OF THE POTTER

None answer'd this; but after Silence spake
A vessel of a more ungainly make:
' They swear at me for leaning all awry;
What ! did the Hand then of the Potter shake ? '

THIS RECORD moves to its close.   In the Royal Academy
Exhibition that year I had two pictures, both nudes.
On the second day after the exhibition opened to the
public a man attacked the larger one, a group of youths
and girls bathing in a forest pool, and cut it to shreds
with a butcher's knife.   Tom Frankell, who by an odd
chance was in the room at the time, saw the whole
thing happen and came round to see me that evening.
He found me quite unperturbed, much I am sure to
his relief, as he wanted to tell the story in its humorous
aspect.   " He was a thin, stooping chap," he said, " with
an iron-grey moustache and beard and one of those
pointed pink-tipped noses which seem to find a favourable soil on the faces of the unco guid.   I was standing
near your picture, looking at the next one to it in fact,
when our friend sidled up and stood for several minutes
staring at your bathers.   He was breathing so noisily
that I turned my head to look at him, and noticed
several other people approaching, apparently attracted
by his odd manner and the noise he was making.   And
then he jumped at the picture, dragging at the top of

his trousers where he must have had the knife and shouting out, 'I protest against this indecency!' he began slashing it. Some one knocked the knife out of his hand, some one else rammed his hat down over his eyes, and a couple of attendants came over and collared him. As they took him off he made the most extraordinary whinnying noises. Clear case of mania, I should say. What are you going to do about it?"

"Nothing. I can't prevent the Academy prosecuting; they'll do that on principle; but I shan't associate myself with it. I shall go out of town for a week or so; probably it will be forgotten in a few days."

The following September I was busy one evening in my studio at work on some sketches for an historical picture. I was painting by candlelight to get an effect I wanted; and apart from the candles grouped about my easel the studio was in darkness.

It was then about half-past nine. I had dined at home, and during the meal I had read in the evening paper that the Prime Minister, who was to speak on our foreign policy at a City banquet the following evening, had a severe chill and that his place would be taken by Sir Piers Rowland.

There was a knock at the studio door and Alison was shown in. As the door closed I turned to switch on the light; but she said, as she came towards me, "Please don't, Julian; and go on with your work; I'll sit and watch if I may."

And so for a full five minutes I painted, scarcely knowing what I was doing, and neither of us spoke. And then, and I heard the sharp intake of her breath, she said quietly, "Julian, take me away."

I did not answer. I stood staring at the colours on my palette. Perhaps no more than a minute of time passed; and then I heard her stir and forced myself to look towards her. But she was already moving to the door. I could not even go to open it for her.

The next evening she was by Piers's side when he made his now famous Thus-Far-and-no-Farther speech on Britain's foreign policy.

Ten days before Christmas I saw Piers in the lounge of The Forty Club. He came over to me and was unexpectedly friendly, even affable. He told me that he and Alison were leaving England on the twentieth for a five-weeks' holiday; and in a burst of unusual confidence he said they were both looking forward to what they hoped would be the happiest holiday they had yet spent together. And then he said, with a smile that had almost a trace of shyness in it, if that were possible to Piers, "Alison is expecting a baby in June."

On January the fourteenth the International Airways flying-boat *Attila* crashed near the Bay of Naples. Among the dead were Alison and Piers.

That was nearly two years ago. I have done no painting since; I have travelled in Europe and I have occupied myself in the writing of this book. And twice I have destroyed it when it was partially completed.

I come now to the point where I must make my revelation or withhold it. But for Alison's death I should have withheld it, should not indeed have written this record. But things have no longer the same values; perhaps they have no values at all.

The truth about my life is that I am a man with a physical disability which renders the act of love impos-

sible. I am incapable. Not of loving (that would have
been merciful) for I have loved Alison since she was a
child; but of love's consummation.

I am a man imprisoned in my own inadequate body.
As other men I am moved and stirred by beauty in all
its guises, and greatly by the beauty of women; but
love, sexual love, the origin and fruition of all beauty,
is beyond my reach.

It was when I was about thirteen that suspicion first
began to stir in my mind; but it was not until a year
after pubescence that I knew I was not as other boys;
and as I grew into and beyond adolescence my infirmity,
my deformity, increased until I became one of those
ghosts, those simulacra of man, inhabiting a shadow
world which is the only place of existence for me and
my kind.

What was the cause I do not know; perhaps it was
congenital, or perhaps due to some injury in early
boyhood; I remember hurting myself badly at play
on the Kendalls' lawn when I was nine or ten. But it
is impossible to say; and it does not matter now.

Always I have been haunted by a self-contempt, a
self-shame, and a fear of discovery and derision. I
did not consult doctors; the idea was abhorrent to me.
But I read everything that had been written upon such
cases as my own, especially the work of Franz von
Neugebauer; and I learned more than the mere fact
that my case was hopeless; for I was made aware of a
small, dark, ugly world of tragedy undreamt of by the
happily normal. And I came to know of the nightmare horrors that may lie ahead of me; I came to
understand that the very pictures I painted with so
much pleasure, so much peace of mind and emotional

release, might well be finger-posts pointing to degradation, if not to actual mania, to insanity.

But I shall not suffer these final torments. It is not that I intend or contemplate suicide; my code, if a ghost may be allowed to possess a code, repudiates that way out; it is not surrender but abasement. I have a kinder comfort than that. I believe, I have forced myself to believe, childishly, illogically, that behind the blank haphazard of the cosmos, somewhere at the back of all things, there exists a sort of vast universal poetic justice which does not permit us to be beaten to our knees. And so I count upon release, sure that upon the tragical farce of my life the curtain will be lowered while I still stand upright. And after it has fallen I shall not care what derisive laughter may follow my exit.

THE END

We hope you have enjoyed reading this book — it is one of many popular titles by established authors published in our Lythway Reprints.

We invite you to write for your copy of our complete catalogue which will be sent free of charge.

LYTHWAY PRESS LTD
Combe Park, Bath
Tel. 23201-2-3